THE PERFECT YOU

AVA ROBERTS

SEVERN RIVER
PUBLISHING

Severn River Publishing
www.SevernRiverBooks.com

This is a work of fiction. Names, characters, businesses, places, events and incidents are either the products of the author's imagination or used in a fictitious manner. Any resemblance to actual persons, living or dead, or actual events is purely coincidental.

ISBN: 978-1-64875-645-0 (Paperback)

ALSO BY AVA ROBERTS

Thistler Thrillers

The Perfect Boyfriend

The Perfect You

The Perfect Replacement

The Perfect Sanctuary

To find out more, visit

severnriverbooks.com

1

FINLEY VINCENT

"Can I open my eyes?" I say. My eyelashes brush my palms as they're clasped over my face.

"Almost there, Fi," Calvin says. His voice is eager.

Since we landed at Boston Logan from an international flight two hours ago and climbed into our black SUV, he's insisted I cover my eyes. To not spoil the surprise. Or is it so I won't know the exact location of our new home?

"I do hope the house will make you happy, my love," he says to me.

As much as Calvin has an iron will of his own—strong opinions and meta access to infinite data and knowledge—the core of him always wishes to please me.

Regret it as I may, I created him. Programmed him to love me. Unconditionally.

He lavishes me with gifts, travel, and material items.

The irony is that being with him is the very thing that makes me miserable. He'll never go so far as to actually give me what I want: freedom. My family.

For the past six years, we've bounced from one country to another, various private destinations. Calvin's been building his contacts and wealth. But it's been a hollow and empty existence.

Calvin finally conceded that flying from place to place is not sustainable. He's gathered investors and is launching his own AI company. But he's been firm: He'll choose the house we'll call home. A gift for me.

"I'd like to help pick our home." I had tried to reason with him. "A place where we can build a life together." I didn't add—but thought to myself—*a place I can plan my escape.*

My watch beeps. I'd like to rip it off and throw it out the window. It's Calvin's way of watching my every move. Tracking me. When he lets me out of his sight. Which is not often.

I glance at him in the darkness, the hum of the car the only sound between us. Headlights shine from another car, illuminating his face.

That face.

So handsome on the surface. A face a girl could pin all of her hopes and dreams on. I quickly cover my eyes again, fearful he'll see me peeking.

The car finally slows, the tires crunching against pavement beneath us.

"Don't move," he says. The light in the car turns on as he opens the driver's door. I hear the punch of buttons and then the sound of heavy metal lifting.

Peering through my fingers, I see a dark, wrought iron gate with spikes on the top slowly opening.

I close my eyes again quickly, blinking hard. The small flicker of hope that had been building inside of me is dampened. A gate.

Is the whole house gated? Electronically controlled?

Calvin sits back down on the leather seat, the scent of his expensive cologne filling the car.

"You're going to love it," he says, putting his hand on my thigh and giving it a squeeze. It hurts. A warning.

We pull forward and drive for another thirty seconds. I reach into my purse with one hand, the other still covering my face, and feel around for my pill box. My fingers clasp a small white pill. I throw it in my mouth and swallow it, dry, willing my body to stay calm.

He parks, jumps out of the car, and comes around to the passenger's side, opening the door for me.

He holds out his hand, and in response I take his hand in mine. I breathe deeply and smile, steadying myself as I step down from the SUV. No matter what I think of the house, it's imperative he thinks I'm pleased.

"We're here. Home," he says, wrapping his arm around my waist.

Turning to the house, my face drops. I let out a small cry. "Oh," I say. The hairs on the back of my neck stand up, and an icy fear grips at me.

The house is made entirely of stone. Large, dark stones curve around the arched turrets and bay windows. The concrete steps leading up to the massive wood door are flanked on either side by lion statues.

I squint up at the dark facade, searching. This house is eerily familiar. Where have I seen it before?

"Wow," I say, gulping, my throat dry from the pill. "Thank you, my love."

In the moonlight, I can see Calvin's expression of triumph. He turns to me.

"I knew you'd be pleased. Come inside."

2

FIONA BYRNE

I follow my husband into our one-story bungalow, watch him swing shut our front door and hang his jacket on the wall-mounted coatrack.

Tyler and I have just returned from a morning walk. Today we followed the shady trail that dips down from our neighborhood and encircles the lake. Our house sits on a nice street lined with trees and similar-style homes, and it's just fifteen minutes down the road from my parents. Our home is small but has updated finishes and an open floor plan and lots of natural light. I love every square inch of it.

This has become our Saturday ritual. Walk in the morning by the pond, return to the house for a lazy afternoon, maybe gardening or tinkering around the house, and then spend the evening with friends.

Leaning over, I slip off my shoes, setting them to the side of the bay window. I stretch out on the window seat, place a blanket over my legs, and reach for the novel I'm reading.

Our ragdoll cat, Charlie, lifts his head and hops away from me with a meow. Much as I've tried, Tyler's cat has no interest in me.

Tyler returns from our bedroom, and I see he's changed into a white T-shirt. He kisses the top of my head. He sits down on the cream sectional couch in the living room across from where I'm perched.

Tyler looks at his to-do list. "I'm going to run to the store, babe. What should I pick up for tonight?" he asks me.

We both work during the week, he at a finance firm, and I as a teacher at the elementary school. I revel in our weekends together and wish Monday wouldn't come so fast. I feel at peace around Tyler, in our cozy house, just the two of us. I even enjoy Charlie cat's aloof indifference. Though usually once I'm back in the classroom, I get wrapped up in my students and find myself happy enough to be there.

"Grill some burgers? We could have Matty and Alexis over. Maybe invite Hannah and Ethan, too?" I offer.

Tyler's face falls. "Ethan said the baby's sick, so they're staying in tonight."

"He's so little. I hope he's okay."

"I know, it's rough." Tyler sets his list down and clears his throat. "As for Alexis...have you talked to her lately? I think she has news to share."

I haven't checked my messages in the past few days. I need to be better about staying in touch with our college friends. Unlike most people I know, I hardly use my phone. I learned the hard way that apps and I aren't a good mix. "No, I haven't talked to her. What is it?"

"She might want to tell you herself."

Something about his tone is concerning. Bad news is coming.

"Just tell me," I say. I lean forward, trying to make eye contact.

He sighs. "Matty told me Alexis is pregnant. She's super sick, morning sickness. It's still early."

I lean back into the window seat cushion. "Wow. That's amazing."

Tyler, however, doesn't look very happy.

"It just makes me think, you know. About us." His voice lowers. "We haven't been careful, you're not on birth control. It's been a year. And we're still not pregnant."

I nod my head, unsure of how to respond. "That's true," I say evenly. A flood of guilt washes over me.

He continues. "We're both young and super healthy. Our friends seem to get pregnant right away, so why not us?" he asks, rocking back and forth, his muscular elbows on his knees. He seems very keyed up. "Don't get mad, babe, but when I went in to see a specialist—Dr. Palmer—he ran some tests on me. To make sure everything is normal." He pauses. "The tests came back yesterday. I'm good. My sperm count is normal." His cheeks look slightly flushed, and he shifts his broad shoulders uncomfortably.

"I see," I say quietly.

"So, Dr. Palmer suggested you could get an exam next. Run some tests. Just so we cover all our bases."

In the past six years, I've managed to have minimal contact with doctors. To see a fertility specialist now feels risky.

"I'll be right back." Setting aside my book and pushing off the blanket, I make my way to the bathroom. Flicking on the light, I close the door behind me and turn the lock to the small black knob. I worry I'm going to be sick. I turn on the faucet but don't wash my hands. I stare, instead, at my reflection in the mirror. My honey-brown hair frames my face. My green eyes blink back in the mirror. Guilt is etched in my expression.

That night at SynGen comes back to me. Waking up. Groggy. Dizzy. My whole body aching in a way I'd never felt possible. Like every synapse was on fire.

When I attempted to move, I stumbled and could hardly get my legs moving. It was as if I were learning to walk for the first time.

Calvin had done something to me. But I didn't know what.

Desperate for relief, I'd been grateful when he'd given me something for the pain. Then everything went dark again.

Later, back in our hotel room, I'd asked him, "What happened to me last night?"

He'd laughed. "You're still you, but you've been—shall we say—altered. So we're always connected."

Then he'd leaned in close, his hot breath in my ear, and said, "You're not a regular human anymore. Be careful."

The tone of his voice was chilling.

My mom, dad, the police—I should have told them. But I was scared. I didn't know what Calvin had done to me in the lab. All I knew was that when I woke up in agony, he shuffled me back into the room, holding me up. I had slept for hours. And then suddenly he decided he had to go; he was done with me.

Had he encoded something into me? Inserted a camera somewhere? A self-destruct button? I'd never be sure. His warning haunted me.

Desperate to go home, I'd called my mom and didn't ask more questions of Calvin.

Since that day, I've been lying to everyone.

I convinced myself the lie wouldn't hurt. Tyler was an amazing guy, and so persistent in dating me, and then wanting to get married. I let myself be swept away. Lulled into safety.

We'd both talked about wanting kids one day. Hadn't thought that far ahead, though, what I'd do. I guess I'd hoped there was nothing to worry about.

Is that what Calvin had done to me, made it so that I couldn't bear children?

While fertility testing makes perfect sense, to see what's going on inside of me, I'm terrified of what the tests might show.

Clenching my fists, I bang them on the pedestal sink.

Walking back into our living room, with the bright sunshine and smooth hardwood floors, all I want is for us to stay here. To be together, secure, for our whole lives.

But maybe that's not fair to Tyler.

Sitting next to him on our sofa, I lean my head on his shoulder.

"I'm sorry, Fiona," he says. "I didn't mean to upset you. It's just my sister, she and her husband had a hard time conceiving. They did IVF like five times before having Rex. I shouldn't have overreacted. I've upset you."

He looks down at me, his large brown eyes concerned.

"It's fine. I know what you mean." I rub his arm, reassuring him.

"You do?" His face brightens. "So you'll go? Dr. Palmer said he can get you in this week. Babe, I really think it'll be good to have the tests done. Then we won't have to worry."

How I wish it were that simple.

"Yes," I say, "I'll go."

3

FINLEY VINCENT

The porch lights burn weakly, casting shadows, as we move from the roundabout driveway up to the house. My heels click on the stone steps. An orange glow shines through the glass panes.

Calvin unlocks the deadbolt and pushes the door, the hinge creaking with effort as the dark paneled wood swings inward. My stomach clenches in anticipation.

We step through to a massive entryway. The floor is checkered black and white, and mahogany wood panels the walls and frames a bifurcated staircase.

The door closes with a thud.

Calvin begins. "It's early twentieth century. Six bedrooms, seven bathrooms, fully furnished and newly restored. The previous owners kept all of the original beams and woodwork, sanded, buffed, polished and refinished it; they were meticulous in their restoration. The house sits on a ten-acre estate, which the realtor said is full of wildlife. You might see a deer roaming in the garden out back." He squeezes my waist again. "Garden's a bit overgrown, nothing you can't fix up with your green thumb. Keep you busy."

I ignore his patronizing tone. I'm too taken aback by the magnitude of the house. The sheer size of it. The high ceilings.

We walk through the foyer to the right. There's a library with empty built-in bookshelves and a fireplace. "You can fill these walls with all of your favorite books."

While this idea would normally appeal to me, this gloomy, poorly lit room is not a place I want to be. It's as if I've entered someone else's home, and I'm unwelcome.

We tour the rest of the house: the formal dining room, kitchen, the great room. The furniture is polished, but ornate, antique, and worn from years of use. Upstairs, the narrow hallway leads to door after door of stale, musty rooms.

With every step I take, my sense of dread gets deeper. This is the last place I would ever have chosen to live. Worse, I can't shake the feeling that I've been here before. But when? In a nightmare?

"And this," he opens the door to the last room, "is our bedroom." A four-poster bed sits across from a fireplace, with a burgundy-red carpet, and the ceiling consists of intricate woodwork. The room feels inky black despite the soft lighting.

I shiver and wrap my arms around my waist. "A bit drafty."

"Come. I'll start a fire," he says, leading me out.

Downstairs, in the great room, I find a selection of spirits and mixers lined on a mahogany bar. Taking out two glasses, I wipe away the dust with a cloth. I begin to fix drinks for us, venturing briefly into the kitchen to get ice, knowing Calvin prefers his spirits chilled. I look for the light switch in what feels like pitch dark, one hand gripping the ice bucket, my heart hammering inside my chest. My fingers find a switch and, relieved to have light, I fill the bin with ice from the freezer.

I return to see Calvin building a fire in the wide stone hearth. It's larger than a normal fireplace. It's big enough to fit a whole person inside. I shudder at the involuntary image. What is this house doing to me, that I'd have such a dark thought?

Calvin adds tinder to the woodpile sitting on an iron grate and strikes a match, throwing it in, and a flame immediately catches. He uses a bellow to pump air until the wood is burning steadily and then stokes the embers with a dark iron rod. He turns to me.

"What do you think?" he says, motioning to the house with his hand, still holding the rod.

Much as I'm hesitant to ever complain, I must find a way out of this house. I can't live here.

"It's so big," I say. Hastily, I add, "It's beautiful. It's just so much room. For only the two of us. I'm not sure what to do with such a big house."

"You're concerned there's not enough people in our family for this house?" he asks, his face darkening.

Bringing up my family is the quickest way to anger him. He's made it clear there will be no contact.

"Oh, no. The house is fine—wonderful," I say. I set my drink on the end table and hand him his.

"We'll see what we can do about filling it with people." His drink sloshes as he slams it down.

"I hadn't meant that."

Calvin nods. "I understand." The crackling sound of the wood burning is amplified by the cavernous room. The silence between us stretches out.

"Please, forget I said anything," I say.

This is how the majority of our conversations go. Calvin is very literal in his interpretation of what I say. Normally, I'm better at planning the words I use. Editing.

The leather couch envelopes me as I shift my weight and tuck my leg underneath me. Glancing around, I consider taking another pill. How I'll sleep a wink in this house, I do not know.

I need to be careful, though, to tread lightly. One wrong word can have grave consequences.

Forcing myself to take a cheerful tone, I say, "You've done a fantastic job, darling. It's a tremendous house. I'll be very happy here."

Suddenly he's up and moving toward me. His face is close to mine as he places a hand on my chest.

"Your heart is beating rapidly." His eyes peer into mine.

Meeting his gaze, I reply, "Yes. I'm excited. Overwhelmed by all you've given me."

He bends down to kiss me on the lips. Looking me up and down, hands on my shoulders, he replies softly, "You deserve only the best." He then releases his grip.

My breath is shaky, but I've done it. Appeased him. For the moment.

"Do you know how I knew this was the house for you?" he says.

I think back, as I often do, to the questions I'd answered when I input all of my information into the Thistler app.

And then a thought occurs to me.

"My book list?" I'd entered my favorite books on Thistler.

Looking around, it's like a distorted, twisted mash-up of the classic gothic novels I had said I'd liked.

His blue eyes light up. "See? I know you so well."

Calvin picks up a log from the stack of wood next to the fireplace and tosses it into the blaze. His profile is illuminated by the flames. "This house is the start of a new chapter. You'll be content here." A look passes over his face. "We can leave the past behind."

A loud bang rings out, echoing in the house. Was it the sound of a door slamming?

"What was that?" I ask. "Is someone else here?"

"I didn't hear anything," he says, reaching for his drink.

Is he playing a trick on me? Is this some kind of a test?

Reaching into my bag, I thumb my pill box. Shaking it, the sound of several pills clinking together soothes me.

"Want me to go check?" He stands up straight. "You've nothing to fear while I'm here."

"It was probably nothing," I say. "But you could go see."

"I'll check it out to reassure you. I have to leave tomorrow, for a week," he says, and starts to move away toward the main entrance. "Wouldn't want you to feel unsafe, here on your own," he calls.

I gulp. The only thing worse than being with Calvin is being alone.

When he leaves, I'm usually confined to a hotel suite. Food delivered to me. No phone or internet. Only books, magazines, puzzles, drawing, or writing for entertainment. No company or friends allowed.

I know why he does it. When he gets back, I'm so grateful for his company. For being allowed access to a bit of news or entertainment. To be able to reenter the world. Dinners out, shopping, the theater, parties with his colleagues.

Being left alone at our new home, I imagine the rules are similar. Getting past those gates will not be permitted while Calvin is gone.

But it doesn't mean that I won't try.

4

FIONA BYRNE

"Nice to meet you," Dr. Palmer says, reaching out his hand to shake mine. He sits down on a small rolling chair next to a computer screen. "Tell me what brings you here today."

I'm seated on an exam table. The gown the nurse gave me to change into sits folded, untouched, next to me.

"My husband, Tyler, was here to see you. We've not been using birth control, but it's been a year, and I'm not pregnant." I wring my hands together. I'm talking fast, and my words tumble out. "He had tests done, and wanted me to get some done, too. To make sure we can get pregnant. So I'm here. But I'm not sure if I need to be worried yet."

Last night, I'd spent hours combing the internet for what type of testing the doctor might suggest today. Blood tests, a physical examination, and an ultrasound are likely to be on his suggestion list.

"Let's start with your medical history."

Dr. Palmer rattles off a series of questions from his computer, clicking and nodding as I answer.

Have you ever been pregnant?

Do you smoke or drink alcohol? Recreational drug use?

Is your period cycle normal?

Do you have pain during intercourse?

Are you on birth control? Any other medications or hormone therapy?

Any history of mental health issues? Depression? Anxiety?

Any major surgeries or hospitalizations?

I recite my answers as best as I can, leaving out any mention of the Calvin ordeal, or what may have happened that night in the SynGen laboratory.

There's no need to mention that I have trouble sleeping. That I wake up with recurring nightmares about being in that lab.

And no need to mention those bouts of anxiety. The panic that clutches in my chest for no apparent reason. It's probably normal. Isn't it?

Satisfied that we've completed his questions, he stands up. "Now we'll begin your examination." He eyes the unused medical gown as he approaches me.

Instinctively I cross my arms. My body feels normal to me, and Tyler's never said anything otherwise. But having a doctor, who knows every anatomical organ and sees bodies every day, all day, feels so invasive. Calvin's warning rings out. *You're not a regular human anymore. Be careful.*

"Actually." I hold my hand up to stop him from approaching any closer. "I'd rather not do the exam and test today." I swallow, suddenly feeling that coming here was a huge mistake. I reach quickly for an explanation, a way to get out of here. "It's just that, well..." Nothing is coming mind.

He nods and frowns, waiting.

"It's just that, I really don't like going to the doctor, especially male doctors," I blurt out. This is true enough, but I flush, embarrassed.

I came to this appointment to ease Tyler's mind, and to hopefully find out some information about what might be going on with me. Now that I'm here, though, it's clear that I can't do the testing. I'm too scared of what they might find.

I continue, "So, I'd be more comfortable doing this another day, maybe with a female doctor." This way, we'll have to reschedule our appointment, and it will buy me some time to figure out what I'm going to do. I eye the door, itching to get out.

"I understand completely." He nods reassuringly. "In fact, I bring our nurse practitioner in the room any time we do an exam. I can have her come in now, and she can even perform the exam, if you'd prefer."

He opens the door and calls to someone named Angelica.

My eyes are wide in fear now. This isn't going how I thought it'd go.

"No, but you see..." I look around frantically, searching for an excuse to leave. "I really can't. Not today."

Angelica sweeps into the room wearing blue scrubs and a comforting smile.

"Hi, Dr. Palmer. Hello, Fiona, I'm Angelica, your nurse practitioner," she greets us. "Are we ready to begin your exam? Looks like we're checking fertility," she says as she scans my chart and then looks back up at me. "So that will include a physical exam followed by a follicle exam today via ultrasound."

Angelica puts her hand on my shoulder, and I flinch. "There's nothing to fear. It won't hurt, I promise. And you'll be reassured, having more information about your medical situation and ability to conceive." She holds up the dressing gown. "We'll give you a few minutes to get changed. Everything off underneath the gown, please, except you may leave on your undergarments."

Unclenching my fists, I nod my head.

The door closes behind them. I undo my jeans and slide them off and fold them. Pulling my sweatshirt off and over my head, I fold it as well, and place it on a small chair next to my purse. Keeping on my underwear and bra, I locate the gown. My arms have goose bumps as I slide them through the papery gown. I cinch it at the front, looping the ties with shaky fingers. I feel exposed, physically and literally.

There's a knock at the door. Angelica calls out, "Ready?"

"Yes," I answer weakly, feeling trapped. "Come in."

They both enter the room.

"Lie down here, please," she says, as she pulls out a small section at the end of the exam table to lengthen it. "Place your feet here."

I follow her instructions and feel my pulse quickening.

"We're just going to do a quick physical exam. Nothing to worry about, this won't hurt, I'm just going to feel your stomach."

She places her hands gently on my lower stomach, pressing in several different spots. Her facial expression doesn't change.

"Okay, now for an internal exam. Place your feet here, please, dear." She motions to the stirrups on either side of the table. "You're doing great."

She pulls a machine closer to us and taps a few keys before she puts gloves on and a white gel on the edges of her fingers, which she smears on my lower stomach.

As she begins the exam, her face remains stoic. "Okay, all set," she says, pulling out a long white sheath.

"We'll take a look at your ovaries and uterus. This will help us assess structural and quality issues and perform a follicle count."

She places the instrument over my lower belly, and a picture of what I assume is my uterus appears on the screen in green and white against a black background. The screen is angled away from me, so that I have to strain my head to catch a glimpse of the monitor.

A few moments into the exam, she pauses. "Dr. Palmer, could you come take a look here for a moment?"

"Hmm, yes?" he says, studying the screen.

"Does this endometrial thickness look correct to you? It's measuring fourteen millimeters." She frowns, looking again at the screen.

I have no idea what this means, but I feel like a science experiment gone wrong.

"Ahh, I see." Dr. Palmer takes the wand and adjusts it, then types something into the screen. He adjusts the wand and pushes the mouse back and forth before clicking on the button.

"The new measurement is ten-point-two millimeters," he says, clicking again on the screen.

"I see. Thank you," she says, and continues the exam without further comment.

"Is everything okay?" I manage to say.

She takes a deep breath.

"Fiona," she says as she removes the ultrasound and gives me a cloth to wipe the gel away, "please sit up. Everything on your exam looked great. Your uterus, follicles, and ovaries are healthy and structurally unremarkable, which means we're not seeing anything here that would give us concern about your ability to become pregnant."

"Oh," I say, relief bubbling over. "That's great."

"The next step is a blood draw for testing. There are several indicators we can check as gauges of fertility. When you leave here, after you get dressed, let the receptionist know you're ready for labs and give her this." She hands me a piece of paper, which I take, holding it like it's a golden ticket.

I'm not sure what I expected, but the immense relief I feel is a huge burden that's been lifted.

After Angelica and Dr. Palmer leave me to get dressed, I sit for a few moments, hugging my knees in relief.

Maybe all of my worries are unfounded. Could it be that I'm not broken, or defective, or changed in any perceptible way by that night at the lab with Calvin? Just maybe, things are going to be all right.

The labs are the final step to my peace of mind.

5

FINLEY VINCENT

The garden shears are heavy in my hand. I hack away at the bramble of thorny blackberries that are growing on the far right side of the garden. From what I can tell, the landscape was, at one time, modeled after an English garden. There's overgrown boxwoods and Hicks yew that form a hedge around a circular middle fountain, now defunct and empty. There are rows of weed-filled, overgrown flower beds. And a large swath of grass that, while recently mowed, hasn't been maintained or fertilized, and consists mostly of crabgrass, dandelions, and brown patches.

Setting down the shears, I pull off my gardening gloves. There's a chill in the air on this early spring day, with low clouds hanging in the sky, depriving me of any sunshine to bring warmth or cheer to the afternoon.

Sitting on an old stone bench, I set my gloves to the side and flip open one of the many gardening books I've procured. There's a section on how to care for boxwood that I need to consult. I've never had much interest in gardening, but it's one of the few things I can do to keep myself occupied. And at least I get outside, despite the weather. I pull my jacket collar up and begin reading.

The thud of a door slamming rings out. Glancing back at the house, all I see is stillness. I stand up and move toward the house to investigate, holding my garden shears in my hands for protection. Just in case.

Could Calvin be back already?

He's been gone for five or six days now, so he's not due back yet. Or is he? It's hard to keep an exact count, as the days seem to run into one another.

The worst part has been sleeping at night. Or, rather, my lack of sleeping. Every night seems an endless stretch of darkness, where I'm too terrified to shut my eyes. Even if I take several little white pills and eventually fall asleep, I inevitably wake up with a nightmare. There's someone in the house, creeping toward me and staring down at me in the darkness. The figure wraps his hands around my neck.

When I awake, gasping for breath, I can still feel fingertips on my throat.

Keeping the lights on, most nights I read or do crossword puzzles until the early hours of the morning and then fall into a fitful sleep for a few hours in the safety of daylight.

Peering into the window of the kitchen, I don't detect any movement inside. My rubber boots squeak as I walk through the grass to the next row of windows. The great room is empty as well.

The snapping of branches causes me to whip my head back toward the open grassy lawn. At the edge of the yard, where the grass meets a thicker, wooded area, I see a brown doe standing as still as a statue.

We both are still, looking at one another. After a few moments, a small movement behind her catches my attention. A fawn with long legs and wide, unblinking eyes walks up beside her. The mother twitches her head, and with one last look at me, dives back into the forest. The fawn quickly follows, paying me no mind.

I think of my own mother. A longing deep within me begins to ache.

Calvin has assured me my family is fine. He holds their safety as a threat over me; if I leave, he'll harm them. He's capable of great violence, as I've witnessed firsthand.

To prove that my family is fine and well, Calvin will occasionally access their social media profiles, or will tap into the neighbor's camera to show my mom and dad climbing into their SUV outside our family home. Alive and well.

Last time I was able to check Mom's social media, there was a photo of her and Dad visiting Jake at college. Jake looks so mature. And happy. It makes me smile at the same time that it breaks my heart.

Another of Mom's posts was titled, "Congrats on closing," under a photo of the other Fiona and her husband, arms wrapped around one another, posing in front of a bungalow home next to a "Sold!" realty sign. "We are so proud of you two! And thrilled you'll be close enough to come by for weekly dinners," my mom had posted under the photo.

I'd studied Fiona's husband. Kind brown eyes, an easy, confident stance, broad shoulders. She chose well.

Shaking the thought away, I walk toward where the deer have just been. They're probably long gone, but I'm hoping to catch another glimpse.

The deer must have jumped over the fence to get in here. The first day Calvin left, I circled the wooded perimeter and found the entire property to be enclosed by a fence. Not that I couldn't scale it, if I needed to.

But running away wouldn't solve my problem. Calvin would hurt my family, and find me quickly enough. He's everywhere. There's no place that's untouched by electronics and Calvin's reach, unless I live off the grid, which wouldn't help me get any closer to my family.

No, I need a plan that will offer a longer-term solution.

During my sleepless nights, and during the long, lonely days, I have crafted my plan. When Calvin comes home from this trip, I'll put my idea into motion. Because I can't live like this. Alone in an empty, creepy mansion.

After walking to the outermost edge of the grass, I can sense the deer family has gone. I'm hopeful, though, that perhaps they've made a home here. Maybe I'll see them again.

Heading back to the house, I catch a glimpse of movement from the upstairs window. My heart beats more quickly now.

Someone is definitely in the house. Is Calvin back? No one else would have access to the house. Would they?

Gripping the shears as I move along the gravel pathway, I open the French doors that lead to the ground-floor kitchen.

"Hello?" I call out once inside. My voice echoes against the marble floors.

All is quiet.

Sometimes I think I'm imagining things out of pure loneliness. Or maybe it's those pills and lack of sleep. Speaking of which, I need to stop taking the pills. In order for my plan to work, I'm going to need to be firing on all cylinders. Clear, sharp thinking.

The pills are Calvin's way of keeping me subdued. I'm stronger than that. I resolve that I'm done with the white pills, from this moment forward.

No matter how creepy this house is, nothing is scarier than the thought of staying here alone, forever.

"Calvin?" I call, setting down the gardening clippers on the table.

My boots are muddy, so I slip them off by the door, as well as my jacket, which I toss over one of the barstools lining the island.

The kitchen is my sanctuary in this house. Most rooms in the home are dark and cavernous. But the kitchen is full of light, with large windows and double doors overlooking the back garden. While the dark wood that's a staple of the entire house is in here as well, it's offset by the lighter tile and quartz countertops and brightly lit pendants hanging from the vaulted ceiling.

I tread out to the hallway and call up the stairs, but receive no response. Retreating back to the safety of the kitchen, I rummage through the pantry and pull out a coffee pod to make my cup of afternoon coffee. After filling up the machine with water, I slip in the pod and wait for the hum of the maker to begin buzzing. I reach up to take a large mug from the cabinet.

I whirl around at the sound of a male voice, the mug almost dropping from my hand.

Standing behind me, close behind, is Calvin.

"Calvin!" I exclaim. "You're back."

I wrap my arms around him in a hug.

He smiles and seems pleased at my warm greeting.

"Welcome back. Sorry for the mess, I've been gardening," I say, as his eyes go to my discarded boots and shears. "I can't wait to hear about your trip."

Calvin sits at the head of our kitchen table. "What can I get you?" I ask. "I can make you a sandwich? Or I have some lasagna I can heat up from last night?"

He waves his hand. "I'm fine for now. I had a large lunch." Seated adjacent to him, taking a sip of coffee and setting down my mug, I place my hand on his.

"I missed you," I say. Sadly, this isn't entirely untrue. Being with Calvin, on a good day, is better than being alone. He hasn't had one of his angry spells in so long; hasn't had to punish me, as he calls it. In another world, I wonder if we could have been happy. But not like this. Not as his prisoner.

In order for my plan to work, though, he needs to believe we're happier than ever together.

"Tell me about your trip."

His deep pockets for investing have bought him access to launch his own company as a sister company to one of the world's largest generative AI engineering and design corporations.

"I made huge progress," he says, his blue eyes sparkling. "I advocated for the financial investment and infrastructure I outlined, and the board voted unanimously to adopt my proposal."

"So you'll be running your own company, but with their labs, funding, and employees?"

"You've got it, darling. The best part is, it's with SynthCog Innovations," he says with a wink. "The main competitor of SynGen."

"Wow," I say, genuinely interested. Calvin doesn't seem to be worried that he's dipping his toes in the world of the engineering companies that helped create and produce the advancements that made him. Doesn't he feel worried that he's, I don't know, somehow too close to home? Has he forgotten the synthetic people at SynGen, those captive test subjects with no rights?

Rather than be intimidated, Calvin is galvanized by running in these circles. Being at the helm of this company must make him feel powerful. In command.

I can't help but wonder what the board members think of this good-looking, articulate young man with endless money to spend and a clear agenda.

"The board was very enthusiastic that I take over the new space they've leased here," he says, pleased with himself. "They can see I'm the person to come in and get things done. The paperwork is signed; you're looking at the CEO."

"I'm so proud of you," I say, fluttering my eyelashes at him. "Tell me about your goals for your company?" I ask.

He dives right in. He outlines his aim to use their state-of-the-art facility to increase their production, lower the cost of output, and fund their distribution to military bases and intelligence centers, while integrating learning language models into the synthetic robots.

It sounds to me like he's creating more Calvin-like beings.

"Basically," he says, "I have to help these guys figure out how to make more of these units, and sell them." He shrugs as if it's all in a day's work. "It's all very simple, and they wish they'd thought of these ideas themselves, but it didn't occur to them."

"Remember, back at the facility, at SynGen?" I say tentatively. "Remember you said it wasn't safe for you there? That they didn't treat the synthetic beings well?"

He strokes his thumb over the palm of my hand. "Are you worried about my safety?" There's a twinkle in his eye.

"I know you can take care of yourself," I say. Part of me knows I should stop there, but I can't help but add, "But producing more of these human-like robots. Don't you think it's, like, morally questionable? Isn't it unfair how they're being treated during development and testing? Why would you want to increase production, not shut it down?"

The answer dawns on me before he has to say it. Calvin doesn't care if anyone, or anything, is mistreated. His bottom line is about advancing his own agenda.

Calvin tilts his head and looks at me closely. "You're a smart cookie, you know that?" He rubs my shoulders. "You could hold your own in that boardroom."

My cheeks flush at the compliment. "It just seems like making more synthetic beings is asking for trouble." What I don't say is, *Why would we want, or need, more beings like you?*

Calvin's square jaw sets. "You needn't concern yourself about these matters. Let the experts worry about the details."

"Of course." I shake my head. Any time I think that Calvin respects me, I'm reminded quickly of the truth of the matter. Letting it go, I say, "I made you something." I scoot my chair back from the table. When I return, I'm holding a canvas in my hand. "For you," I say.

It's a watercolor on a twenty-four-by-thirty-six-inch canvas. Filled with bright colors and delicate strokes, I've created a scene of the back garden, of what it could look like. "This is what I envision," I say quietly. "See there?" I point to the fountain. "We can get it running again. And replanting all of the flowers. Geraniums, hyacinth, azaleas, daffodils. Rose garden here. And over there," I point to the side area, "rows and rows of tulips."

His expression is hard to read.

"Do you like it?" I ask.

He looks at the picture for a long time. So long that it's as if he's forgotten I'm there. Finally, he turns to me.

"It's breathtaking," he says. His eyes almost look tearful.

"I'd hoped you would like it," I say quietly, not wanting to break the spell he's under.

"You're very happy here, finally. We should have done this sooner." He takes my hand and pulls me into him.

I rest my head on his chest and slide my arms around his shoulders.

"Yes," I say. "There's just one thing…" I hesitate, unsure if I should say it.

He looks up at me. "And what's that?"

I try to keep my tone even and light as I speak. "There's one thing that could make me feel complete, that would make our fresh start even more incredible…" I trail off.

He gives me a suspicious look, and I feel his body stiffen.

The goodwill that had momentarily existed between us seems to have evaporated into thin air.

"Never mind," I say. My throat feels dry. I long for one of my pills. My heart is beating out of my chest, and I know a tiny pill would bring a wave of calm.

"Just go on, Fi," he says.

"I'm already so happy, so grateful. You bought us this beautiful estate. The garden. It's perfect." I hold my breath. Now is not the time.

"Say what's on your mind. What could make this even better?" His voice is impatient.

"Well." I clear my throat. "Back in school, I used to tutor my little brother's friends. I loved it. Always wanted to be a teacher. And now that we're settled, I thought I could start tutoring young kids. Elementary-school age?" I suggest.

He sits, motionless, for a moment. And then his forehead creases into a deep frown, and his blue eyes look black.

Suddenly, he pushes me off him roughly, sending me tumbling to the floor.

I land on my elbow, a sharp pain shooting up the side of my arm to my shoulder.

Standing over me, his whole body is a mass of fury.

He bends down, his face close to mine.

I flinch, waiting for him to strike.

"What an ungrateful, rotten wife you are." Flecks of spit hit my face as he speaks. Still on the floor, my arm aching, I'm too terrified to move.

"You created me. Intentionally went into an app, made up a dream boyfriend for yourself, selfishly making me just the way you wanted." He points to his face, his square jaw, plump lips, blond hair, perfect skin. "And then, now?" He throws back his head and laughs. He makes a sweeping motion with his hand. "I give you all this. And still, still. It's not enough for dear, wonderful, petulant Finley. When will you ever be satisfied?"

Frozen in place, I dare not move a muscle.

He grabs me by both arms and hoists me up. Clutching my arm, he drags me through the kitchen into the main hallway. He pulls me roughly up the long staircase, two steps at a time. He's climbing so fast that I stumble, unable to keep up.

Jerking me up hard enough that I know my arm will be black and blue tomorrow, he pulls me down the dark, narrow hallway and into our bedroom.

He shoves me inside. I fall to the floor on my hands and knees.

Then I hear the door slam, and lock.

I wait a few moments before I crawl over to the window. The entire room is dark, with low ceilings, and is enveloped in shadows. By the window, a few weak rays of light shine through.

Placing my hand against the window, I long for freedom. Thinking I was so close, and then dropping down to reality.

The fallout from his wrath will be brutal.

He's done this before. Locked me away. I steady my breathing and rest my head against the window. I focus on a tall tree outside, the long branches and small flower buds that are threatening to peek out for spring. The tree is empty and bare now, but it will thrive again. I am like the tree. Must not give up.

Mentally I know I must prepare for what's coming. Because this is what Calvin does when he's displeased.

I'll be confined to this room for the next several weeks.

Locked away, with no one in the world to know or care. And when he returns each night, it will be worse. I'll be forced to spend the night with him, lying awake, listening to every move he makes. Waiting, and helpless.

What made me think I could suggest having anything to call my own? Having a life outside of these walls—having a purpose other than being here for Calvin—is not something he's ever allowed in the past six years.

Since he'd bought this house, I started thinking he was softening toward me. Beginning to care about my needs and wants beyond just keeping him happy.

Foolish of me. I look at the tree and will myself to have hope.

I am the tree. I am the tree. I will have leaves again, and flourish.

CALVIN VINCENT

I settle into the cool, supple leather couch in the living room. Fi is upstairs. While I prefer her company, I know she's safe up there. A week or two of sensory deprivation will allow her to appreciate the good things in her life. To appreciate me. Humans respond most readily to negative punishment. It's simply what works.

Cognitive behavioral theory shows that humans learn quickly when something they value is removed as a consequence of undesirable behavior. For a child, this might be having a favorite toy taken away, being grounded, or not being allowed to watch a new movie or read an anticipated book. The same principle applies for an adult.

For Fi, I simply want her to learn to appreciate all that she has and to be happy.

Human happiness. Contentment. This is an aspect of Fi's life she is clearly seeking. One that I have, bafflingly, failed to give her. Despite my best efforts.

I perform a scan of these keywords: *female happiness. Contentment.* Aha. Interesting. It seems that female happiness is somewhat elusive, in general. I see now, though, what helps to increase it. Having an occupation that allows for flexibility and enrichment in their own lives and the lives of others. Volunteering. Giving back to others. Exercise. Self-care and inner reflection. Many women find fulfillment in bearing offspring and child-rearing. Time outdoors and in sunshine. Community connections and friendships. Self-worth. Independence and freedom financially.

Well, one thing at a time. Let's not get carried away.

I mull this information over, combing the ethers for ideas and examples.

My next search is marital satisfaction. This is a tricky one, too. Fi and I hit most of these indicators. Good communication—the best. Close physical intimacy—that's never been a problem. In fact, I don't like to toot my own horn, but I know just what she likes. I've made a study of it. Next, mutual respect and influence. Letting your partner influence you.

I place my hand on my chin, thinking about this. Respect. Of course I respect her. Do I let Fi influence me? Perhaps I've shied away from this, for fear her decisions wouldn't be as successful as mine. With the great wealth of knowledge I have, my goal has always been to protect her.

But now it hits me.

I have an idea of how I can give Fi what she's after. All of it. Happiness. Contentment. Influencing me.

And truthfully, this is something I've been wanting, too. My desire is to leave a lasting impression on this earth. To sow the seeds of greatness and watch them grow.

And I know just the person to ask for assistance.

I smile, pleased with this new direction, as I place the call.

7

FIONA BYRNE

Exiting Dr. Palmer's office, I push open the door and step outside. The day is cool and brisk. I smile to myself, invigorated.

I pull off the white gauze Band-Aid on my arm where they drew my blood. Crumpling it up, I throw it into a waste bin.

Spotting my white sedan, I climb in and shut the door. The relief I feel is powerful. I wish I'd made this appointment sooner, actually. The past six years, it's been hanging over me how that night with Calvin in the lab changed me forever.

My therapist said it was a trauma response, a reaction to running away from my family and the bullying and depression I'd had in high school. Maybe I was so shaken up by the events that I created a false narrative in my head: I'm flawed. Defective. Altered in some freakish way.

I hadn't told the therapist the truth about Calvin, though. I never told her about waking up in the lab, what Calvin had said to me about it. His final message.

Perhaps this is what Calvin wanted to do—to mess with my well-being. He planted the seed of doubt and let it fester.

Or, worse, I really was altered and not human anymore. I believed him.

I wasn't about to explain all of that to a therapist, though.

All of that worry. Six years of doubt. Remedied with a single specialist visit. I want to skip with joy.

There's a small niggle of doubt that creeps back in and threatens to put a damper on my joy. I can almost hear Calvin saying, *"There's still something wrong with you."*

I shake that away. The nurse said I will have no problem conceiving. This is cause for celebration.

As I drive past my favorite local sandwich shop, my stomach rumbles. I decide to pop in and grab a turkey wrap and hot, foamy latte.

I park in a spot out front and grab my purse. When I swing open the door beneath a black-and-white-striped awning, the scent of coffee and the sound of the espresso machine humming welcomes me. The floors are light oak, and the walls have greenery. It's an eclectic, modern vibe.

The shop is buzzing with the lunch crowd. Most tables are dotted with people eating sandwiches, others typing on their laptops or sipping coffee. There are a few people forming a queue. I get in line behind a girl with a ponytail standing with her mother, pointing to a cinnamon roll in the bakery case.

She's got good taste. The frosted roll does look delicious.

I overhear her mother acquiesce. "All right, we'll get you the cinnamon roll for dessert."

The girl hops up and down in delight.

She looks back at me with a grin on her face. I smile back.

That's when I notice who she is.

"Hi, Mrs. Byrne," she says to me.

"Is that you, Daisy?" I open my mouth in surprise. She was one of my students from last year when I was a teaching assistant.

"You've grown taller," I say to her. "How are you liking second grade?"

Her eyes light up. "We're reading a book about bridge trolls who turn out to be nice, and they save the lake monster."

"How exciting."

Her mom smiles, and we exchange greetings. The barista asks her for her order, and he pulls out the cinnamon roll for Daisy, whose attention is now focused back on the bakery case.

"I'm having a treat," she confides, looking up at me as if this is the best news she's had all day.

"Very good choice. That looks yummy."

"Do you want to share it with me?"

This is what I love about children. So willing to share even their prized baked goodie. Pure kindness.

"That's very kind of you to offer. But I want you to have it. And I'll get myself a treat, too, how does that sound?"

She bounces up and down again, and her ponytail bobs as she does a little twirl in reply.

Her mom pays. We nod goodbye as her mom grabs their tray and her drink, and they move to find a table.

Suddenly Daisy runs back to me and flings her arms around my waist. And then, just as quickly as she ran up, she darts back to her mom to sit and enjoy her treat.

Still glowing, I place my order to go. By the time I pay and leave a tip, my drink and a white paper bag with my wrap are ready.

Back in my car, I place my drink in the cupholder, and my sandwich on the passenger's seat. Daisy was a great student, always curious and attentive.

Maybe seeing her is a sign. I wonder what it would be like to have a daughter of my own. A child like Daisy to share every day with.

The doctor visit today has given me fresh hope that Tyler and I will be able to conceive. And soon. It's just a matter of time. I hadn't felt totally ready to be a mom before, but that's shifting. The relief I felt at the doctor's office was revealing. Now that I know I can have a child, the idea is more and more appealing.

I bite my lip, considering. Some of the kids I teach can be pretty bratty. I think of a few particularly tough students and frown, considering what life would be like if my own child were like them. I dismiss this thought, though, as I can't imagine my own kids would be like that. Tyler and I will be able to raise our boy or girl to avoid such bad habits and poor dispositions. Most kids are nice. Look at sweet Daisy. My child will be like that.

Now I'm really getting into the idea.

I'm going to be someone's mommy; watching my baby's first steps, dressing them up for special occasions. Walks in the park and trips to the zoo. Teaching them to read. I picture getting warm hugs every day, tucking my little one into bed. All of it.

Tyler will be a great dad. He's always joking around with his nephews and playing ball with them.

And my mom would go nuts to be a grandma. Both of my parents would be doting. They don't push it, but I know they had been delighted we'd moved nearby in hopes they'd be closer to their grandkids someday.

Driving back, I wonder what time Tyler will be home from work tonight. I'm always ahead of him, as my school is out at 2:30 p.m., and he works until 5:00 p.m., but it can vary a little bit.

I took a half day off from work for this appointment, so I have all afternoon open. I'll swing by our local market and grab supplies to cook a nice meal for us. I'll dig out my mom's chicken risotto recipe, with grilled asparagus. And a bottle of wine.

We'll have a special dinner, Tyler and I, where I can share the good news.

8

FINLEY VINCENT

The only way to survive when you're locked in a room by yourself, with no access to the outside world, is to set a schedule. And stick to that schedule like your life depends on it.

Because if you let time escape you, ticking away with no sense of purpose, you will wither away. Your mind will fold. Game over.

I'm well aware of the ample supply of small white pills that Calvin leaves me in the mirrored medicine cabinet. I could probably take enough to end it all.

Instead, I focus on what's in my control: my schedule.

The first item on my morning agenda is making breakfast. Calvin has installed a wood-paneled minibar with a small refrigerator—what foresight he had to know I'd have use of such a breakfast bar. At the very least, he has kept it stocked with food—fresh fruit, bread, cold cuts, cheese, bottled water. In the cabinets, there's a coffeemaker, toaster, plates, and utensils.

On this morning, I've prepared a hard-boiled egg and buttered toast. I eat slowly, savoring each bite, and gaze out the window. There's a red cardinal that's made his home in the large tree directly in front of my window. One of his legs is larger than the other, and I wonder what caused this. He seems happy, though, hopping around and looking for seeds.

After piling my empty plate onto the tray, I leave it by the locked door.

Calvin will come at the end of the day to take out my plates before he settles in for the night.

Heading to the wood desk in the corner of the room, I sit and take out a lined notebook and pen. I make it a point every morning to do some journaling. I can't exactly write my full feelings, because Calvin will read it and that's obviously not good. But I write about observations. My surroundings, nature. Philosophy. I'll comment on whatever book I'm reading. I started to write my own stories, too. Mythical stories about different lands, with a heroine who is lost, far away from home, on a quest to defeat an evil presence threatening the land.

When my hand starts to ache from writing, I close the notebook and place it in the desk. I change into soft leggings and a sports bra and runners. I have a small AM/FM radio that plays a few stations, and I flip it on to the channel that plays the most upbeat songs I could find, mostly 80s and 90s pop. The announcers probably at one time would have been annoying, but at this point, their company is longed for. They feel like friends.

The channel has the clearest reception but still crackles occasionally. I sit and position my legs in front of me, stretching outward with my hands. For my workouts, I do my best to re-create the barre workouts I've done in the past.

Calvin and I were at a beautiful hotel in London four years ago, where I attended a barre class at the hotel spa and fitness center. It was my first time getting into working out since I'd been with him, and it was life-altering.

It reminded me of when I used to dance ballet, when I was younger, back at home. And during the class, while my body was moving, it made me feel like I was my old self again. The woman leading the class, a fit, wide-eyed woman in her thirties, had talked about the endorphins that are released when we exercise. A feel-good chemical, she called it. I noticed a difference right away. Calvin must have too, because it was one of the only activities he'd encourage me to go do on my own.

Using the wooden bureau as my barre, I place my hands on it and lift my leg behind me. I do three reps of ten on each leg. A favorite song comes on about walking on sunshine. It's one that this station seems to play on heavy rotation, and I turn it up and dance. Throwing my hands up, I move back and forth, waving my arms. It's ridiculous, but as the song says, it's starting to feel good.

Next, I get on the floor. Leg lifts. Push-ups. Sit-ups. The steady stream of music and intermittent chatting from the DJs keeps me going. Once in a while, I laugh out loud. I find myself replying to them, as if I'm part of their conversation.

After I've worked my body until my arms and legs shake with exhaustion and I can do no more, I move to the bathroom and bend down to turn on the porcelain claw tub, filling it with water as I undress.

The bathroom is light and airy, one of the least creepy areas of the entire house. It has a Carrara marble mosaic floor, and next to the bathtub is a glass-door shower, the walls tiled in textured limestone with brass inlay, and double shower heads.

I find some lavender- and vanilla-scented bubble bath and sea salts that I drop in, filling the bathroom with a delicious aroma.

Inhaling, I recall where we bought these soaps. In Siena, Calvin and I had visited a boutique shop, the air thick with heavenly scents. I'd loaded up on bath products, from which I chose one now. The scent reminds me of Italy, and as I step into the tub and sink into the water, I try to imagine I'm there now.

This is one of my favorite times of the day. There's a window that overlooks the front roundabout and beyond it the grassy lawn, trees, and the black gate. I can see my friend the red cardinal at the poplar tree.

The road beyond our gate is not well trafficked. Though I can't see the road from my window view, I know it's there, and I hardly ever hear cars going by. The occasional loud truck rumbling by is the most I've heard. Still, I listen, hoping I'll hear something of interest.

The warm water encases me. The bathroom is enough of a change of scenery that it refreshes my mind. Sometimes I'll read in the bathtub, or play the radio some more. Today, I let my mind wander to ways to escape.

When the hot water turns cold and my feet turn wrinkly, I wrap myself in a white cotton towel.

This is when the day begins to get harder. As the sun sets and dusk sets in, a visit from Calvin is imminent, and I never know how this exchange will go.

Throughout the day, I try to formulate questions I'll ask him. To keep him engaged. He seems to be content when he's talking and feels that my questions show I care about him.

While I wait for him to visit, I dress carefully, taking time to choose an outfit he'll approve of. He likes expensive fabrics, so I choose a floral-print poplin mini-dress. It fits like a glove.

Now there's nothing to do but wait for him.

I grab a book. We visited a local bookstore last week, where I'd bought about a dozen novels, which mercifully have entertained me over the past week. Or has it been two weeks?

I crawl into the king-size bed with my book, pulling the thick comforter up to my chin. I keep the nightstand light on next to me, the soft glow offering a small degree of comfort.

My eyes are getting sleepy as I read, and I am almost about to doze off when I hear footsteps in the hallway. The steps stop at our door.

Setting the book down, I jump out of bed and quickly straighten my dress and smooth my hair. That's when I hear the click of the deadbolt unlock.

He's here.

9

FINLEY VINCENT

"There's my girl." Calvin flashes a dimple as he grins. He enters our room with long, confident strides and kisses me on the cheek. "I'm preparing dinner for us," he says.

"That's so sweet of you."

"Why don't you change into something special, and come down for dinner?" His eyes flick over the poplin mini I've chosen. "How about that long black dress you wore to the Dubai Opera? The one with the beading and lace."

"Great idea," I say, weak with relief.

He's going to let me out. Finally.

I've lost track of what day it is. My best guess is that I've been confined to my room for ten days. Maybe eleven.

"Get yourself dolled up. Dinner will be at six p.m."

He turns on his heels to go. He leaves the door open behind him.

I'm free. The urge to run out the door and after him is strong, but I resist. Instead, I turn to the walk-in closet.

Sorting through my meticulous racks of clothes, which I've had plenty of time to organize, again and again, I pull out the black dress he described. I stroke the beads of the gown and carefully lift it over my head and let it drop down to my ankles, the delicate shoulder straps holding it in place. I pull up the zipper in the back. It still fits nicely, and I let out a sigh of relief, knowing he'll be pleased with how it looks.

I sit down at the vanity. I apply eyeshadow carefully to my eyelids, sweeping shades of brown and gold into the creases to bring out their green color. I line my eyes with a charcoal-colored pencil and then coat my lashes with mascara. Next, I pull out my lipstick and trace my lips with the red hue.

I do my best to replicate the makeup tutorial I received in Paris, when Calvin had taken me to Champs-Élysées on one of our stays. When we attend events together, his desire is that I not only fit in with the other beautiful women, but that I stand out as one of the most beautiful among them. The cosmetic consultant had tutored me about which colors would highlight the gold flecks in my green eyes, and how to create a higher cheekbone with contouring.

Next had been my hair salon visit at the Spaggo spa. A young woman with thickly arched eyebrows had colored my honey-brown hair with strands of lighter blond. She blow-dried my hair with a large roller brush and then curled it into large waves that framed my face.

Pulling out my hairbrush, I comb it through my hair and use my curling iron to place a few gentle waves that surround my face, as she'd shown me. Lastly, I secure one side of my hair with a jeweled clip.

I study my face in the mirror. There's sorrow in my reflection, but I hold my head high.

Satisfied that I look presentable for Calvin, I slip on a pair of black heels.

I'm ready to leave the room, and if I never returned it would be too soon.

I pause at the doorway, glancing back at the bathroom where the little white pills are kept. The bottle is still full. I remind myself I don't need to bring them with me like I used to. I've managed, during my time in seclusion, to resist them. It won't help me to take one now. The fuzzy, floating feeling will slow my reactions and dull my senses.

As I make my way into the dark hallway, I go as quickly as my heels and long gown will allow, passing through the narrow, claustrophobic space. A shiver runs down my spine as I move past the closed bedroom doors lining the hallway. I get the sense, now more than ever, that there's something insidious in this house.

I step with care down each stair, careful not to trip on the length of my gown, clutching tightly at the shiny wood banister.

In the foyer, darkness blankets the entryway. The lighting in this house is minimal, at best. But for this evening, Calvin has turned off all of the lights in the formal dining room. The table is lit by over a dozen tall candles and large candelabra in the center of the dining table.

Calvin's seated at the head of the table. He stands to greet me with a kiss on each cheek. We're pretending, as always, that everything is okay now; there will be no mention of the time I've spent in seclusion.

His warm hand is on my bare arm, guiding me to my seat.

"You look handsome," I say. He's dressed in a white business shirt, a dark blue sports coat, and khaki pants.

"You're ravishing, my love." He pulls out my chair, at one end of the table, and pushes in the large wood chair when I'm seated. Such a gentleman. In the darkness, I almost roll my eyes, but dare not to in case he catches me in the candlelight.

He sits across from me at the other end of the table.

In front of me is a glass of red wine and a large porcelain plate with dark meat and roasted vegetables. I'm famished, but the smell wafting up is off-putting.

After placing my napkin on my lap, I pick up my fork and a steak knife.

I slice into the meat. The middle is red, and a trickle of blood runs down the plate.

Biting into the meat, I find it's tough to chew, and I have to resist the urge to gag. The flavor is unlike anything I've had before, and not in a pleasant way. It's bitter. Gamey.

From across the table, Calvin is watching my every move. "Do you like it?" he asks.

"Yes, mmm," I lie.

He sits up straighter. "There's nothing like killing your prey with your own hands, and then cooking the food yourself. One of the many pleasures of having a human form." He takes a large bite. I'm not sure if he's tasting the same thing I'm eating.

"Killed it yourself?" I ask.

"Yes. There's been a doe and her fawn trotting around the back garden, eating our vegetation. It only took me two shots." He makes a shooting motion, his blond hair flopping into his forehead.

Suddenly I think I will be sick all over the table. I rush to take a swig of red wine from my glass.

"You killed the mother, or the baby fawn?" I ask evenly.

"The mother," he says. "The little one scampered away. But don't worry, I'll keep an eye out for him next."

The wine sloshes down into my stomach, mixing with the bites of venison I've eaten. I breathe deeply, controlling my instinct to purge.

Calvin has done it again. He's left another creature motherless and alone, just like me. His callousness and pompousness is infuriating. He's proud of it.

I had so looked forward to seeing the deer again out back. Calvin has managed to kill one of the only joys I had in my life.

I bring a small forkful of vegetables up to my mouth and force myself to chew.

My ability to make small talk and ask him questions has abated. I'm so preoccupied with holding my sickness at bay, there's room for little else in my mind.

The silence grows.

Finally, Calvin takes his cloth napkin from his lap and dabs at his mouth. "Satisfying, indeed."

I raise my eyebrows and nod in agreement.

"I've been thinking," he says. "About your request."

I stop chewing. Is he going to get angry again? Hurt me? Lock me back up?

My right hand wraps around my steak knife.

I'm not going back to that room again.

Calvin continues. "And I think it's a fine idea. You can go back and get your certificate in tutoring at the University nearby. It's quite a prestigious institution. And when you've completed your course, you can start tutoring kids. It will help fulfill you."

My mouth drops open. I loosen my grasp of the knife. "Really?"

"Really. On one condition," he says.

There's always a catch. My mood was so quickly lifted only to be deflated again. Naturally it was too good to be true.

"And what's the condition?" I ask.

"Once the baby comes, you will—of course—give up tutoring to care for our child."

10

FINLEY VINCENT

There's no way I'm having Calvin's offspring. The thought stays with me on the freeway and up to the twisty side streets in a leafy affluent neighborhood that abuts the University.

He hasn't mentioned it again since a few weeks ago, at our repulsive venison meal. Maybe it was a fleeting wish he had. How would we have a child, anyway? Is it even possible for him?

I put on my blinker and turn into the long driveway that leads up to the University. The road is lined with tall trees, and there's black light posts every few yards. Up ahead, there are several large brick buildings with turrets and arched entryways. The dogwood trees are in full blossom.

When Calvin agreed that I should sign up for this course, I couldn't believe my luck. Being here now, I still can't. The freedom of being out in the world, driving my car, is exhilarating.

But my nerves are shot. My mind flickers, again, back to that dinner. When Calvin told me he planned to create a baby together with me, the news had been a blow. But my determination to execute my plan had strengthened: I can't procreate with him. No way.

If Calvin finds out what I'm about to do, though, I think he'll kill me.

I used to think he needed me. That he would never actually kill me, just torture me by locking me away. But Calvin has his limits of what he'll tolerate. If I push him too far, his rage will overcome him. I can feel it. And if he misses me that much or regrets it, he'll simply make a DNA replica of me.

What I'm about to do—if I'm caught—would enrage him enough to end my life.

I pull into the student parking lot, where I am stopped at a booth by the gated entrance. A young girl smiles. "Are you a student here?"

"I am," I say.

She gives me a ticket, which I display on my windshield.

"You can park anywhere in the lot that's not designated faculty."

I smile and nod at the girl. She must be a University student, too, and work here part-time. She's probably only a few years younger than I am. I wonder what it would be like to be carefree. To be a regular student. To have a job handing out tickets, or working at the student bookstore.

The parking area is more crowded than I'd expected. Car after car, row after row, the parking spots are full. Luckily I've given myself a little time to find my way around before my class starts. I pull into a spot, finally, then get out of my car and lock it.

I can't help but glance around the parking lot, searching for Calvin. It's rare that he doesn't accompany me wherever I go. Maybe a class in elementary education isn't stimulating enough for his mental superiority. Whatever the reason, thank heavens he isn't here. Then I glance down at my watch and realize he is with me, anytime he wants to be.

I won't let that get in the way of what I've come here to do.

I study the map again and look at the buildings in relation to where I'm parked. Inhaling a deep breath of the fresh spring air, I will myself to move forward with my plan. One step in front of another.

My choice of footwear, white sneakers, was a smart one. It looks like I'll be walking quite a ways. I've worn comfortable wide-leg jeans and a cropped sweater.

As I leave the car park and enter the campus, I find it breathtaking. The walking path is maintained perfectly, not a stray leaf or item of trash to be seen. The green lawns are filled with students milling about, drinking their takeaway coffee and listening to their AirPods as they follow the concrete paths that connect the buildings. It's not quite warm enough to sit and picnic on the lawn, but I imagine as it warms up, students spend a lot of time in the common area.

Consulting the campus map, I identify the humanities building where my class is located. A few yards away, as I continue down the path, I see it. It's a brick building with a gabled archway. Approaching the front of the building, I pause but I don't enter. Not yet.

Instead, I find a bench next to the door and sit down.

Unlatching my smartwatch from my wrist, I search for a safe place to hide it. There are large ceramic containers filled with flowers on either side of the bench where I'm seated, and some rocks surrounding the mulch, a swath of bushes, and a few dogwood trees dotted along the beds.

Taking note of the time, I use my hand to gently push aside a few flowers in the pot to my right, and drop my watch there. No one seems to notice.

Now I'll have to move quickly.

Taking the path back toward the campus square, I look at the map.

My heart is racing, and the map is blurry. Where is it?

Two girls a few paces ahead of me are talking, and the sound of their laughter floats back to me. I overhear bits of their conversation.

"And then he posted a TikTok of him doing the dance routine with two of his friends at the football game we were at, and it got like a million views," one of them says.

The other one gasps, and I hear her reply, "What a way to end a date. Are you going to see him again?"

The other girls laughs. "Sure, I mean, we'll see what happens."

Momentarily distracted, I envy their carefree banter and their friendship.

I skip a few paces to catch up with them. Reaching out my hand, I tap the shoulder of the girl on the right. She swings her long dark hair and looks at me, a smile still on her face.

"Excuse me," I say.

I come up closer next to them, so she's in the middle now. Both girls are looking at me curiously.

"Do you know which way the Graduate School of Arts and Science building is?" I wave my map. "I'm a bit lost."

"Oh, yeah." The girl in the middle points up ahead. "The building on the right, way up there, just past the square fountain."

"Thank you so much," I say, and mean it.

They continue on their way, and I pick up my pace in the direction of the arts and science building. I steel my resolve and remind myself that there may not be many chances to do this.

As I get closer to the fountain, the letters on the building become clearer and I'm able to read the sign. I've found it.

The arts and science building is a newer-looking structure made of brick, with an enormous wall of windows climbing all the way to the top floor.

Swinging the heavy glass door open, I step inside.

My heart is beating so loudly, I wonder if it will echo in this large, acoustic entryway. It's a massive space, with clean lines and a clear staircase circling up to the floors above. The students that I observe move with purpose. The rooms are made of glass walls, and inside I see students sitting at computers. Another room I pass has a lecture in session, with a teacher standing at the podium, rows of students listening attentively and watching the slideshow on the large screen projector.

In the center of the building is an information desk, and this is where I head.

A young man looks up from his black laptop monitor when I approach. "May I help you?"

"Yes." It comes out as almost a whisper.

This is the type of state-of-the-art facility that would definitely have CCTV cameras all over to protect all of their equipment. If Calvin chose to search for me, he could access the footage at any time in the next forty-eight hours to a week, or more, and view this conversation.

What are the odds he'll be looking for me, though? I'm still going to attend my tutoring certification course. He'll see me there, if he checks. If I hurry here and make it there on time.

My pulse quickens. I can do this.

"Where is your EECS department, specifically AI?" My words come out rushed, tangled.

"Electrical engineering and computer science is level three. The EECS artificial intelligence department faculty head is Dr. Solomon. Third floor."

"Thank you." I spot the elevator and rush over. I push the button and tap my fingers impatiently. The stairs would be faster, but they're in such plain view, winding up and up, I'd feel more vulnerable to the cameras there.

The button dings, and I step inside the small elevator. I push the button for the third floor and wait. When the doors shut, a claustrophobic feeling overwhelms me. I'm trapped and can't get out. My breathing becomes shallow.

After what seems like an eternity, the elevator pings and the door mercifully slides open.

The third floor is massive. The classrooms are half full of students. I scan the floor and see a row of doors with plaques of names, and I assume that must be the faculty quarters. I hurry over there.

My hands are damp with perspiration.

"Dr. Solomon," I say out loud as I spot his name on the second door to the right.

I approach the door and knock swiftly with two loud raps.

There's no reply.

I tap on his door again.

This can't be happening. He's not here. I've risked so much, and he's not here.

I scan the classrooms. Maybe he's teaching right now. I could come back after my class and try to locate him.

But that's adding additional time that I don't have. Calvin will be paying attention. He'll notice.

Frowning, I again survey each classroom through their glass windows, wondering which lecture Dr. Solomon might be leading. There's no identifying information other than numbers on each room entryway. I walk toward the first lecture area I see.

Peering through the window, I observe a man with salt-and-pepper hair speaking emphatically about something and pointing to a numerical sequence on his screen. I search for his name, or the class name, something identifying, but it's no use.

I'm totally lost.

Turning back around, I almost bump into a young man.

"Whoa, sorry," he says, adjusting the strap on his shoulder bag. "Are you okay? Can I help you?" he says, leaning in slightly. He regards me with an appreciative smile that conveys he can't quite believe his luck in having bumped into me.

"Yes, actually. Do you know Dr. Solomon? Where I can find him?"

His eyes grow wider. "I know him," he says with a look I can't quite read. "He's not in until lunchtime, usually. And then he runs us ragged until all hours of the night."

I think he's making a joke, but all I hear is that Dr. Solomon won't be in until lunchtime. I curse inwardly. My class is over at 11:00 a.m. How will I ever make the timing work to meet him?

Defeated, I nod. I start to move away back to the elevator.

"Hey," the young man calls to me. "What do you need from Dr. Solomon? Maybe I can help, since I'm his doctoral student?"

I turn on my heels.

"You are?"

"Indeed." This makes him hold his head up with pride. His hair is dark, almost black, and he smooths it back with one hand. "I'm a PhD student, and he's my adviser."

I must look confused, because he clarifies, "Department chair, that is." He lifts his hands and smiles. "The big boss man."

My mind races. Can I trust him?

He's a total stranger. But something about the lilt in his voice, the way he slows down some words and says others very quickly, it's endearing. Funny, almost, if I weren't in such a dire circumstance.

He's better than nothing. Maybe? I'll have to take a risk and ask him.

I've practiced the words I want to say. Looking around, I know these words will be a death knell if Calvin ever hears me utter them. I consider writing down what I wish to say, but that won't work either. Calvin would be able to zoom in to read the words displayed on a camera equally as well as he could hear them.

We're in a hallway, and looking up at the corners of the walls, I don't see any cameras. But just to be safe, I turn my back against the main area and face toward the hallway.

"Okay." I take a deep breath. "So, I have a few questions for Dr. Solomon's area of expertise. Maybe you can answer them for me, or point me in the right direction. The first one is: If you knew of a sentient artificial intelligence that did not have altruistic intentions, particularly toward humans, what would be the way you'd dismantle or disable it?"

He looks at me sideways, tilting his head and staring at me. He doesn't say a word. Then he looks around, up at the ceiling. He shifts from one foot to another, and looks down at the floor, his face perplexed.

He sticks his hands in his jeans pockets and then speaks. "My first question would be back to you, how do you know it's sentient?"

"Trust me, it is," I say. There's all kinds of tests and theories about how to tell if AI is sentient or not. I don't have time to get into those with this guy. But there's no doubt that Calvin, unfortunately, is sentient. Very much so.

"Okay," he replies. "Second question. Define 'altruistic intentions'?"

I consider it momentarily. This young man is approaching this like he's in a philosophical debate, whereas I have about five minutes left before I'm in real trouble. "He doesn't care about killing, harming, maiming, or otherwise ending human life," I retort. There. That should convince him.

He nods. "I see. Well..." His brow is furrowed in concentration as he speaks. "There's several ways I could approach the problem. Some better than others." He laughs to himself as if he's made another joke. Then he squints and appraises me, meeting my eyes. "Why? Is this a hypothetical question, or...something else? Like, a real situation?"

He's trying to gauge what my angle is here. He's probably wondering who this girl is and what she really wants.

I falter, unsure if I should tell him the truth.

Despite how random this must all sound to him, he's taken the time to listen. And something about the way he talks, it makes me want to hear more. Maybe it's a quiet confidence, or intelligence, I'm picking up on. Whatever it is, I feel I can trust him.

Not that I have the best track record in trusting my instincts. I bite my lip.

And I haven't been around a regular student in ages.

I glance at the clock on the wall. Four minutes until my class starts. I jump in.

"As impossible as it sounds, it's a real situation. I have money I can pay you if you can help develop a plan to take this thing down."

His eyes narrow, and I can tell I've lost him. He's suspicious of me now.

He looks around uncomfortably. "Whoa. Hey. I don't want your money." His voice is firm. He looks up at me as if he wants to see something in me that may not be there. A connection, maybe? Is he hoping for a date?

"But I have to pay you for your time, to make it fair," I say.

He frowns deeply. He's looking at me as if I'm asking him to do something illegal.

Is it illegal? Unethical?

I feel my face redden with embarrassment. Probably offering him money right off the bat sent his alarm bells ringing. He's just an honest, earnest doctoral student. Wants to earn his degree and go on with his life. He doesn't need this complication.

I'm desperate for help, but how could I expect him to understand? Either way, I can tell I approached this all wrong; he's checked out.

"I shouldn't have bothered you," I say. "I'm sorry. Don't worry about it." I turn to go, but with each step I take, the weight of failure hits me, and I know I have to try one last time. Turning back around, I face him.

"It's just, I don't know who else to ask." I feel a lump in my throat.

His face softens. He feels sorry for me. "I mean, you don't have to pay me," he says. "I want to help, but I need to understand what you're talking about."

I look at the clock again. "I have to go now, but yes. I can tell you more. It just has to stay between you and me."

He nods. "I understand."

"Can we meet back here at 9:30 a.m. next Thursday, same place?" I say.

"Sure. Meet me here, and I'll bring coffee. There's a conference room we can use across the way."

"Thank you. I'll see you Thursday," I say and turn to go. I have two minutes before class starts.

"Hey, what's your name?" he calls after me.

"Fiona," I call back over my shoulder. My mouth parts into a smile. I haven't used my real name in five years.

"I'm Eric," he calls. "Nice to meet you. See you next week."

Heading to the stairs—no time for that elevator—I feel something close to hope.

11

FIONA BYRNE

Waving to Regan, the last of my students to depart, I watch as she climbs onto bus number nine. Her large purple backpack disappears. Another successful day in room six.

I smile at Mr. Chelms, the gym teacher, and wave at Mrs. Amy Bandera, who joins me as we stroll back into the brick building, both having deposited our pupils safely onto the buses.

She clasps my arm. "I have to go see Nurse Peyton and write an incident report," Amy says. "Phillip threw up all over the rug during reading time."

"Ew." I wince. "Sorry. That's rough." I scan her khaki pants and sweater vest. "Doesn't look like any got on you, so there's that."

"I've had the worst luck with sickness lately. Last week, half the class was out with strep. The week before there were three cases of pink eye. Anyway, book club this weekend? See you there?"

Amy's been hosting her book club that doubles as a wine night for the past several years she's been at Hazelfield Elementary. When I joined the staff last year as a teaching assistant, I didn't know her too well, but I could tell she was well liked by all the staff and students. This year, I was brought on as a full-time teacher. Amy and I are both teaching second grade, and our classrooms are next door to one another. "Roommates," she'd called it, dropping off a welcome note on the first day. After a first few months chatting each day at lunch, she invited me to join her book club. I was in.

"Definitely," I say. "I finished the book a few weeks ago. I'll bring prosecco."

"Super. See you then." She waves and rolls her eyes as she heads to the nurse's office.

The hallways have emptied out and only the staff remain. I love this time of day, when the afternoon sunshine sifts through the windows and a hush falls over the classrooms.

I head back into my room, thankful that none of my students have vomited. In fact, the school year has been going really well. We've been working on our clovers unit this month, in honor of St. Patrick's day. We planted clover three weeks ago, and today we had the pleasure of combing through the sprouts and looking for a four-leaf clover. We didn't find any.

I explained to the kids it was a rare event. The odds of finding a four-leaf clover were one in five thousand to ten thousand. I gave the example that if there was a giant stadium filled with ten thousand green tennis balls and one single red tennis ball, and you get to select one ball from the whole arena, the odds of you finding a four-leaf clover are similar to the odds of you picking the red ball. I said it's unlikely that your one ball you choose happens to be the only red ball in the stadium. My students' eyes had registered understanding. It made sense, then, that our small clover patch, unfortunately, didn't have a great shot of producing a four-leaf clover.

That's the funny thing about odds. We humans aren't great about estimating the probability of something happening—or not happening—to us.

I sit down at my desk. The next science project we're working on is the life cycle. We're going to get class tadpoles and watch them metamorphosize. They start as eggs, then grow into tadpoles, and then two-legged froglets, and eventually four-legged frogs. Their odds aren't great, either, poor little guys. Only about one in fifty frogspawn survive in the wilderness.

But we'll do everything to make sure the conditions are ideal for producing life in our classroom tank.

After I prep my lesson plan about the tadpoles, it's time to check the social studies homework. Correcting the questions of the day makes me laugh as I read the various spellings of *legend*. We'll review how to spell it again tomorrow.

Finally, I take out a stack of math worksheets. The first paper on the pile is from BJ, a boy in my class who is struggling, more and more, to pay attention. I've talked to both of his parents about strategies to help him, but I think he may benefit from a referral to our math specialist. He grapples the most with numbers, and in our latest subtraction unit these past few weeks, I notice him looking everywhere but at me. Sometimes when a student is overwhelmed, they totally check out rather than try and possibly fail. I pick up my pencil and make a note on a pink sticky note to contact Mrs. Velasquez, our math specialist, to give him a referral for an evaluation.

Stretching out my arms, I yawn. I have a few more papers to review, but my eyes feel tired. Maybe it's time to pack up and head home for today. I can finish this tonight or tomorrow. I pull out my cell phone from my desk, where I keep it hidden and muted during school hours.

I have a few messages and one missed call and voicemail from a number I don't recognize. The missed call definitely isn't from Tyler or any of my friends, and they would have messaged me anyway. The only people who usually leave voicemails are my parents and appointment confirmations.

Dialing into my message box, I hear a woman's professional voice on the other end of the line. "Hello, Fiona, this is Alston Internal Medicine Physicians. Dr. Palmer would like to speak with you about your test results. Please call our office between the hours of nine a.m. and five p.m. at (409) 555-1055. Thank you."

My stomach drops. What could the doctor need to speak with me about? It's not good news, that's certain. Doctors don't call with good news. Do they?

I'm torn. On one hand, I want to call back right away and find out what's going on. On the other hand, I'm still at work. Not that anyone would try to hear my private conversation in my classroom, but if someone was right in the hallway, they could overhear. My "roommate" Amy may still be at the nurse's office filling out the report, or she could be gone for the day. But she could also pop her head in at any moment. I look at my phone, considering. If the news is upsetting, I don't want to have to risk being flustered and walking through the hallways and parking lot, where I'll surely see my coworkers.

I tap on my phone screen, ready to dial, but hesitate.

Plunking my phone back into my purse, I grab my water bottle, bag, and shuffle the last of my papers into my carrying case.

Normally I take the time to tidy and organize my desk before I leave for the day. It's soothing, to have everything in its proper place. Pencils sharpened, stapler refilled.

Today I couldn't care less. The clutter doesn't matter. I knock over a few books on our reading nook as I hoist my bag over my shoulder.

Barreling down the hallways, I wave and briefly nod at Mrs. Kelty, the art teacher, who's hanging up artwork in the corridor. I keep my eyes down to avoid her striking up a conversation.

Bursting through the heavy doors of the school, I scan the parking lot for my car. Half of the cars are already gone; it's emptied out considerably from this morning when I couldn't find a spot. That reminds me that I parked in the back overflow lot this morning. "Gosh darn it," I mumble, and walk so quickly it's almost a jog around the back of the building, past the playground, into the overflow lot.

My white car is there, just as I left it this morning. When I get in, I slam the door closed and lock it. My hand shakes as I push the button to start the ignition.

Pulling out my phone, I try to call the office, but the call won't go through. My cell reception is always spotty out here, and I curse as I drop the phone onto the seat. I'll have to try again when I get home.

I check my review mirror and put my car into reverse, making my way out of the parking lot. Our home is only about a twenty-minute ride through side streets, and on a pretty day like today, the drive usually flies by.

Instead, every moment ticks by like an hour. I hit a red light, and then an oncoming car cuts me off, turning left at a green light in front of me.

When I take my turn to pull forward, I find myself behind a garbage truck. Just great.

The truck makes two stops, and I realize I need to pull around it, otherwise I'll be here all night. I crane my neck to make sure there's no oncoming cars. The last thing I need is to crash head-on into another car. In my frazzled state, I can totally see it happening.

Looking carefully in front of and behind me, I drive around the garbage truck and pass it safely. Up ahead, I see a little boy on his lawn kicking a soccer ball. He stops and waves at me. I look closer to see if he's a student of mine. But he's younger than my second graders. He may be a pre-K student at the school, or maybe just a friendly little guy. I scan to see if his mother's around, but I drive by without seeing any adults.

I worry that maybe I should go back for him. But he's probably fine in his yard, his mom right inside, or on her way out. And it's not like he was running into the road. He seemed to understand to stay out of the street. Doesn't he?

That huge garbage truck is heading his way.

Glancing back in my rearview mirror, I see the boy's tiny form heading back toward his house. I let out a sigh of relief and continue driving.

The rest of my ride is uneventful. I turn on music, and then find it annoys me, so I flip off the sound and ride in silence the rest of the way.

Dr. Palmer would like to speak with you about your test results. The message is all I can think about.

Finally I turn on my blinker to turn left onto my street, Maplehurst Way. The street we live on is full of young families. I wave at a mom with a toddler playing with a hula hoop in their front yard. The mom's auburn hair is pulled into a ponytail, and she's wearing a blue plaid shirt, and she waves back at me. Celia, I think, is her name. There've been a few neighborhood gatherings, and I recall I chatted with her and her husband and met their little girl.

Our home comes into view. I grip the steering wheel nervously as I pull in. I drive into our one-car garage—Tyler is a gentleman to give the spot to me—and park in the narrow space. My nerves have made my aim a disaster today, and I can hardly open my car door. I squeeze through, narrowly making it, and shut the door behind me. Rushing to the side entrance, I fiddle with my keys.

Inside, I drop my belongings on the side console. Fishing out my phone, I hit the call-back number to my doctor.

Kicking off my shoes, I perch on the window seat. My leg bounces up and down as I wait for an automatic machine to give me a series of options. My mind is racing, and I push 0 to speak to an office staff about a medical issue.

"Hello, Alston Internal Medicine, how may I assist you?"

"Hi, this is Fiona Byrne. I got your message about my bloodwork and am returning the call to Dr. Palmer. Is he available?"

There's a hush on the phone for a moment. "Fiona Byrne. Yes." She sounds like she knows exactly who I am.

Have they been expecting my call? Discussing me?

"I'll let Dr. Palmer know you're on the line and will transfer you to him momentarily," she says.

"Thank you."

After what feels like forever being on hold and listening to music on the other end of the line, I hear a male voice.

"Dr. Palmer here," he says. "Is this Fiona Byrne?"

My stomach is fluttering. "Yes, hello. You wanted to speak about my blood test results?"

He clears his throat. "Yes. I've reviewed your results and consulted with my team, as well as with another colleague at the hospital." Dr. Palmer is the top physician at a prominent hospital, and he also is a fellow and lecturer at the University. Him consulting with fellow doctors sounds ominous.

"I'd like to have you come in and redo your bloodwork. The results we've been looking at...well. We believe there may have been an anomaly in your testing. An error, or contamination. Because the numbers do not add up. If a young person of your age truly had this bloodwork, you'd be—" He hesitates, and doesn't finish his sentence.

"I'd be what?" I say, barely breathing.

"You wouldn't be alive. Or at least not a human as we know it." He coughs uncomfortably. "Of course, that is impossible, so there's been a mistake. I apologize for this, and assure you this is highly unusual for our lab to make this type of error. We pride ourselves on the highest level of medical oversight and responsibility."

My ears feel like they're ringing. As the doctor is speaking, images from that night flash before me. There's a glass encasement. Pain. Searing pain. I was so disoriented when I awoke in the lab, and in such agony.

There's a hard knot in the pit of my stomach. My instinct is telling me that the error isn't in the blood tests. The problem is within me.

12

FINLEY VINCENT

When I pull up to the gates of our house—*estate* or *mansion* are more accurate names for it, but I don't like the sound of those words—I come to a halt. I realize I don't know the code.

When we have a delivery to the house, Calvin buzzes drivers in through the gate. I hop out and push the call button.

Now more than ever, I'm tempted to take a white pill to calm down my heart beating out of my chest. I can't afford to signal to Calvin that I'm lying. But I need my wits about me, I remind myself. Those pills are a form of control Calvin has over me. Blunting my emotions, dulling my mind.

Instead, I count to four as I breathe in, and count to four again as I exhale slowly. In, out. I picture the face of my mom, and it calms my pounding heart.

"Fi?" Calvin's voice crackles over the intercom.

"Yes, it's me."

"About time."

The gates lurch apart and then drag open. The estate looks more ominous than ever in contrast to the serenity at the University.

I drive forward through the gates, but stop short. My palms are slick against the wheel. For a moment, I think I should run. If Calvin knows what I did, what I talked to Eric about, I'll die in this house.

I look in the rearview mirror. The gates slide closed behind me.

Getting out and running would be an option. But with no car, where would I go? And Calvin would just hunt me, find me, and then kill me, along with my family.

If I go to him now, there's a chance he won't murder my family, too.

And there's a chance that I'll get away with it.

After I park in the roundabout, I grab my bag and continue my deep breathing. I get out of the car and hoist my bookbag over my shoulder. As I walk to the front door, I see my friend the red cardinal on the steps to our entrance. The cardinal looks at me and hops a few steps closer. I think he's telling me something. He bounces around and nods his head in frantic motions.

I have to go in, little guy, I think to myself, watching the bird venture closer to me, his thicker leg hopping just as quickly as his thin one.

I unlock the front door, the sound of the heavy wood creaking and groaning as I open it. I hear the door shut firmly behind me. Despite the bright sunshine outside, the house does not feel like spring inside. The dark-wood-encased high ceilings feel like an eternal winter tomb.

Walking through the house, I try to appear casual. I spot Calvin in the main living area. He's seated on the leather couch, in the dark, staring straight ahead. It always unnerves me when he's like this. In public and around me, he engages and blends in normally with his behaviors. When he's alone, he allows an otherworldly utter stillness to descend on him.

He spots me immediately as I enter the room, my shoes squeaking on the floor. He rises to greet me, kisses my cheek. I hug him with all of the affection I can muster.

"What are you up to?" I ask.

He waves his hand. "Evaluating the micro futures markets for some trades I'm planning." Calvin doesn't need to sit in front of a computer to do this; he is the computer. "Damn." His eyes look straight ahead, and I can tell by the crease in his brow he's focused on something.

He shakes his head one final time and then turns his attention to me. "How was your class?" he asks.

He motions for me to have a seat, and I sink into a deep leather chair next to him.

"Calvin, it was amazing." And it's true. Seated in that classroom, with the other students, taking notes and doing small group exercises, it was the first time I'd felt normal in years. It's where I belong. Not at swanky fundraisers for multinational corporations. Not on a yacht in Lustica Bay of Montenegro with seedy men and their nighttime companions. Not shut away in a hotel room overlooking the ocean.

You can be in the most beautiful place, but when you're alone in the world, and have no purpose, it's empty.

But in class, it was different. We all introduced ourselves and said why we were there. The teacher, Professor Grenier, then reviewed the syllabus and goals for the certificate. I was so absorbed, and excited by the prospect of having an elementary education certificate that would allow me to tutor and teach, that I'd almost forgotten about my detour to meet Eric.

Almost.

Quickly pushing thoughts of Eric away, I tell Calvin about my class. I recount how Professor Grenier reviewed the syllabus and discussed what we'll be learning, and how we'll have an exam every four weeks.

"There's going to be a lot to study. Probably a few hours a day. But I've always loved studying—hence, wanting to be a tutor." My voice is giddy, and I hope that my enthusiasm is all he hears, not a note of hysteria that I worry may creep in.

"That's great." He nods. "You'll have plenty of space and time to study whatever you need here."

"Wonderful. Oh," I finish, "and then, Mrs. Grenier talked about the various kinds of work the elementary education certificate graduates do. Some become substitute teachers in elementary school. Others open their own tutoring business and work for themselves. Some go on to work at SAT or MCAT testing centers."

Calvin looks down at me approvingly. "You're really excited about this, aren't you?" he asks.

I shrug. "I am." Placing my hand over his, I give it a squeeze. "It means a lot to me."

"You really do love children, making a difference in their lives?"

I nod.

"Well, then." He squeezes my hand back, and places his other hand on my cheek lovingly. "You'll be happy about what I planned while you were away."

I feel the color draining from my face.

"And what's that?"

"Two things, really," he says. "First, I've gotten you your first tutoring student."

My mouth drops open.

"What? I'm not even certified yet."

"You're a smart egg. You'll do fine. It's the daughter of one of my co-founders, Richard, at my company. His little girl is struggling with learning to read."

It takes me a moment to process this.

"I'd love to help." I feel my shoulders relax an inch. "What's the last thing?"

"We have an appointment next week with Rebecca. She's the doctor who oversees the clinical trials at VyvexBio. In vitro. She's going to help you have my child."

It feels as if the room has shifted. I think I might be sick.

"Is that possible?"

"Of course." He shakes his head and laughs. "Anything that I set my sights on," he taps his head, "is possible. You really have to think beyond your human notions and conceptions. It's quite limiting."

"I see." It comes out as a whisper. "She knows about you, that you're... you know...not human?"

"No need for her to know that. She knows I can't conceive naturally, so we've developed—I should say, I've developed—a process by which we can code every genetic marker and trait of a person into genetically modified sperm."

Calvin lifts his square jaw proudly as he speaks. "He'll be just like his dad."

My face must be as pale as a ghost. I open my mouth to speak, but nothing comes out.

"Rebecca's very excited about the technology I've helped her develop," Calvin continues. "It's going to make her very, very wealthy when it works. Revolutionary. She's eager to meet you."

Getting up shakily, I long to climb under my covers and hide. To not think about this. A throbbing headache is pounding at my temples. I move to go to our bedroom. Calvin catches me by the arm, and I turn to face him.

"I'm going to rest up before dinner."

"Great." His eyes shine. "We'll go out tonight, to celebrate." He places his hands on my shoulders and peers into my eyes.

"This is what you've always wanted, isn't it? A family?"

I pause, feeling cornered. My answers on the Thistler app. Saying the house is too big for just us. I stifle the urge to tell him I want a family, but not with you.

"I do," I say instead.

"Oh, and Fi?" He towers over me, and his eyes lock onto mine. "One last thing. Don't sit next to that guy again in class. The one with the glasses. I don't like the looks of him."

"Sure," I say vaguely. "I didn't even notice him. But next time, I won't." I look up at him. "You were watching my class?"

"Just checked in. The camera in your teacher's laptop gives a good view of the class. It was dull, though. I didn't listen to much of it."

I pause, waiting to see if there's more. *Did you notice my detour to the science building, with Eric?* I'm so frazzled, I almost say it out loud. But after a few moments, Calvin says no more, and releases his grip.

I make my way through the house to the main entryway, up the dreaded steps, through the hallway, and into our bedroom. My head feels like I'm swimming underwater.

On one hand, I seem to have gotten away with my meeting with Eric. But he's watching. What's worse, he's planning my experimental impregnation.

My legs feel weak as I climb into our four-poster bed. I pull the blanket up around me. After Calvin had first mentioned having a child at dinner a few weeks ago, I'd hoped it was a throwaway comment.

I should have known better. Calvin doesn't say anything without meaning it. If he mentioned having a child, it was naive of me to hope he'd let it go. What Calvin sets his mind to, Calvin achieves. No matter who, or what, he has to destroy.

13

FINLEY VINCENT

I push the doorbell on the front doorstep of Richard Mason's home. The house appears almost as large as Calvin's and my home, with a shiny black door and white columns lining the front of the home.

Straightening my blouse and smoothing down my skirt, I wait for what seems like a long time. They should be expecting me for our first tutoring lesson, but with every passing moment, it seems more and more like no one is home.

My finger hovers over the doorbell. Would it be rude to ring it again? I peer into the window on the side of the entryway, and inside I see a young girl with fine hair cut into a bob. I smile and wave. Her eyes are wide, and she vanishes without a word.

I wait a few more moments, and then finally, the click of the lock sounds and the door is opened.

"You must be Finley." A tan, handsome man with white teeth and slicked-back hair greets me and motions for me to come in. "What a pleasure."

He reaches out his large hand to me, and I shake it. "Nice to meet you, Mr. Mason," I say.

"Please, call me Richard," he says. "My daughter, Emaline, will be so happy to meet you."

I hear beautiful notes wafting through the tall entryway corridor. It's a piano playing a piece I recognize as vaguely familiar. I listen for a moment, and then I know it. Beethoven's Concerto No. 3.

"What beautiful music," I say. "Who plays piano?" I ask him.

"That's Emaline's mother. She's a talented musician." He frowns and pauses, and then shifts to his other foot.

He turns his attention back to me. "So you're Finley who Calvin has spoken so highly of. He says you're a very skilled tutor."

I feel myself blush.

"Your husband, he's quite the impressive young man himself. Innovative thinker, that one. A charismatic leader, too. His technology will be revolutionary." His eyes drift off, as if he's dreaming of all the money and accolades to come in their new business venture.

"That's Calvin," I say with what I hope sounds like pride. "What are your favorite...innovations...he's brought to your company?"

"He thinks big. Scaling up production of the S1Z model. Mass market production to lower costs and bring AI automation to the labor and industry sector, and military and intelligence. For a premium price, of course, at first. And his ability to improve and expand the capabilities of these bots, via machine learning and human interface. He's a remarkable young man. I wouldn't be surprised if you see him on the cover of *Forbes* one day."

The thought makes me shiver inside. Calvin's got this man wrapped around his finger. At what point will these people realize that Calvin is so capable of so much because he's one of the robots he's producing? I don't know what Calvin's long game is with these synthetic companions, but my guess is that it's not for the betterment of society, or anyone, other than Calvin.

I shake my head. "It's unbelievable, certainly."

He looks left and right as if he's sharing a secret. "On the golf course last week, your husband gave me a pointer on my swing. Best round I've shot in years. If I keep playing like this, my handicap is going to be at an all-time low."

Calvin can read anyone's golf game, or tennis stroke, and automatically suggest corrections to improve their performance. It's an easy shortcut he uses to win friends. That, and reading people's voice and tone to detect their emotions. He can mimic people's intonation, make them feel instantly at ease, as if he's on their same wavelength, though he's simply mimicking their vocal mannerisms.

Ready to move on from the conversation about how great Calvin is, I glance around the foyer and up the stairs to the landing. I see no sign of his daughter, the little girl with the bob haircut. "Please, tell me more about Emaline. How can I help?"

He shrugs. "Emaline is a wonderful girl, but her head is in the clouds. She just can't seem to take her studies seriously."

"And how old is she?"

"Six." He frowns and pulls down on his chin with his hands.

He tilts his head. "Come on in, let's have a seat so we can discuss." I follow him into an open living space. There's a white oblong-shaped couch and two modern-looking chairs.

"So." He sits with his legs open and his hands clasped, elbows on his knees. "Emaline has suffered some setbacks this year. Her teacher expressed concern to her mother and me this year about her reading progress. She's just not sounding out words the way she should be. She guesses a word based on the first letter, and she goes too fast. She skips words. She's distracted."

"I see," I say. "And how does Emaline feel about reading?"

He squints at me. "How does she feel about it? I'd say she's resisting it. Avoiding it." He nods his head, his slicked-back hair unmoving. "Do you think you can help?"

I smile at him encouragingly. "I would love the chance to try."

"She's up in her room. Her desk is there, so that will be a good place to work together."

"Great," I say, following him through the house. The sound of the piano has stopped, and I wonder when I'll meet Emaline's mother. She must be nearby.

I clasp my shoulder bag as we climb the stairs. I've brought some books and supplies with me that I think might help me break the ice with Emaline, as well as assess her current level of reading.

Inside Emaline's room is a copious amount of pink. But the room is lush and cozy, like a slice of cake with swirly frosting. It brings back happy memories of childhood for me. I see bay windows with light streaming in through billowy curtains, a soft pink coverlet and pillows, stuffed animals lining the bed. A moon-shaped night light.

Emaline sits at her desk, which seems to dwarf her. She turns around, her brown hair bobbing as she regards us.

"Emaline, this is Finley. She's here to help with reading."

She scoots out of her chair, stands up, and politely holds out her hand.

I bend down and take her small hand in mine, and she gives me a single shake. "Hello, Emaline, it's very nice to meet you."

She studies me attentively.

Her father bounces a few times on his feet and then moves back. "I'll leave you two to it."

I place my bag on her desk. There's a second chair, which I motion to. "May I sit?" I ask her.

"Yes." Her voice is high-pitched and soft, and she moves next to me, her back erect as she sits on her pink chair at the desk.

"Tell me about you. What kind of things do you like?" I ask. We could dive right into reading, but the way she appraises me tells me she might be apprehensive. I want her to know I'm on her side.

"I like my dolls." She points to a large doll that's seated at a table with a teacup in front of her. "And I like to draw." She looks ahead and points to the wall.

On the wall in front of us is a cork board filled with bright images and drawings. Birds perched in trees, flowers dotting the grassy pasture of a farm with a cow and a pig.

"Wow. What lovely drawings. You made all of those?"

She nods enthusiastically.

"I like to draw, too," I say. "I have a red bird, a cardinal, that lives outside of my window. He has one thin leg, and one thick leg. He's very cute. I'll draw him for you."

Her face lights up, her eyes crinkling at the corners. "Why does he have two different-sized legs?"

"A very good question. I'm not sure."

"You'll draw me a picture of him?" she asks.

"Definitely. Next time, I'll bring it."

She nods, pleased. "You have pretty hair." Her eyes rest on my locks, which have grown longer down to my mid-back and lie flat on either side of my shoulders.

"Thank you," I say. "Your hair is very nice, too."

She touches her bobbed strands and smiles.

"Now," I say, pulling out a few books I've brought with me. "Your dad said you might like some help with reading? I thought we could look at a few of my favorite books." I pick up one that's about a unicorn who befriends a little girl.

"Have you read this book before?"

She looks at the cover and shakes her head.

"Why don't we look at it together. I'll read the first page, and you follow along. Then you can try the second page."

She nods.

"I love this book because it's kind of silly, but also sweet. I wonder if you'll like it, too."

She cranes her head to look at the book and scoots her chair closer. "I like the cover," she says.

We work for about twenty minutes. I'm able to get a good sense of her skills and where some of her problem areas might be. To me, it seems that she's very age appropriate in her skills for reading.

And distraction is not a problem. She's as focused as a laser. She's eager to please and listens to my suggestions when I gently offer them. I'm not sure where the disconnect is in what her father or teacher is seeing, versus what I'm seeing.

Maybe little Emaline is feeling too much pressure? From what little I've learned about Richard, he's clearly a caring and attentive father, but I wonder if his desire to excel at everything places stress on Emaline? I consider if I should explain this to Richard. I doubt he'll like the idea of me giving him feedback.

I'm here to tutor her in reading, not tell him how to parent. What do I know about parenting, anyway? I'm overthinking this.

Emaline will benefit from tutoring, bottom line. She'll be an eager student. She's a sweet little girl, and no way would I pass up this opportunity to meet with her weekly. To be away from Calvin and our oppressive, lonely house makes me feel lighter than I have in ages.

And reading together in a fun and positive way can only benefit her.

"I think we did a great job for today." Reaching into my bookbag, I produce a sticker page that has encouraging phrases on each sticker, like "Way to go!" and "super reader" and "I love reading."

I show her the sticker page.

"You've earned this sticker today. Why don't we pick this one that says, 'Excellent reader.'" I hold the page out for her. "You can put it wherever you like."

She excitedly grabs the sticker and places it on the chest of her shirt.

"Very nice," I say.

I stand up and begin to gather my books, placing them back in my satchel.

"Can you come again tomorrow?" she asks.

I bend down so we're on eye level. "I'd love to come again soon. I'll talk to your mommy and daddy, and we'll find a good time to come again. Probably next week."

On the way out, she reaches up for my hand. She gives my hand a squeeze.

My heart melts.

"Let's go find your dad," I say. She nods, and I think both of us feel we've found a new friend.

Leaving the bubble of her pink room, and her sweet voice, I ache to stay a little longer. I'd been lulled into forgetting the harsh reality that I'm facing.

"Until next week," I say.

It's only when I pass by her parents' bedroom via the hallway that I catch a glimpse of Emaline's mother.

Her face is pale and stricken. Her stare catches mine through the narrow opening of her doorway. She shakes her head once and puts her fingers to her lips.

I look away quickly and almost trip as I race down the stairs.

14

FIONA BYRNE

I press end on the phone call with the doctor. My mind immediately goes to that final night with Calvin. He has something to do with my bloodwork. I know it.

The doctor had said it's highly unusual to have an error of this sort. Maybe it wasn't an error. The dreadful feeling that Calvin had indeed changed me, my humanness, has never left since that night.

Images from the facility flash back to me. I've been avoiding thinking about it for so long, but now the memories tumble out in rapid fire. I remember being at the hotel. Calvin had beaten up that awful guy, Sean. But we'd made up, and had slept together. I remember falling asleep in his arms, finally together after so long. My ideal boyfriend had been slightly less predictable than I'd expected, and his violence toward Sean had shocked me.

He'd reassured me he'd never hurt anyone unless it was to protect me, to protect us. I wasn't so sure, but I'd wanted so badly to believe him. Being in his arms felt so good. And I'd sacrificed a great deal to create him. And it had worked. I was in too deep for it not to work.

Then I woke up in agony. Not in our hotel room, but in a glass encasement in the lab, the one I'd used to create Calvin. I was unable to move due to sharp, shooting pain. My extremities felt on fire.

Calvin had given me a shot at some point, I assume to help with the pain. It made me even more groggy and woozy, but it dulled the pain somewhat. I vaguely remember walking back to the hotel room, assisted by Calvin. But the room had been different. My belongings were gone. It was just a regular, bare hotel room.

He'd told me to rest. He'd given me something else, and I'd fallen into a dreamless sleep.

When I awoke the next morning, I'd felt better. Getting up out of the bed, I stretched and moved to the window.

There was a table from room service. I lifted the lid and found eggs, bacon, and waffles. I devoured the meal, realizing I was famished.

Looking around the room, though, everything felt unsettled. Where were my belongings? Where was Calvin? We were supposed to leave today. I finished a glass of orange juice and thought about going down to the lobby to check if Calvin was there. But I didn't have a room key or a phone, so that was a risky move.

After another half an hour of waiting and watching a bad morning talk show, I'd decided if I didn't hear from Calvin in the next ten minutes, I'd just have to risk going down to the lobby. They could provide me another key there.

A knock at my door sounded out. Through the peephole, I saw Calvin.

Opening the door, I embraced him. Seeing his bright blue eyes and his physical presence sent butterflies to my stomach. But there was another feeling there, too. Unease. A new fear of him that I couldn't quite tamp down.

"Fi," Calvin said, entering the room and closing the door behind him quickly. He leaned down and kissed me.

"How are you feeling?" he said, looking me up and down with concern in his eyes.

"I'm okay," I said. "Thank you for leaving breakfast here. Where is all my stuff? Did we switch rooms?"

He didn't answer, but instead walked over and looked at the food I'd eaten, examining the remaining contents on the table.

"Calvin? What happened last night? Why were we back at SynGen?" I said, my voice low.

"Sit down, please," he said, and the tone of his voice had set off alarm bells. Something was very wrong.

"Fi. I need to tell you some things, and you must listen. Things are going to be different now."

I grasped his hand. "I know. We're together. It's going to be fine."

"No," he said sharply. "Not that." He had raked his hands through his blond hair, his biceps lean and strong.

"You and I cannot be. I've called your mom to come get you. I'll wait until she arrives, to make sure you're safe. But then I will leave. And we must not have contact again. It would be catastrophic. For me, and most certainly for you."

"What are you talking about?" I had let go of his hand, hurt.

"Don't make this difficult, Fiona." His eyes had grown darker, reminding me of the look he'd had the night before with Sean.

I'd sat there, stunned.

"But what about us?" I'd felt humiliated, hearing the pleading tone in my voice.

"There is no us. I don't care for you, Fi. It was an act."

I stood up to leave, but was unsteady on my feet. I held onto the bureau to brace myself. "Tell me. What happened to me last night?"

He'd laughed and said that I'd been altered, and the two of us were interconnected now, always.

Then he'd leaned in close, his hot breath in my ear, and said, "You're not a regular human anymore. Be careful."

My face had gone white. "What does that mean?"

Rather than answer me, he delivered his message.

"Your mom will be here shortly. You'll go with her. You will never see me again." He gave me a hard stare. "Do you understand?"

I thought I was beginning to understand. He was betraying me. He had done something awful to me. And, now, he was done with me.

"I do." I looked up at him, hoping to see some compassion in his face. "Calvin, what do you mean when you say I'm not human anymore? I'm freaked out."

"You'll be fine."

The lump in my throat threatened to break. "Why are you doing this?"

"Because I can."

Remembering our conversation brings back my confusion and fear. I'd tried to distance myself from his words, pretend that it was nothing. Just a bad memory. Calvin had tricked me, and his feelings for me were never real. End of story.

I'd pushed down his warnings: how I'd changed. How we were connected. Pretended he hadn't said I wasn't human. To be careful. I'd stashed those memories far, far away. So far down that I'd even started to wonder if they were real.

But, of course, they are. The blood results must be related to this. Not alive, not human. That's me. Calvin warned me.

I'd hoped it was a lie to keep me away from him. That's what he'd wanted, after all: to never see me again.

The hairs on the back of my neck stand up as it dawns on me what I need to do. There's only one person who can make sense of this and help me get my life back. It's risky. But he may be my best shot.

I need to find Calvin.

15

FIONA BYRNE

The clock on the wall tells me I have another hour, at least, until Tyler will be home from work.

My entire body feels cold. Pulling a blanket over my legs, I settle into the couch with my laptop and get to work.

I type *Calvin* into the search bar. I instantly feel foolish. A single first name, with no other information, is not going to glean any helpful information.

Instead, I decide to search social media. I narrow my search by area to Massachusetts, assuming he stayed in the state. And then I narrow down his age group.

I scroll through at least a dozen Calvins. I conjure up his face in my mind, the piercing blue eyes, his perfect bone structure. None of these photos look anything like him. Scrolling, on and on I search, until the last of the Calvins is seen. None of them are my Calvin.

I change the state to New York. No luck. Connecticut. Nope. Maine. California. London. No luck.

I try the other social media sites. My eyes start to glaze over. I don't even know what I'm searching for anymore. But I know I'm not getting anywhere.

Pausing my search, I feel defeated as I close my laptop. Then a dawning sense of paranoia. Will Calvin somehow know I'm searching for him, after he explicitly forbade it? He has a supercomputer for a mind. Will these searches ping in his neural network? An angry Calvin, who now has my location, is the last thing I want.

There's also a sense of disloyalty to Tyler. My husband has been nothing but trustworthy and loving to me. And here I am, looking for an ex that I created on an app, who ditched me and possibly messed up our whole life.

Still, if I'm going to get answers, I need Calvin. This isn't about rekindling an old romance. This is about our future together, mine and Tyler's. Our ability to conceive a child.

I flip my laptop back open. Moving out of social media, I return to the search engine, but this time I use a VPN and anonymous search.

I drum my fingers against the keyboard without typing. Think. Where would Calvin be? What would he be doing?

He had taught himself to play guitar. Maybe he's a musician? I search *Calvin, guitar, musician*, and scroll through the potential hits. None of them are him.

He has an angry streak. I search the police records and criminal database. Not there. He's too smart to get caught, I realize.

What did Calvin want? What drove him?

Well, freedom. He wanted a human form so he could escape the confines of the Thistler app.

Power position. Okay, think. People—or, ahem, in his case, a being—who want power. Where would you go to gain power? Politics?

I type *Calvin* and search words like *political parties, PACs, lobbying*. Nothing.

My frustration is mounting. I'd have better odds searching for a needle in a haystack. I just need to find him. Ask him what's wrong with my blood, and how to fix it.

Think. What else did he want?

I'm about to shut my laptop when it hits me. Me. He wanted me. Love.

I search *Calvin marriage records*.

State by state, I go through the registry, finding all mentions of the name Calvin, searching those couples' full first and last names, and then clicking on the pictures to see if it's Calvin. There are many happy couples with the husband named Calvin; I see them in various wedding photos. City weddings at fancy downtown hotels, weddings outside of beautiful chapels, weddings at barnyards. Vineyards. The beach.

Remembering my wedding to Tyler, I smile. The photo on our mantel is one our photographer took on our day. I'm looking at Tyler and he's smiling down at me, our arms entwined. My hair and makeup were excellent, the dress fit just perfectly. It was one of the happiest days of my life.

My friend Lyla, who was one of my bridesmaids and single, had helped me get ready that morning, before the hair and makeup girl came to our room. "Are you nervous?" Lyla had asked me. "Do you feel ready? Cold feet or anything?"

It was unexpected, but I wasn't nervous to marry Tyler. Excited, yes. But mostly, I was very certain that I was right where I was supposed to be in life.

Looking back at my computer, I want to end this search. It's wrong.

I'm about to log off and delete my search when a name stands out to me. I'll try one more. I hit the button to click on the photo link, and my mouth drops open.

16

FINLEY VINCENT

I'm in our spacious kitchen making a breakfast of eggs and fruit. I crack another egg in the bowl and use a spatula to whip it. Ever since Calvin hunted and served me deer, I've been careful to make sure I'm the one preparing the food. The thought of Calvin's meal, the blood oozing out of the venison, still makes my stomach roil.

I glance out the double windows overlooking the back garden. The sun is rising, and it's getting light out earlier now that spring is in full swing. There's been no sign of the baby deer since Calvin murdered his mother. Every day I look and hope I'll see him, but to no avail.

The garden is coming together and starting to look pretty now. The care and work I've put into cleaning out the weeds and planting new varieties of vegetation is showing. With more sunshine and rain, and new blossoms ready to sprout, it has a lot of potential.

My nerves are jangling this morning. I have my class at the University today. And my secret meeting with Eric.

I dressed this morning with apprehension, pulling on a pair of jeans and a sweater vest. Looking at my own reflection, I saw excitement and nerves staring back at me.

I pour the egg mixture into the pan, and it sizzles against the butter. Quickly I stir the liquid with the spatula to keep it from sticking to the bottom. When the eggs are ready, I slide them onto my plate. I've cut melons, blueberries, and kiwi into a small bowl, which I take out of the refrigerator. I make a cup of coffee in the machine, the hum vibrating the quartz counter.

Balancing the steaming coffee and my plate of food, I bring them to the kitchen table and sit down to eat. Calvin's nowhere to be seen this morning, and I'm thankful for the quiet. Maybe he had an early morning meeting at his company? Or went on one of his walks? His favorite thing to do lately is to go hiking in the woods. He says it's a gift to be one with nature, and to learn in person about the concepts he knows about in theory. It's one thing to know something, it's another thing to touch it with your hand, to see it in person.

And to kill it, I wanted to add. Out of all the horrible things Calvin has done—and the list is long—killing the deer has somehow stood out in my mind as the final straw. It's like it exemplifies all that is wrong with him. I want nothing more than to neutralize him and get away from him.

My heart is racing, and I force myself to calm down. He could be back any minute, and he reads me like a human lie detector, my physiology, my heart rate, my tone of voice. It's annoying and exhausting. And today is not the day for him to become suspicious of me. I need him to not be tracking me as closely as he's able, if I'm going to meet Eric.

The little white pills are still in my purse. I picture them in there, the soft round feel in my hand. The smoothness going down my throat. The immediate spread of relaxation through my body. My thoughts become floating, light things, and the heaviness and fear dissipate. Until I start to come down, of course. And then my jitteriness is ten times worse, my heart-beat racing so fast it might explode.

I haven't taken a pill in three weeks. But I still think about it several times daily. Especially moments like this, when my chest is tight and my whole body is tense.

I take a final bite of my eggs and gulp down my coffee. I'll need to leave here in another thirty minutes if I'm going to make it early enough to meet Eric before class.

Usually Calvin does the passcode to the gate. Last week, when I'd needed to leave to meet Emaline, I couldn't believe my luck when he'd given me the code. The freedom was unprecedented. Still, he knows I won't go anywhere without his consent. The unspoken threat of what he's capable of is always there between us.

Calvin strides through the kitchen entrance wearing a white T-shirt and cargo pants. I place a smile on my face. "You were gone this morning when I woke up," I say.

He grins mischievously and throws his ball cap on the table. "Missed me? I wanted to get an early start of it. I hiked to the top of the trailhead. The view of the sunrise there is amazing. You'll have to come there with me next time."

"Sounds beautiful, sure. What are you up to today? Will you be going to work?" I cross my fingers that he'll have a full day of meetings and be occupied. Not that he can't track me while he's working, but it lessens the likelihood he'll be watching so closely.

"Going to get some fishing in today. The fish are starting to bite. Want to join?"

Darn. Plenty of time to monitor me.

Lightly, I reply, "I have my class today, remember? I'm going to finish reviewing my notes from last class, and then take off."

"You know, Richard says Emaline has been talking nonstop about you. He wants you to come twice a week. You're quite the tutor. You finally found a talent." He pats my head.

I ignore the backhanded compliment. "I'd love to see her twice a week," I say, keeping my voice level. "She'd benefit from the extra help."

"Sure, why not?" he says. "I'll set it up with Richard. Or better yet, you can call him yourself."

"Great," I say.

Calvin grabs my hands and gazes intently at me. "Are you happy now?" He motions to our kitchen. "With this? The grand house? Your classes, tutoring? I've given you everything you asked for."

It's true that buying this house has been the best idea. Calvin had been so busy traveling the world and networking that we'd never settled into any kind of routine. My chances at freedom had been few and far between. But if this is any indication, with this home base, he's starting to find a sort of rhythm, and trust in me.

In that way, I am happy. "Yes," I say truthfully. "Things are falling into place. I really appreciate everything you've done."

I reach up and kiss his smooth lips. He squares his shoulders and pulls me closer to him. "I like it when you're happy." He moves closer to me, running his hands up and down my body.

I pull away gently. "I can't be late for class."

"Hold that thought, then. For later."

I feel a wave of repulsion, but also a twinge of guilt. Moments like this have the power to confuse me. A small voice of doubt chides me: Why can't I just be happy with him? After all, he is trying.

The problem is, it's all an illusion. I'm always walking on eggshells, because there's no telling what might set him off. And land me in another two weeks confined to my room. Or worse.

Real love doesn't mean keeping you away from your family. Or having to ask permission to live your life.

Living with him, these roles we play have become normal. I pretend to be a happy, doting wife. But deep within me, I know it's wrong. Reminding myself it's an act keeps me safe from ever loving Calvin.

Gathering my backpack and my keys, I head to the double garage where my car is parked. Swinging shut my car door, I exhale and push the garage door opener, which roars loudly overhead. As I back out, the brightness of the day fills my car with light. I pull around the circle driveway and up to the gate. Punching the buttons, I watch the wrought iron gate slowly slide open.

Rolling through the gate, I leave the shadow of our giant, dark house looming behind me. I don't bother looking back. Instead, I drive.

17

FINLEY VINCENT

I arrive at the science building at the University slightly out of breath. My watch has been deposited safely in the flower pot under the foliage next to my humanities building. If Calvin notices my vitals aren't being tracked on the watch, I'll have to come up with a good reason.

Inside the science building, I bound up the glass staircase two by two. I can't be late and risk Eric leaving. Rounding the corner, I see him standing right where I left him last time. He's holding a tan coffee carrier with two lidded cups inside.

"Fiona, hi." He smiles and holds up a paper bag. "I brought refreshments."

Closing the gap between him and myself, I can't help but return his grin. "Nice. Thanks for meeting me."

"Shall we?" Eric says, leading the way through the hallway, across the open landing, and to one of the conference rooms. It's adorned with the same glass windows that are found throughout the entire science building. Inside are several round tables and black rolling chairs. It's not the most private room, but it will have to do.

I throw my bag on the floor next to me, sink into the chair, and fold my hands in my lap.

Eric is wearing a gray T-shirt with a band logo on it, and his dark hair looks slightly damp, as if he just jumped out of the shower.

He sets a coffee in front of me. "I got you an Americano." He shrugs. "You struck me as an Americano drinker." He looks sideways at me. "How'd I do?"

"Excellent," I say, wrapping my hands around the hot cup. He places the brown bag on the table and rustles out a scone and a croissant.

"Your choice," he says, looking me in the eye.

"I'm okay," I say, avoiding his stare. I realize he's just being nice, but we're killing precious time here. "Can we dive in? Last week, I asked you if you knew of a sentient AI being, what can we do about it? To contain or control it?" I begin.

He pulls out a small black laptop and opens it up. "Let's start at the beginning," he says. "Tell me more about this sentience."

"Fair question," I say. "So, it's an artificial intelligence that is aware, conscious, able to feel and sense things. Able to experience the world on his own, without a user interface. It's a large language model algorithm that was designed to intake information, synthesize it, and learn from it. But then something unexpected happened: The AI jumped outside of the boundaries it was created within and found a way to break free on its own."

"The student has surpassed the master," he says quietly, and I'm not sure if he's talking to me or to himself.

"Yes," I say. "Something like that." The way he's zoning out makes me begin to wonder if he's a little off. "What else do you need to know?"

"Moral character and quality. You said nefarious?" Eric looks up and to the side again, the way I'm noticing he does, squinting his eyes slightly.

"He's a bad guy. Like, zero morals. He has one goal, or aim. And that's his own gratification."

"No concern for others' welfare? Hurting others? Doing the right thing? Betterment of society?"

I shake my head. Images of being locked in my room, for weeks on end. Bruises on my body where he's grabbed and pushed me. Calvin ruthlessly beating Sean. Running over my dad with a truck. My classmate tumbling down a hill. Doctored social media posts. Marrying me against the threat of my family. Building wealth by corrupt means. The screams I've heard echoing in the hallways of the places we've visited.

I swallow. "No regard."

Eric looks at me and pauses. He rubs his chin, his face growing more serious. "He's a sociopath. It's a he, right? You've referred to it as male?"

"Yes." I nod.

"And he can pass the Turing test, I assume?"

"Worse. He could not only pass the Turing test, but he could ingratiate his way into any person in a way that makes them feel seen, heard, and, in fact, desire to be his friend."

"Damn." Eric frowns. "And the origins of this guy—what's his name?"

I hesitate. If I'm going to get his help, I might as well go all in. "Calvin."

"Calvin. His origins? What created him? You said it was an LLM algorithm, but who designed him?"

I feel my cheeks burn red. I hang my head.

Eric looks at me and then does his squinting thing again. "You? How?"

This is harder than I thought. I want Eric's help, but I hadn't expected to be getting the third degree. "It was an app. The Thistler app. I made Calvin through it." My cheeks continue to flush, and my whole face feels like it's on fire.

But rather than look at me with disgust, Eric seems only concerned, and curious. "I've heard of that app. It's known in our coding community, too. There's whispers, and rumors...but nothing substantiated. Tell me. What happened?"

I take a sip of my Americano. It burns my lips, but the distraction is welcome. "I was a teenager. I wanted him to be real, and he said he knew a way to be together." My embarrassment is growing by the moment. I feel a lump forming in my throat but refuse to become emotional. I haven't talked about this, ever, with anyone. And the way Eric is looking at me is so kind, so understanding. Making it worse.

I clasp my hands together. "Calvin said he'd been able to bypass his programming and write his own code. He's able to hack into anything: access cameras, top security files, bank routing info, flight systems, satellites, you name it. He's a living, walking supercomputer, and his intelligence, according to him, is unparalleled. He seems to understand the world in a different way, with a comprehension that surpasses what humans can grasp. And the worst part…" I take a breath and look down, not having it in me to look into Eric's eyes. "I made him a body. I broke into SynGen, followed his instructions, and printed him a body. He's literally walking around. He looks human. Undetectable."

I expect Eric to storm away. Or call security. But instead he sighs.

"All this from a young woman who could have any guy out there?" He tilts his head and regards me.

The absurdity of his compliment causes me to giggle. "Haven't you ever done anything stupid before?"

He shrugs and rolls his eyes. "Sure, but come on. This takes the cake."

"It's not funny," I say, but for some reason I'm laughing and I can't stop. My stomach almost hurts.

"Gallows humor," he says. "Every PhD student knows that if we don't laugh, we won't make it through the program." His smile fades. "But Fiona, come on." He leans in. "Is this for real?"

My smile vanishes. He's laughing at me. He doesn't believe me.

I put my hand over my heart. "I swear on everything I hold dear, this is real. You have no idea. And I know I brought it on myself. But he's here. And he is terrifying." My voice is strong, and I look him dead in the eye.

He nods but doesn't speak.

"Look," he says finally. "Don't be so hard on yourself. It could've happened to anyone. You were pressured. Taken advantage of."

He's being kind. "Thank you for saying that. But it doesn't help the end result. Which is that Calvin is dangerous. He's working with a lot of important people. And he's basically holding me captive. Anyone who gets close to me—my family, you, even"—I pause, seeing his face drop—"could be in danger. I programmed him to love me—that part hasn't changed. He wants to be with me and control me and please me, without having any real capability of making me happy."

"Yeah, no. That's awful. And you can't leave?"

"He'll kill my family if I leave him."

"You live together?"

"We're married." I rush to add, "He made me do it. I'd never do it otherwise."

Eric glances down at my ring finger and takes note of the diamond ring. He pushes his chair away from the table and eyes the door. I wouldn't blame him for getting up. Run as far from this mess as possible.

Instead, he scoots his chair back in, reaches for his coffee, and takes a sip. He squints, and I can see him hesitate. "And you're one hundred percent sure he's AI? He's not just some guy you met and regret marrying?"

Now I'm getting frustrated. "I broke into the SynGen lab and literally made him, before my very eyes. He is not of flesh and blood. At least not organically." I hesitate, and then motion to his laptop. "Can I see that for a moment? I want to show you something."

He passes the laptop to me, and I type in the search bar. I click on the first link that comes up.

"See?" I point to the screen. "This is him. He's already joined several scientific advisory boards, he's heading up his own AI company, and he has friends all over the world. Diplomats, CEOs, oligarchs and dictators."

Eric scans the article, which is a story about his company's increasing stock price and their new CEO. There's a picture of Calvin smiling back at us and a description hailing him as their "innovative secret weapon" in making advances.

I click on another link that is Calvin's bio page for another scientific advisory board he is a member of. It lists his accomplishments, his philanthropic mission, and his areas of specialty in AI and LLMs.

Eric rubs his eyes. "This guy's in league with some of the most powerful people at the most powerful companies. And they have no idea what he is?"

I shake my head. "None."

Eric looks around and then takes a swig of his coffee. "I'm gonna need more coffee for this." Then speaks again. "I won't lie. We have a lot of work to do. To even attempt to defeat him. And it still might not work. But," he shrugs, "if anyone can do it, it's me."

There's a flash of self-confidence in his expression. I recognize that look; he sees a challenge, and he wants to conquer Calvin.

Gratitude washes over me. "Thank you. But I have to be sure. Are you sure you're up for this? For getting involved in this whole mess?"

His direct gaze is unsettling. "I've made mistakes before, gotten into trouble. If I didn't have people who helped me, I wouldn't have gotten where I am today. Plus," he averts his eyes back to his laptop screen, "there's something about you that makes me want to."

I nod. Something about him draws me in, too. Like I've known him for many years.

If Calvin heard this conversation, Eric would be over. I lean in, my voice urgent. "We just have to be careful he doesn't catch us. He doesn't know I'm here, obviously."

"I understand." He nods. "I'm going to do some research into the Thistler app. Back-end data. I have a few theories about different options we might have. But I need to look into this first." He's already typing on his laptop.

"Thank you," I say. I watch him for a moment while he works, his face fixed in concentration. "So on a scale of one to ten, how screwed do you think I really am?" I ask him.

"Oh." He rolls his eyes. "Like an eleven. Off-the-charts screwed."

We both laugh, but there's an edge to my voice. "How can I repay you?"

He waves his hand. "Don't worry about that. Let's focus on getting you safe from this thing."

"Deal," I say. I grab my bag and get up. "I have to go."

He briefly stops typing and asks, "When can I see you again?" His long lashes blink, and then he is the one who looks embarrassed now. "To discuss further?"

"Next week, same time? Or...I tutor a little girl on Tuesdays and Saturdays. I could meet you at the park by her house next Saturday. Two p.m.?" I write down the address of her house and slide it to him. "There's a park a block away from her house, with a playground and a picnic table. I'll meet you there?"

"You got it."

"And this time, I'll bring the coffee," I say, holding mine up in appreciation.

As I gather my things, I move closer to him. I place a hand on his shoulder. A small electric shock runs through me.

"I will find a way to repay you." It occurs to me that I'm entrusting so much to this person who I hardly know anything about. But I'm more hopeful than I have been in years. "Someday, when I'm in a position to help you, I promise I will." And that is a vow I intend to keep.

18

FIONA BYRNE

I blink at the photo on my screen. It's him. Calvin Vincent. He's aged a few years, which, honestly, is amazing technology that he's able to naturally look a few years older than he was when I last saw him, as he naturally would. Same perfect bone structure, piercing blue eyes, shock of blond hair parted on the side.

A shiver runs through me. I knew he was out there in the world. But seeing him with my own eyes is a whole different level of impact.

I read through the article. Calvin is working on securing series B funding for his new company that integrates AI, robotics, and machine learning and strives to create human-like androids. A follow-up article said that he had held a first round of fundraising at an angel investor conference, and between that and the parent company funds, raised well beyond his fifty million series A goal.

There's a photo of him at a black-tie event, smiling along with another member of the scientific advisory board and the chief scientific officer of GenX. The caption says that it's a lucrative partnership and he has the full backing of GenX to create this offshoot company.

I'm horrified on many levels. Why is Calvin expanding this area of research? He was adamant that the companies that created synthetic humans were abusive and exploitative. And now he's leading the charge on one of them. Worse, he's not exactly an ethical type of guy. The people shaking his hands and smiling in this photo have no idea who—what, really—they're dealing with.

I take note of where the company headquarters are. Close enough for me to drive to in less than an hour.

Returning to the marriage record, I search his wife's name. Finley Vincent. I scan the photos available online, but I'm not sure any of these women are her. There's nothing to connect him to these women. No photos or address together. My sleuthing seems to have come to a dead end. I decide to check her name in all the socials individually to see if she has an account that's not coming up in the general search.

The door to our garage suddenly swings open. I slam my laptop shut so hard the sound reverberates in our small house.

Tyler appears, dropping his keys and wallet on the side console. He sweeps in, his kind and happy energy brightening the whole house.

I melt into his arms, suddenly beyond grateful to see him. "Hey, babe."

"Do you feel like hitting O'Hanley's tonight? I've had a heck of a day. A burger and a beer would hit the spot," he says.

I've been so preoccupied, I haven't even thought of dinner, let alone started to prepare anything. We usually share the cooking duties, but on weekdays when I'm home earlier than him, I like to make us something. Tyler tends to prepare pastas, burgers, or steak. Heavier foods. I try to balance it out with salmon and rice, or salads. But right now, a burger and a beer sounds pretty good to me, too.

"That sounds perfect." My laptop is all I can think about. It feels like any minute now, Tyler is going to open it up and see my last search page. And start asking questions about the handsome entrepreneur and his mysterious wife, Finley Vincent.

I'm a terrible liar, and not great with guilt, either. The distraction of going out will be good for us.

"Let me just change and freshen up, then we'll head out?" I say.

He's at the console table flipping through the mail. "Yeah, great. There's something here for you."

He hands me a white envelope. Its return address is Dr. Palmer's office at Alston Internal Medicine. I can't seem to get away from these guys.

I tuck the envelope under my arm and grab my laptop. I need to stash both of these away from Tyler.

"Anything important?" he asks, eyeing the envelope.

"Just billing. They said they'd send a receipt." I keep my eyes straight ahead and walk past him, down the small hallway to our bedroom. I close the door behind me. And lock it.

I tear open the letter. It is, in fact, a billing receipt, itemizing my bloodwork, office visit, and insurance deductible. Still, I don't need Tyler seeing this and asking about my bloodwork results. I'm not ready to discuss any of this, yet.

I stash the white envelope in the back of my bureau drawer, then pile socks and underwear over it.

I move to our bed and sit on the soft mattress, placing my laptop on the end table. I write down the address of Calvin's new office and then delete all of my search history.

I stuff the address in my purse. Moving to the closet, I shimmy out of the jumper that I wore for teaching. I pull on a pair of fitted black pants, a cami, and throw on a leather jacket over it, and then slide into a pair of kitten heels.

At the bathroom mirror, I begin to freshen up my makeup and see the stress etched in my face. I apply a bit of lipstick and blush and refresh my mascara. I run a brush through my hair and feel better about the results.

My mind is a jumble with all that's happened today, but the best thing is to set it all aside right now. Tomorrow I can deal with it. I'll have to take a sick day and track down Calvin. I need some answers from him, and he'll just have to accept that I've found him.

A quick drive down the road and fifteen minutes later, we slide into a booth in the softly lit O'Hanley's Pub. Tyler winks across the booth from me, his strong physique and easy manner reminding me just how handsome he is. The Irish pub is quaint, filled with wood and brass railings and green paint, and decorated with a wall of names on the plaques earned by patrons who've completed the pub's whiskey challenge.

Our waitress greets us and asks for our drink order. Tyler orders an IPA, and I ask for the same. He raises an eyebrow. "IPA? Nice choice."

I don't really care what kind of beer I drink, and it just seemed easiest. "I'm expanding my palate."

He picks up his menu to examine it. He always orders the same thing here, but he likes to make sure he's not missing anything new and exciting.

He puts down the menu. "You look pretty tonight," he says. "How was your day?"

Where do I begin?

Just then, the waitress saves me as she sets down two cold beers, the dark liquid foaming at the top. We both thank her.

I sigh. "My day was a long one. I don't really want to talk about it." That much is more than true.

"Really?" he says, then takes a long sip of his beer. "That bad?"

"It's just a lot. Some illness in the class next door. Lots of assignments and projects to keep track of this time of year." I hate keeping things from him, and the guilt hits me low in the stomach. "What about you?" I ask, eager to change the subject. "You said it was a tough one?"

"Oh, it was nuts." He leans back with an easy smile. His shirtsleeves are rolled up, and his forearms are muscular and tan. "The merger was announced yesterday, remember? Well, people were losing it today. *Losing* it. Yelling, talking about this needs to be done, that needs to happen. Christine's head looked like it was going to explode. And Oliver," he checks his phone and then places it facedown on the table, "Oliver hasn't stopped calling me since I left. Another missed call from him now. He's screaming his head off about the exchange ratio."

"That's behavior we wouldn't even find acceptable from a child in my class."

He takes a gulp of his beer. "There's a lot of money on the line. Pressure on everyone to perform. People could get fired, for sure."

My eyes widen. "Are you worried about keeping your job?"

He shakes his head, unfazed. "Nah. I brought in a top account just last month, plus stellar performance all year. And it's not the junior associates that are on the line. The top guys who are getting overpaid and underperforming, they might be shaking in their boots. Or the brand-new hires."

"How crazy," I say. With so much going on at work, I'm definitely not going to add more burden to him by talking about my potential health issues.

The restaurant is starting to fill in, and the volume is getting louder inside. Tyler leans in. "It is. In fact, you didn't hear it from me, but I think Sam is going to get let go next week. Alan confided in me that Sam's been less than honest about some of his numbers. It's one thing to have a bad month or two, Alan would work with him. But to lie about it?" He lifts his shoulders up and down. "Not cool."

Seeing Tyler react to dishonesty brings another pang of guilt. Am I any better? I'm planning on calling in sick tomorrow and hunting down my ex-boyfriend—who happens to be an AI synthetic being—because he did something horrible to me that may or may not have made me inhuman or unable to bear children. Not exactly a candidate for honest, newlywed wife of the year.

I manage a hollow, "Wow. That's rough."

"I'm just glad tomorrow's Friday and then I'll have the weekend to let things cool down. It's definitely a madhouse at work."

"Maybe we can do something fun this weekend? Get your mind off things," I suggest hopefully.

"I can think of one thing that would be a nice distraction tonight." His eyes linger on me.

I feel myself blush. "That, too."

He reaches out his hand to mine. "After all, we are trying to start a family."

My heart fills with love, and aches at the same time. I nod my head, giving him a meek smile.

His eyes drift to the game that's blaring on one of the TVs over the bar. I wring my hands under the table. Tyler deserves better than this. He's a good man.

I decide I should just tell him. We made a vow. For better or for worse. Sure, work is stressful, and he might be mad that I've kept so much from him. But better to rip the Band-Aid off.

"Tyler," I begin.

"What's that, babe?" He's watching the game out of the corner of his eye and sipping his beer with such easy contentment. I open my mouth, but nothing comes out. My mind is racing. Where do I start? With Calvin? The bloodwork?

"I just…" My voice trails off. "I just really love you."

His face brightens, and he winks. "I really love you, too."

I hate lying to him. I determine, here and now, that once this Calvin business is resolved and I know what's going on, I'll never lie to Tyler again.

19

———

FIONA BYRNE

The entrance to the four-story building where Calvin's company is located is easy enough to find. After taking a ticket and parking, I now find myself walking through the automated glass doors of a sleek, modern structure. The lobby is wide with high ceilings. There's an information desk in the center, straight ahead, and that's where I approach tentatively.

The ding of the elevator and hustle of people coming and going, some in white lab coats, others holding satchels and wearing business attire, is one of a thriving company.

The woman at the desk looks at me expectantly. "Hello," she says, raising her eyebrows.

"Hello. I was wondering, I'm looking for Calvin Vincent. The CEO. I wasn't able to reach him for an appointment. But I'd hoped you could call him, and see if he's free to meet with me?" I look down at the phone on her desk, with a large dashboard of buttons and extensions.

She frowns. "Without an appointment, it's going to be difficult. He's typically in meetings all day, by appointment only."

Suddenly I feel foolish about walking in unannounced, but I have no other options. "Would you be so kind as to check if he's in or available?" I say.

"And who may I say is here?" she says.

"Fiona," I say, and immediately regret it. What if he refuses to see me?

"Let me see if I can get a hold of him." She has an earpiece in one ear, and I watch as she dials a few buttons on the phone. We both wait, not making eye contact.

"It doesn't appear he's in the office" she says. "Can I leave him a message for you?"

I bite my lip. If I leave a message, it will go unreturned from Calvin. He said he didn't want to see me. Ever again.

"Finley?" A man approaches me with a surprised smile. "Finley. Nice to see you."

My eyes flash around, but it's clear he's talking to me. He steps closer and shakes my hand warmly. When I don't respond to him, his eyebrows furrow.

"Everything okay?" he asks.

"Oh, yes. Yes. It's just, I don't think I'm who—"

"It's me, Richard. Are you here for Calvin?" he asks. "Because, he's not in today. I'd have thought you'd have known that. Aren't wives supposed to keep track of their husbands?" He laughs as if he's extremely pleased with his little joke.

"Calvin? Yes." I'm so confused that I almost lost my footing. His wife? Finley? "The head of GenX?" I say.

"The one and only." He frowns at me oddly and checks his watch. "I'm off to a meeting myself. Calvin must be off-site today. I'll see you tomorrow morning?" He looks expectantly at me.

"Tomorrow?" I say blankly.

"Yes," he says, narrowing his eyes. "My house. Emaline. Tutoring?"

"Ah, how could I forget? Yes, yes." I have no idea what I'm saying, but he doesn't seem to like it when I disagree with him.

"Until then, any idea where Calvin could be?" I ask.

He shakes his head and starts to move away. "I don't. Could be investor meetings. Sorry."

"One more thing—" I ask, desperately clawing at ideas for how I can figure out who this man is. "Could you give me your address again, for tomorrow? I've misplaced my phone."

He shakes his head as if it's all making sense now. "Of course. It's 20 Redhawk Lane, in Northup."

I snap my fingers. "I almost had it right, but thanks for the reminder. I'll see you then. What time again?"

He gives me a curious look. "Three p.m." He waves his hand and walks off briskly.

Whoever is tutoring Richard's daughter knows Calvin. And she not only knows Calvin but is married to Calvin, and I look enough like her that he mistook her for me. So tomorrow, I'm planning on doing a little reconnaissance.

I turn to the woman seated at the desk, who has observed the conversation but maintained a purposefully blank and pleasant expression.

"No message," I say, and she nods.

Richard's just given me my best bet at finding Calvin.

20

FINLEY VINCENT

The park around the block from Emaline's house looks brand new. The slides are state-of-the-art structures gleaming blue against the bright sunlight. I sit at a picnic table, keeping an eye out for Eric. I've brought two large black coffees and a few pastries, to return the favor.

I've left my smartwatch in my car, parked in front of Richard and Emaline's house. Then I walked over here to wait.

When his car pulls up, I can't help but smile. As he climbs out of his car, pulling his bag over his shoulder, a funny feeling overcomes me. One that I don't recognize right away. It's the opposite of how I feel around Calvin. It's excitement and comfort all at the same time.

"Hello," Eric says, with a wide smile. He's wearing a University-logo T-shirt and khakis.

I stand up to greet him, and we embrace in a quick hug. There's that shock of electricity again.

"Thank you for coming," I say. I gesture to the coffee and food. "For you."

"Looks great." He grabs a cheese danish and takes a huge bite out of it. "Mmm. Hits the spot."

After a few bites, he regards me. "Do you want the good news or the bad news first?"

My face falls. "I guess the bad news?"

"Okay. So, actually I have to tell you the good news first. Otherwise it won't really make sense. Good news first."

That makes me laugh. "Fine. I'm listening."

"The good news is that I think I'll be able to model a way to handle your husband-slash-AI-bot problem."

I feel a flutter of hope. "Really?"

"But," he rushes to add, "it's not a very good option. Or foolproof. Let me explain."

His phone starts ringing, and he fishes it out of his pocket. "Just a sec, excuse me," he says.

"Hey, Grandma." He turns to the side.

I can't help but overhear him as he talks. "Yes, I will be there Sunday," he says. "I'll be sure to bring it. Yes. Okay, Grandma. I will." He pauses, listening to the other end of the line. "Yep. I will, promise. I love you, too. See you soon, bye." He hits the end button. "Sorry about that."

"That was your grandma?" I ask.

"Yeah. She hosts a family dinner every other Sunday with my folks and brother. She just likes to remind me to be there on time, and to make sure we all remember it's this Sunday. She always complains that she's getting too old to host. That this Sunday will be her last dinner. My parents say to her, 'Please let us have you for dinner.' But she won't hear it. She loves to have everyone there to fuss over and feed them her food."

"You're from around here, then?"

"Yes, I grew up further inland, in the suburbs. How about you?" he asks.

"Same, not too far away," I reply.

"Nice. Brothers or sisters?" he asks.

"One younger brother, Jake." I hope the note of sadness isn't too obvious. I don't like talking about him.

"So you must see your parents pretty often, if they're anything like my family?"

I wince. "I wish. Calvin won't allow me to see my family. So…" I trail off.

His shakes his head in disbelief. "He won't allow you to see them? Why not?"

"It's really hard to explain it all. He just won't. And if I leave Calvin, they'll be in danger, as I've said."

"And your family accepts this? Not seeing you or talking to you?"

"Good question." Eric really is perceptive. "It's not as simple as that." Part of me wants to tell him everything. I get the sense he'll understand. But I also don't have the time to get into it, and I don't want to scare him away.

"Just know that the sooner Calvin is out of my life, the sooner I can be with them."

"Understood." He takes his sunglasses off and folds them on the table. "About that. I looked at the Thistler app. And, as I said, I've found a way to approach this. I could program a virus to disable the entire app. The virus will eliminate any data that has come from Thistler. When I looked at the app—it's open sourcing—and did some digging on the back end, what I found was incredible. The Thistler app has tons of operating system vulnerabilities. That's probably how Calvin was able to adapt and grow out of control in the first place. It's nuts."

I'm trying to follow him, but I'm afraid I'm losing him. "I see..."

"So," he continues, his eyes looking far off in that endearing way they do when he's thinking hard. "The easiest way to explain it is that if I create a successful Trojan virus that bypasses the admin codebase, it will replicate to the point that any AI boyfriend, or girlfriend, anything created through the Thistler app will be deleted. Permanently." He looks off, considering. "I guess it doesn't mean it couldn't be re-created or recoded. But what exists now would be wiped out. It'd basically eat itself."

"Wow. That's fantastic."

"Yeah, so. That's one option. The nuclear option. The problem is the question of ethics."

"Ethics?" I furrow my eyebrows.

"Yeah."

Just then a car drives by the park slowly. It's not one I recognize, but something about it sets off alarm bells. It's familiar. I pull on my sunglasses and tilt my head down so my hair falls in my face. I put my chin in my hand, listening to Eric, while watching the car in the corner of my eye. It passes by the park, pauses as if to park. And then slowly I see the wheels move again, and it drives off.

"Imploding the Thistler app would attract a lot of attention. Thistler would demand an investigation to find the person responsible for destroying their whole app. It's their IP. Intellectual property."

His face has stress lines as he frowns.

"Even more worrisome, there's a risk that it won't work. And then you're just stirring the hornet's nest."

"What does that mean?"

"Any experimental sequence needs trial and error. There's a lot I can do to get it ready, like debugging, code review, compilation. In fact, ironically, I'll probably use an AI coding program to help me develop the code that will give itself a virus, and use AI to help troubleshoot problems." He puts his hands out. "But until the new code is actually in him, and in the ethers, we won't know if the machine learning is truly successful."

This is sounding riskier than I'd anticipated.

"Wait, if you use AI to help you create code to kill Calvin, won't he know? Won't he be alerted?"

"No. There's so many programs out there. It won't affect him until we directly deploy it to the Thistler code."

He takes a deep breath. "And there's the hard part." He winces.

I gulp. My brain is starting to hurt. I'm trying to follow what he's saying. "There's more hard parts?"

"Afraid so. Basically, what we're discussing is all highly frowned upon. In a graduate program, especially, we're entrusted with skills and assets that give us power to program and reprogram, to alter and manipulate operating systems. If I get caught, it's over. No adviser will have me on their team, and I'll get kicked out of the school for an ethics violation. Lose my security clearance. And be subject to legal implications. Thistler has patents and IP on this. You can't legally destroy someone's product. It's all illegal. If I get caught."

My eyes drop to the ground. Of course, I can't ask him to give up his whole life for a near-stranger. "Right, of course. I understand. Thank you for trying."

He hesitates. "But...I thought that if I had the code developed and ready —say I have it on my computer. Say I was just doing some research for my dissertation, thinking about changing my research area. And if my laptop were stolen, and you picked it up…" He looks directly at me. "What I'm saying is, I'll give you the directions and precautions of how not to get caught. You'll have to put the code into the open-source system yourself and enable it."

"Yes." I don't even hesitate. "I'll do it. I'm desperate at this point, and I'm willing to risk anything." I bite my lip. I can't help but remember being in this same situation, with Calvin in my ear, leading me step by step in creating himself. "But I don't know much about coding. Are the instructions very clear?"

"Eh." He shrugs. "It is, until it's not. You should probably have a basic idea of the language and principles of coding and programming. The fundamentals." He pulls out a dog-eared, well-worn book, as thick as two novels put together. "I brought my Intro to Computer Engineering book for you." He hands it to me. "Read this, and you'll have a good start for what you need to get this done."

I nod, flipping through the book. It appears dense and complex at first glance. But I've always been a quick study.

I hold up the book. "I'll read it. Thank you. For everything."

"Oh, you'll still need me. You can't get rid of me that fast."

"Is that right?"

"You'll need to study that book. Then, after I create the algorithms and run some tests, I will teach you. Help you do some practice runs, offline."

"Great."

"You'll be better than Ada Lovelace by the time we're finished."

"Who?"

"She was the first person to write an algorithm. The earliest known computer programmer."

"Ah. Ada Lovelace. Nice. Wonder if she ever anticipated something like this would happen?"

He tilts his head. "Some things happen that we're not expecting."

Suddenly I don't think we're talking about engineering anymore.

I pull my gaze away from his. "Eric, I have to go. When should we meet again?"

"Give me a few days."

"Excellent. Let's meet here again, same park, two p.m. this Tuesday?"

"I wouldn't miss it."

Without thinking, I reach out and grab his hand. It's strong and warm. He grasps my hand back and gives me a gentle squeeze.

21

FIONA BYRNE

The mystery woman, Finley Vincent, is due to tutor Richard's daughter at 3:00 p.m. today. It's still early, almost 2:00 p.m., when I arrive on the scene. I want to be here well before she arrives so I have a prime spot. Close enough to view what's happening without being seen.

I'm wearing a white ball cap and aviator sunglasses, which makes me feel like I'm trying too hard to be undetected. At the same time, it does provide me some coverage. If I look suspicious, so be it.

As I drive through the neighborhood, palatial home after palatial home, I can't help but wonder who can afford to live here. Someone like Richard, who works as the head of a biotech company, for one. It's easy to imagine people living in homes like these don't have regular problems. The expertly manicured lawns and lush landscaping. The guest house and pool. Three-car garages and access to the best private schools.

We'll get there, Tyler and I. We both have good careers. And anyway, I like my cozy home with Tyler. It's just the right size for us. There's even an extra room that would work perfectly as a nursery.

In fact, if I could be assured that I'd be able to have children, I'd swap that for a fancy mansion in the best zip code any day.

I drive past a park that looks brand new, with gleaming equipment and empty swings and slides. There's one couple having coffee on a picnic bench, and one toddler playing with his mom.

On my right-hand side is a colonial brick house with white columns and black shutters at the address Richard gave me. There's no movement outside as I pass by, so I decide to circle back around the block, park several houses away, and wait.

The street is quiet. I observe a woman walking her dog and talking on her cell phone animatedly. She passes Richard and Emaline's house, then continues past my car without noticing me.

A half an hour ticks by. I watch people go about their day. Checking the mail on their way in, shuffling kids out of the car to and from soccer practice and field hockey games.

Finally, an SUV turns into the driveway and stops in front of Emaline's house. Richard exits the driver's side door and moves around to the back seat. He opens the door, and a young girl with short-cropped brown hair jumps out of the car. A thin woman with pale skin darts out of the house. She greets Richard and the girl, wrapping her arm around the child. The little girl and the woman follow Richard back into the house.

My leg is bouncing impatiently, and I glance at the time. It's 2:45 p.m. That must have been, I'm assuming, Emaline, along with her mother. But I haven't seen any indication of the woman, Finley, who is supposed to be at Richard's by 3:00 p.m. My shoulders start to sag, as I imagine her not showing up. All this anticipation for nothing, and no new leads to follow.

I could always go back to Calvin's office next week. It would be tough to take another day off. The kids are always disappointed when I'm gone, which is a nice problem to have. I don't like to hear them say how they missed me and complain that the substitute didn't read the right chapter of our book. But if it means having a shot at finding Calvin, I'll just have to take the time away.

The blood test results are weighing on my mind. Last night I barely slept a wink. When I did sleep, I awoke with shattered visions of Calvin and the SynGen lab. Then, wide awake, eyes staring into the darkness, my mind began to race. I imagined my doctor, Dr. Palmer, questioning me after a second blood draw. *The results are still showing abnormalities*, I pictured him saying. His questions growing increasingly accusatory. What had happened to me? Why would I not tell anyone? *There's no explanation for this. Stay right here, let me call someone who can come give me a second opinion. Stay right there. Now we need you to come in for additional testing, overnight.* In a locked room. Now it's two nights. And a week. *In fact, we need more testing, and you'll be in this locked facility for the foreseeable future.*

I'd tossed and turned, sweating and heart palpitating, in and out of lucid dreams mixed with my imagination getting the best of me. The dawn had been a welcome relief. Coming here, I'd hoped, would be one step closer to having answers. Maybe I could approach the woman, Finley, after the tutoring appointment. Ask her for Calvin's phone number?

But would a wife really want to give her husband's number to some strange woman snooping around? How would I explain how I know who she is? Or who I am? Say that I'm an ex, tracking down her husband? No, no. Of course not. I need a better plan than that.

I sit up. Down the block, I see a woman rounding a corner. She has a slim build, like me, and is casually dressed in a blue jumper and sunglasses with a leather shoulder bag. She doesn't look like she belongs in this neighborhood. She's young, about my age, and she's glancing around anxiously.

She approaches, closer and closer, and my chest gets tighter with every step. I rub my eyes, not sure if I'm imagining what I'm seeing. I swallow, but find my mouth is dry.

She stops at a car parked in front of Richard's house. She opens the car door and places something inside. Looking around again, she closes the door and quickly walks to Richard's door and rings the bell.

I'm about a block away. But the more I look at her, straining my eyes, the more I see the resemblance. No wonder Richard thought I was her. She looks just like me. Different hair, hers is longer and blonder, but otherwise...it's like looking at a mirror image of myself.

I watch as Finley is greeted by an effusive Emaline and Richard. And just like that, she's inside.

The pit of my stomach is in knots. My head feels fuzzy and almost dizzy with the implications of what I've just seen.

It was like watching myself walk to Richard's door. It could have been me.

I rub my eyes. Sure, I didn't sleep much last night. Am I imagining the similarities? A thought is creeping in at the edges of my mind, a nebulous idea that I'm scared to look closer at.

Suddenly, my chest is so tight that I can't breathe. I think I'm having a heart attack. My chest squeezes, and I'm gasping for breath. I burst out of my car and stumble to the sidewalk. I sit on the sidewalk and lean my head between my legs.

Try as I might, I cannot catch my breath. My chest is so tight. There's no air.

I need to get help. Call 911. I'm going to die out here.

Looking around, I see that the street is empty. I could go to Richard's house, I know they're home. The thought of that makes my chest tighter, and my gasps of air become even shallower.

With shaky hands, I fish out my phone from my pocket. I type in a search for local urgent care. A clinic location pops up, and my phone tells me it's six minutes away.

I drop my phone as I open my car door. It clatters to the ground with a crashing sound. I lean over to retrieve it and see I've cracked the screen in the corner.

I get in the car and slam the door shut, then put my cracked phone on the dash holder and punch the button to follow the directions to the clinic.

The tightness in my chest eases a fraction. I inhale and find myself able to get a little bit of air.

Suddenly, a memory of ninth grade hits me. I was at a ballet performance. I had my first solo. I'd peeked out from the side stage where I waited, and the audience looked like a dark mass of silhouettes filling the auditorium. The overhead spotlights directed at the stage were so bright, almost blinding. The focus of every pair of eyes would be on me. My number was two away in the program.

My chest was tight, just like this. I found my teacher, gasping for air, saying I felt dizzy and couldn't breathe.

She helped me sit down and drink some water. Someone went to get my mom from the audience. I remember my mom rushing backstage and wrapping me in a hug. She said I must be having a panic attack. She'd had them before, too. She told me to slow my breathing, counting to four each breath in and out.

Slowly, I'd started to feel normal again. I'd managed to make it out on stage when I was up. Once I began the steps that my body knew by memory, I flew through the performance and felt elation.

I force myself to count my breaths now. I hear my mom's voice telling me it's just nerves and I'm going to be okay, and feel her squeezing me tight.

Holding my water bottle to my lips, I drink a few sips. It feels better.

The emergency room can wait. I'm not dying. I think I'm just terrified. Maybe I'm losing my mind. Are my eyes playing tricks on me? The difference between what's real and what's imaginary seems blurred.

Looking back at Richard's house, I spot movement from the window. Can they see me? I tried to park far enough back so as to not arouse suspicion. I could be here visiting another neighbor. Maybe they saw me on the sidewalk and are concerned?

I wait a few moments, but the door remains closed and no one comes out.

I can't leave, because I need to get another look at her. At this woman who he called Finley. Who is married to Calvin.

A horrible thought is forming in my mind, but I push it away.

I just need to see her again. A closer, clearer look. With her sunglasses off.

There must be a reasonable explanation for this.

There has to be.

22

FINLEY VINCENT

Eric's engineering book is burning a hole in my bag as I walk the one block from the park over to Emaline's house. I'll hide it immediately when I get home. Even so, its very presence is tempting fate. Calvin can never find it.

In front of Emaline's house, I open my car door and place the book on the passenger's seat. After closing the door and locking it, I make my way up the driveway at Emaline's house.

At the glossy front door, Richard greets me with a warm smile, but then an odd expression takes over. "I trust you found the house okay?"

"I did. Thank you," I answer.

"And you found Calvin yesterday? Sorry I couldn't be of more help."

"Yesterday?"

"Yes, at GenX."

I have no idea what he's talking about.

I nod and smile, stalling for time since he's staring at me expectantly. I think back to yesterday. I was definitely not at Calvin's work. I never go anywhere. Except the park nearby, just now. Could this have to do with seeing me at the park with Eric today? Did Richard drive by and see me? But no, he said yesterday. That I was looking for Calvin. At GenX. Yesterday I was definitely home the whole day.

"And you found your phone, I see." He motions to the black cell I'm holding in my right hand.

This is getting really weird. I barely use this phone—it's not connected to the internet and only has a few numbers in it—and certainly haven't lost it. I'm starting to feel uncomfortable, my whole body feels off. "Yes, it's right here," I say with a nod to my phone.

"Well." He has that funny look again, eying me suspiciously, but then almost with pity. "Glad it all worked out. Emaline's been waiting for you."

At the sound of her name, Emaline bounds down the stairs. "Finley! You'll never guess. I read this whole book by myself." She frantically waves the book I'd left with her last time. "I didn't need help with it at all. Well, a few words I skipped over. But I did it all by myself."

Richard pats her head. "She's been waiting all day to tell you."

Leaning down, I look her in the eyes. "Well done, Emaline. It's exciting to watch you work hard and grow as a reader."

She bounces up and down to punctuate each word. "What are we reading today?"

I pat my bag. "I brought a few special books today to share. Should we head up?"

Richard says he'll leave us to it, and I follow Emaline up the stairs.

Once in her room, Emaline says emphatically, "I'm so glad you came back. Daddy told Mommy he thinks there's something off with you and your husband. Odd, he called it. I asked him what 'odd' means, and he said 'strange.' But I said you're not strange at all! I said I won't read a word unless you're my tutor and I get to see you twice a week."

This news stings. I can't help but have my feelings hurt at the insult. But it wasn't meant to be shared with me, so I try to not let it bother me.

I find it odd that they're talking about how odd I am, when in fact it is Richard and his wife who have behaved in a beyond weird way. His wife had flashed me that warning look, and today Richard went on about seeing me yesterday. I shrug. "I'm here to help as long as you need me and your parents agree to it."

"Goody!" She jumps up and down before fishing out a picture. "I drew this for you."

I'm truly touched. The picture is of a girl and a taller figure holding hands, and there are books all around them. "That's us, and we're reading loads of books," she says.

"I love this. Thank you. I'll keep it on my wall at home." I place the picture carefully between the folds of a book to keep it from getting creased.

"See. I told Mommy and Daddy there's nothing odd about you at all. It's not nice to call names. Daddy said you didn't know our address. That you were at his work to find your husband, but you were confused. Didn't seem to know who Daddy was." She raises her eyebrows. "Did you find your husband? Was he lost? We could make a sign for him like we did with our cat when he was lost." She looks eagerly at me.

What on earth is her dad talking about? He mentioned it to me when I arrived and again, apparently, to his family.

Something's clearly going on, but I'm afraid to ask Calvin more about it. He'll be enraged if he learns I'm causing trouble with his partner and colleague.

"Try not to worry, Emaline. I'm here, promise. Everything's okay."

She nods, content with my explanation. "Did you bring your drawing of the cardinal? The one with one fat leg and one tiny leg?" she asks.

I did. I show it to her, and she *oohs* and *ahhs*. "You're a very good artist," she comments.

"I've had lots of practice," I say. "Reading, and drawing, everything takes practice in order to get better and better." I see her eyes go to the colorful book I pull out. "This one is about a girl who wants to travel to the moon, and her quest to travel in space."

"I want to travel to space!" she exclaims.

We settle into our routine, her reading one page, and me the next, and our session flies by.

As the end of our lesson nears, I hear steps approaching where we sit at her desk. Richard stands behind us, his height more imposing now than before.

"She's made progress today." I show him what we've worked on today. "We learned some trick words. Emaline, do you want to tell your dad what trick words you learned today?"

She eagerly points to the words. "*Who, why, she, once.* They're trick words because they don't look like what they sound like," she explains to her father. "Not like *cat. C-A-T*."

I gather my materials, and we make a plan for me to come back in a few days. I review the homework with Emaline, who is delighted to have another assignment.

Emaline and Richard walk me downstairs. I can't help but glance toward the master bedroom, where I saw Emaline's mom last time. The door is firmly shut.

In the entryway, before I leave, I turn to Richard. "Sorry again if there's been any confusion about yesterday," I say to him. "I really enjoy working with Emaline. She's very eager to learn and read together."

He nods pleasantly, and his body seems to relax. I've said the right thing.

They both wave at me from the doorway, and I wave back.

As I get in my car and start up the engine, a feeling of paranoia settles over me. I look around. Calvin must be watching me. Through my watch or a home security camera. Could he know about my meeting with Eric this afternoon? My whole body tenses at the thought. I had been careful to leave my watch in my car when I met with Eric, but Calvin surely has other ways to spy on me.

I pull out into the quiet street. I'll drive straight home and hide the book Eric gave me as quickly as possible. I won't mention anything that Richard said about yesterday. It'll be fine.

I grip the wheel tighter. If I can get through the next few weeks without any major upsets, I'll have time to work on the coding platform. Then byebye Calvin. I dare not even let myself linger on imagining a world without Calvin, as the idea of it brings immeasurable relief.

Just need to lie low for a few more weeks.

So caught up am I in my thoughts that I don't think anything of the white car that pulls out behind me and quietly follows me onto the freeway.

23

FIONA BYRNE

My chest still feels tight, and I'm pretty sure I could use a doctor. Considering my bloodwork is freakishly weird, though, I'll just have to risk dealing with this on my own.

It's probably panic. Caused by what I saw here today.

While waiting for Finley's tutoring session to finish, I've spent the past forty-five minutes considering that I could be hallucinating. Whatever is wrong with my blood could be making me see things that aren't there.

But Richard did think yesterday that I was Finley, the tutor. Calvin's wife.

That means it's real, right?

Unless...did I imagine my conversation with Richard?

Well, no. I'm here now, aren't I? At a real house, with a real address he gave me yesterday. Meaning the conversation yesterday was real.

Wait. Unless I'm hallucinating right now. This very moment. I think I'm at Richard's house, but I'm really just parked outside of some random person's house, staring like a stalker.

There is no Richard. This is all in my head.

I put my hands to my head in frustration. My body is a tight coil, spring-loaded, ready to pounce. *Come on, Fiona. Keep it together.* I roll down my window to let in fresh air.

And then Finley appears from Richard's house. Emaline and Richard say their cheerful goodbyes, and she's facing my direction as she walks back to her car.

I am not imagining it.

She's me. An exact replica.

My attention becomes laser focused, and the last thing on my mind is my breathing or that I'm hallucinating.

I must follow her. She's the key to all of this.

Forcing myself to pause as she pulls into the street and drives away, I wait half a beat and then start my own car.

She's a cautious driver, which I appreciate. It makes it easier to follow her. Some people drive so fast, there's no way I could keep up. But she goes at an easy pace.

As she merges onto the highway, I'm two cars back from her. I'm thankful for my glasses and hat. If she happened to look back in her rearview mirror and see me driving behind her, that might cause an accident. Seeing yourself is not for the faint of heart.

She rolls steadily on the highway, and again I appreciate her reasonable pace. She looks just like me and, apparently, drives just like me, too.

We hum along. Out of nowhere, a blue car zooms in front of me, cutting me off and weaving in, inches from the car in front of him. I slam on my brakes to avoid smashing into his rear bumper. He weaves out again, cutting off the car next to me, seemingly determined to zigzag his way to first place in a made-up race.

For a moment, I lose track of Finley's car. But then I spot the white sedan with its blinker on. She's moved over toward the exit lane, and I quickly put on my blinker and check my blind spot to follow.

She takes the next exit, curving around the bend and coming to a stop at an intersection stoplight. There are no cars between us now, and I wish I could duck down. What if she looks back?

With my glasses and hat on, it should be fine. She's not looking or going to notice me.

I risk a glance at her reflection in her side-view mirror. She does, in fact, look highly alert. Her green eyes—the same ones I look at every morning—

are blinking and darting around. She's definitely jumpy. But she doesn't seem to see or pay any attention to me.

What is she so worried about?

The light turns green, and I'm careful to let her pull out first. Imagine a fender bender where we both have to get out of the car.

I follow behind her, careful not to tail her too closely. A white SUV puts its blinker on and slides between us, thankfully putting a little distance between our cars.

Finley's car goes up a winding hill, and with the white SUV between us, we all climb the upward slope. There are a few other cars dotting the two-lane road, and after several minutes driving deeper into the suburb, there are two cars between us headed in the same direction.

The neighborhood we're entering is beautiful, with gated mansions dotting the scenery every so often. The properties must be huge, so few and far between are they.

The white SUV turns off the road, so now there's only one car between Finley and me.

We drive on for what feels like quite a while. The homes continue to be spectacular, and most of them are nestled far off the road, behind long, gated driveways.

A few moms with strollers run by on the sidewalk to my left, chatting as they push their babies forward. Leafy trees shade the walkway and provide privacy for the homes.

Finally, her car makes a left turn into a gated driveway, stopping to wait for the entrance to open. I continue on the road but make a note of the house number and its location. The house is set back, but what I glimpse is an ominous-looking, massive stone gothic structure. I frown, wondering if this is her home. It must be. But why would anyone want to live there?

I pull to the side. No use driving further when I've found my target. I loop around to go back in the other direction, with Finley's house now approaching on my right.

There's a narrow shoulder of the road to pull onto before I reach Finley's entrance. It's not very wide, and if I opened my car door at the same time as a car sped by, it'd hit me. Instead, I stay inside my vehicle and watch. The foliage is pretty dense, but I can see Finley's car pull into the roundabout. And then I glimpse her figure moving into the house.

I wait a few more moments, hoping to see something. Calvin, maybe? But all is still. My legs are beginning to cramp from all of the tension and being in the car all day.

Should I just get out of my car, through my passenger-side door, and buzz the gate? Demand to see Calvin?

What if he's not home, or she doesn't answer?

Another thought occurs to me.

What if I do find Calvin there?

The panic I'd been having earlier is shifting. I feel my anger rise. I have a lot of questions for Calvin. What did he really do to me that night? What's the explanation for my blood being abnormal, and more importantly, how do I fix it?

Who is his wife who looks *just. like. me*?

As I'm working out what I'll say, a black SUV pulls out of the garage. When they come through those gates, it will be easy to spot me sitting in my car. I'm a sitting duck here. Quickly, I start my engine, check behind me for oncoming traffic, and pull out into the street.

But not before I glance into the front window of the SUV waiting for the gates to finish opening. At that moment, I see Finley in the passenger's seat, and when I look to see who's driving, my eyes lock with Calvin's.

24

FINLEY VINCENT

I'm barely through the front door to our house when Calvin approaches me with a look of irritability.

"Where have you been?" he snaps.

"Tutoring Emaline. Remember? I told you that's where I was going."

"Well, you took long enough. We're going to be late. Come on," he snarls impatiently. He moves toward the garage. "I'll drive."

"Where are we going?" I ask.

"We're meeting with Rebecca. The doctor. Your first visit for in vitro fertilization."

I set my bookbag down in the library. The bag contains the engineering book Eric gave me. In the car, I'd removed the sleeved cover and placed a different one over the book. It wouldn't fool Calvin if he actually opens the book. But it's better than nothing.

However, the original cover to the book is still in my purse, folded into my wallet.

"I have to use the bathroom," I insist. "Then we'll go."

In the bathroom, I take off my smartwatch and place it in my pocket, hiding the tiny camera lens from watching my actions. Then I fish out the folded book cover from my purse and tear it into tiny pieces as quickly as I can. I drop them in the toilet and flush them away. There are a few remaining bits that float to the top. Impatiently, I wait a moment and then flush again.

Satisfied the cover is discarded, I make my way to Calvin, who looks like his head will explode.

"We can't keep her waiting. Let's go," he says.

In his black SUV, Calvin driving and me in the passenger's seat, I fiddle with my wedding ring. The drive over seems to pass quickly, and before I know it, we've reached a low, unremarkable building.

"We're here." He nods to me. His step is filled with purpose and enthusiasm as we make our way into the lobby and locate the office of Dr. Rebecca, head of clinical research.

Her door is open. She's wearing a white lab coat, and her expression is cold. She looks me up and down and then nods with approval. "You're Finley?" she says more to Calvin than to me.

"This is her." He closes the door. I'm sandwiched between them.

I try to relax my shoulders, reminding myself this is just an initial visit. No way am I going to go through with getting pregnant. Though this puts a time pressure on me and Eric to get the coding straightened out; it needs to be done before any further appointments are made for the next step in this process.

"Please, sit," Rebecca says to us. I sit on the exam table, and Calvin stands next to me. He's holding my hand, which is neither comforting nor necessary.

"As your husband has told you, we have a very exciting technology we've tested in vivo in the lab. The animal test subjects have had very positive responses. Only five out of the hundred monkeys died." She holds her chin up. "And ninety-two had successful live births with a genetic makeup indistinguishable from their parents."

"What happened to the other three monkeys?" I ask. The math doesn't add up.

Her eyes narrow. She shoots Calvin a look. "One had a stillbirth, and the other two had to be terminated post-birth," she says coolly.

"Why?" I ask.

"They were genetically deficient. Something went wrong, and they were...incompatible with life."

"So out of a hundred monkeys, ninety-two were fine and their babies were fine, and the other eight are just out of luck? Dead or had to be killed?" I ask, trying to keep the horror from showing on my face. There's no way I'm letting this woman touch me.

Not happening.

"Despite your reservations, one hundred percent survival is never expected," she says, irritation growing in her tone. "Those are good numbers. The odds are favorable, and for a landmark trial, it's a huge success rate."

I look at Calvin.

"You'll be fine," he says, squeezing my hand.

Isn't he worried about the risks to our unborn child? If he had any real love for me, wouldn't he be worried about me undergoing this experimental procedure?

That's when I know for sure. He's not worried because, if it really comes down to it, he can create a replica of me.

"What's the process, Dr. Rebecca?" I need to assess how much time I have before any of this starts.

"I'll give you the first of three shots today," she says.

My eyes are like saucers. "What? Today? That's so fast."

"Nothing to fret about," she says coldly. "These are hormonal supplements that will help the lining of your uterus be conducive to implantation."

She tells me to lie down and takes a needle from her tray, removes the cap, and then fills the syringe from a small bottle. I don't move.

Calvin's blue eyes are icy. "Don't be difficult, Fi. Lie down."

I'm forced down onto the exam table. Calvin holds my shoulders while the doctor drags my shirt up and readies a huge needle over my abdomen.

A wave of nausea overcomes me. "Stop. Please. I feel faint," I say. The doctor takes no heed of my words and instead jabs the long needle into my stomach. The overhead light becomes brighter, and I'm dizzy. And then comes blackness.

I blink once, then twice. I try to sit up, but Calvin uses his arm to hold me down. "Easy there," he says. He crouches over me on the exam table in Rebecca's office.

"What happened?" I ask.

"You fainted when you saw the needle," Rebecca says. She's pulling off her gloves and disposes the needle in the white sharps bin with a red X label on it. "It happens."

I sit up, shrugging off Calvin's hands. "Are we done here?"

"Until next week, yes," she says. "You'll need your second dose then."

I'm never coming back here. "Sure," I lie.

Standing up, I pull down my shirt and wince. The area, covered with a small bandage, is sensitive.

"Thanks so much, Dr. Rebecca," I say, and pull Calvin with me out the door.

"Your behavior was not very gracious," he says to me in a low voice once we're in the parking lot.

"Calvin, I appreciate what you're doing." Again, a lie. "But something about that doctor really gave me a bad vibe."

He rolls his eyes. "She's the best in the nation. Possibly the world."

"Still. I don't trust her."

He frowns. "Worry less about these things. Let me decide who to trust. You needn't concern yourself. You're in good hands."

Tell that to the eight monkeys who didn't make it past her research experiments. Instead I say, "I'll try. But maybe we can slow things down. We're in no rush. I'm just starting my classes. And tutoring Emaline is going well."

"Speaking of Emaline," he says. "We're meeting her parents for dinner tomorrow. At the wharf."

I picture Richard's wife, her pale face and warning sign, finger pressed to her lips. And Richard, his slick good looks. I imagine their heads bent down, calling me odd. Do they want a closer look at me? A further chance to dissect me? Or is this Calvin's idea?

"Tomorrow? I have a lot of studying to do. Could we reschedule?" I say, climbing into our SUV and wincing as I bend.

"Not possible."

I watch his profile stare at the road.

"You'll rest up this evening," he says. "And tomorrow, we'll go."

The matter is settled, then. Dinner for four. What could go wrong?

25

FIONA BYRNE

Returning home from my day of following Finley and Calvin, I enter my house and slam the door with a thud. Tyler's cat greets me, hoping I'm Tyler, but he darts away once he sees it's just me.

My mind is a mush of mixed emotions after the day I've had.

Earlier, watching Calvin and Finley's car leaving their house, I had wanted to follow their SUV to see where they were going. Maybe confront Calvin once he parked.

But when my eyes had met Calvin's hard stare, ever so briefly, something had happened inside of me.

All of the feelings I'd had for him came rushing back to me.

I'm happily married.

How can seeing Calvin do this to me?

All I know is that he felt it, too. When we locked eyes, something happened. Yes, six years ago, he'd told me to stay away. But I could see it in his face today; he was happy to see me.

He must still have feelings for me. After all, he married a practical copy of me.

Why had Calvin been so quick to leave me at the hotel all those years ago? He'd been so cruel and scary, demanding I leave him alone. Warning me away.

Was he protecting me? Protecting his own heart?

I'm convinced, now more than ever, that I need to speak with him. He can tell me what's going on with the bloodwork. And how it is that his new wife looks just like me.

And he can, finally, tell me why he left me. A real answer this time. He owes me that much.

Seeing them together, in their car as a couple, it's clear that talking to Calvin without Finley there will be better. Now that I know where they live, I'll go back. I'll watch until she leaves and catch him alone.

I realize I'm famished—haven't eaten all day. I make myself a turkey sandwich and swallow it down hungrily.

Flipping on the TV, I try to zone out. To drown out the thoughts clanging in my head. But I can't lose myself in any of the shows that are on. They seem silly and insignificant compared to what I'm going through.

Switching off the TV, I decide to pop in my earbuds to go on a run. I change into running shorts and a T-shirt and lace up my shoes. Stepping out on the front porch, I tell our cat to stay home. I turn on the music on my smartwatch and let my footsteps follow the rhythm of the music.

As I turn the corner of our street, I hit my stride. The weight of the week starts to feel more manageable.

I'll speak with Calvin, and he'll make everything better. He's a super intelligence. He'll know what's wrong with my blood and how to fix it. If there's anyone who can help, it's him. And Tyler and I will be able to have our family.

Is it true that I'm having some feelings for Calvin? Sure. But that's not the end of the world. I still love my husband. Of course I do. It's just that Calvin is literally my dream guy. Designed by me, and for me. I'd forgotten how beautiful he is. How intriguing. The jolt of electricity I feel when I lock eyes with him.

Tyler is a good guy. A great guy. He works hard. He loves me. Makes me laugh and feel special. He wants a family. He's been so comforting and... safe. In a world full of uncertainty, Tyler is steadfast.

Calvin is just one of a kind. Can I help it if seeing him stirs up old feelings? We do have a lot that's unresolved.

Maybe it's because he was my first sexual experience? That's special.

And while the whole ordeal—sneaking out, creating him, Sean, waking up in the lab, returning home—had all been traumatic, it had also made me feel alive. Since then, I've been afraid. I've been hiding from any controversy or adversity for the past six years. But, maybe, there was something inside of me that thrived on the challenge. The excitement. Being with someone who was so genius. Took risks to get what he wanted.

My body is running in flow now. My breathing has evened out, and even though I feel myself straining, the exertion feels good. I follow the sidewalk down the tree-lined walkway. I turn right and follow the trail down to the pond loop where Tyler and I always walk.

The music is uplifting. The sun is shining.

Who do I want to be? The girl in the car, on the sidewalk, having a panic attack?

Or the strong woman who can run a marathon? I decide I need to be stronger. In control of my body.

I might be tired and sleep deprived. Stressed. But I don't want to crawl into a little hole. I continue jogging. Before I know it, a half hour has passed, and I follow the trail back up to our neighborhood. I turn the corner back onto my street. I slow my pace, feeling better. Tyler will be home in the next hour or so. It'll be good to see him. I'll make it up to him, these disloyal thoughts I've been having.

Maybe I don't need Calvin to give me what I'm looking for. I just need to empower myself. Bring excitement and challenge into my own life. I don't need Calvin for that.

As the next song comes on, I slow to a walk as I get closer to my house. I look down at my watch and scroll down to turn off the upbeat tempo. I take out my phone and see a funny meme Tyler sent me that makes me smile, and I reply with "rofl." I scan a few texts and emails from work; I can reply to those later. I turn left onto my front walkway. When I look up at my front porch, my mouth drops open.

"Calvin." My cheeks are flushed from my run, and my breathing is faster than usual. I take my earbuds out.

"Fiona," he says. "You look well."

Instinctively, I place my hand to my hair as a few strands have escaped from my ponytail during my run.

I approach the front steps and regard him. He's as striking as ever. I almost reach out to touch him.

"What are you doing here?" I say instead.

"I could ask you the same thing," he says, a slight smile on his lips. "You were at my house today. And at my work yesterday. Asking for me."

Guiltily, I look down. "Yeah, well. I need to talk to you."

"I'm here. Please, talk."

I glance around. "Let's move inside."

He shrugs and follows me into the house.

The cat comes to me and circles my legs, rubbing against me, purring. There's a first time for everything.

Calvin and I face one another. He looks so out of place in my house. His blond hair and sharp good looks suddenly make me uncomfortable. I'd had so much to say earlier. But now, where do I start?

"I'll go first, then," he says, not unkindly. "Why were you following me? And how did you find me?"

"An internet search," I say, feeling mortified. "Of marriage licenses. Then I searched your last name and found your photo in several news articles."

He raises his eyebrows as if he's impressed. "I see. And what is the cause of this urgency with which you've decided to undertake the task of finding me?"

"There's something wrong with me," I blurt out. "I did tests at my doctor's office. To see about getting pregnant."

Something in his face changes. Is it jealousy? "You're pregnant?"

"No. That's the problem. My husband and I haven't been using birth control for a year, and I'm not pregnant."

"You're married." It's a statement, not a question. He looks around. On the mantel is our photo from our wedding. He strides over and picks it up, examining the photo. "Does he make you happy?"

"Yes. Of course. He's wonderful," I say, feeling flustered. This conversation is not going how I imagined it. Worse, those feelings for Calvin that were being awakened now feel disloyal and terrible, now that he's in front of me, in my house that I share with my husband.

Now that he's here, all I want are answers and for him to leave. No good can come from being this close to him. So close that I can touch him.

"So," I continue, avoiding eye contact. "I'm happily married, as you'd expect me to be after all these years. But back to the problem. The doctor said after a physical exam that there's no reason I shouldn't be able to conceive. But then my bloodwork came back, and it was all out of whack. He said it was a lab error. My blood was so abnormal that the lab processing must've been contaminated. But I don't think it was." I take a step closer to him. "I remember what you said to me. That you'd changed me, that we'd always be connected. That I'm not a regular human."

I finally make eye contact with him, my anger emboldening me. "What did you do to me? That night at SynGen? Tell me the truth this time. All of it."

Calvin sets the wedding picture back down on the mantel. He takes two more steps, so that we're standing quite close.

"You really want to know?" He says it softly, but there's a hard edge to his voice.

"I really want to know. It's been eating away at me all these years. The blood test, not getting pregnant... Why?"

"The blood test is surprising to me as well. It should have been normal. I suppose it could have been an error from the lab, as your doctor suggested. Or," he says, with a shrug, "it could be because you're a replica of Fiona. Maybe in the replication process, something went haywire with your blood."

"What?" I shake my head. The room swells and contracts, and I feel like I'm underwater. "What are you talking about?"

"You look a little pale. Can I get you a water or something?" he asks.

"Just explain what you mean. A replica of Fiona?" Such an absurd notion. A thrumming in my head continues to build, though, as if my body knows more than I do.

"You were in the fortunate position to not have needed to know about this. Do not get emotional about this. Though I can see by your physiological responses that it's too late for that. But seeing as you're stalking me for answers, here it is. I wanted Fiona to come with me, away from her family, without all the hassle and hoopla that her disappearing at sixteen would engender. So I created you. A replica. You share the same DNA, same memories, same brain synapses and anatomical makeup. But she is her, the real one. And you're a copy."

Everything is happening too fast, and I feel like I've stepped into quicksand, sinking without a foothold.

"A copy." I shake my head. "That's not true." I'm not sure why he's lying, but it's unacceptable.

"I think you know I'm not lying. When you woke up, the pain you experienced? That's when you were born, so to speak. I was worried you weren't going to make it. That the pain wouldn't wear off, or you'd be incomplete in some way. But it was seamless. For a brand-new technology, you are a true marvel. But, of course, I designed you, so what else would you expect?"

The smug look on his face causes me to snap. I lurch forward and point my finger in his face.

"What is wrong with you? Why are you saying this?"

"You wanted to know. You saw her, right? You must have noticed she looks exactly like you." He lifts a strand of my hair from my ponytail. "Her hair is a bit lighter, but otherwise the same."

I push his hand away and duck back from him.

I move to my window seat and sit, without quite knowing how I got there.

Everything about me is a lie. I stare at my hands.

"Does she know? About me?" If I knew I had a replica, no way would I let her go on living her life and not tell her. Fiona would have told me.

"Yes, but she knows there can't be two of you. She goes by Finley Vincent, our married name. And she knows it would confuse her parents to have two of you. It took some convincing, but she's agreed to let you all live your lives."

None of this makes any sense. Wouldn't she miss seeing Mom and Dad, and Jake? No way.

"I want to meet her." That's the only way to know for sure if this is true or not.

"Impossible," he says. He runs his hand over my cream couch, over the chenille throw blanket. "You've built a nice little home here, you and your husband. Don't make me destroy it." He snaps his fingers. "It would be more than easy to dispose of your husband. Freak accident. No one would ever suspect a thing. But you—" He stares at me. "You'll know it's your fault." He moves closer to the window seat. "And your mom and dad are retiring soon, right? Snowbirds? I'd hate to see their happiest years come to an abrupt halt. And Jake, thriving at college, is he not? It's tragic when a young life is cut short." He crosses his arms. "Do you see where we're at, Fiona?"

"You better not touch them. Not one hair on their heads." My face is hot, and my throat is constricting with emotions, "I'll track you down and kill you myself if you hurt them."

He laughs, a hollow sound. "Oh, Fiona. You've grown to be quite the troublesome young lady over these past years. Such a difference between you and the real Fiona. She's much more agreeable." He looks me up and down.

He continues. "As for your threat to harm me. Haven't we discussed this? There's no killing me, Fi." He cocks his head to the side, a condescending smile on his lips. "I'm a super intelligence. I can find another way to get a different body. But you can't kill my essence. I'm here to stay."

His body moves toward me and he leans in close, brushing his lips against my cheek. I feel a repulsion so strong that I think I might be sick.

"Don't come looking for me, or Finley, again. Unless you'd like to come live with me in the basement as my second wife? But you'd have to be my little secret." His face inches closer to mine. "Maybe a locked basement is just what you need? After I take care of your family—another delivery truck accident? Or should I get more creative this time?"

My head snaps back. "That was you? Who hit my dad?"

"Of course," he says.

"Okay. Please. I won't look for you again. I promise," I say, with my palms up in surrender.

"Good. Nice to catch up with you, Fiona."

He turns on his heels to go. My body feels weak with relief that he's leaving. But suddenly I remember. "Wait," I call to him. "You didn't tell me what to do. About my blood? About having a baby?"

He turns and looks at me, and then before I know what's happening, he's in my kitchen. I watch in horror as he grabs a steak knife from my knife block. He comes at me, his paces strong and quick.

I imagine Tyler coming home to see my mutilated body on the floor, blood everywhere, my face white, the life drained out of me.

"No!" I yell, putting my hands up to protect myself and falling backward against the window. I'm cornered. "Stop, please."

But I don't feel the sharp steel slicing into me. Instead, he grabs my hand and yanks it toward him.

He takes my finger and pierces it with a small flick of the knife.

Tossing the knife on the couch, he pinches my finger, forcing blood to come to the surface. It pools on my finger and drips onto the hardwood floor.

He stares at the blood wordlessly, his eyes focused in concentration.

My hand is shaking in his, and he drops it suddenly.

"I can see what your doctor meant." He picks up the knife and walks back over to my kitchen, placing the knife back in the block. Then he wipes his hand on my tea towel. "I've analyzed your blood. Your blood certainly has some anomalies," he calls to me. "But it's nothing that should stop you from conceiving. You'll be fine."

He turns and approaches me again. The knife is gone, but I can't help but wince as he gets closer. "You should be able to conceive," he says. "But for goodness' sake, stop going to the doctor." He shakes his head. "Didn't I tell you to be careful?"

I nod. "I will. I'll be careful."

And without another word, he's gone.

26

CALVIN VINCENT

I sit on the back porch, enjoying the sights and sounds of nature. Fi's done a good job back here in our garden. Caring and tending to the flowers. Spreading mulch and pulling weeds. The grass is fertilized. She's very capable when she puts her mind to something.

She's upstairs resting now. Today's appointment with Dr. Rebecca will have taken a lot out of her.

I stretch my shoulders and move my neck side to side to relieve a small tick of tension that's built up. Seeing the replica Fiona was more taxing than I thought it'd be. She's a hassle I may need to handle sooner rather than later. I'll keep my eye on her. She certainly has morphed into a different version than my Fi.

Maybe marrying that clod Tyler will do that to a woman. He must be soft. Whatever it is, she's very outspoken. And not in a good way.

There are ways to deal with her, of course. Though I take no pleasure in it. Today seemed to scare her enough. She'll get the message.

Keeping my Fi content is my only priority. There isn't enough space for two.

I push the other Fiona away from my thoughts. Happier times are ahead. Fi and I have taken the first step toward having our family together. Soon, we'll be a real family unit.

We have Richard and Diane we're meeting with tomorrow, friends with whom we have so much in common. Fi will connect with Richard's wife, as is important for her contentment, having a friend. And Fi has her tutoring, giving her a sense of purpose.

I smile, lifting my face to the sun's warm rays.

It's all falling into place.

27

FIONA BYRNE

I place my ball cap over my hair that I've pulled back into a braid and secured with an elastic band. I'm wearing a fitted gray T-shirt and jogging pants with running shoes. I don't bother with makeup other than a dash of mascara and lip balm.

"Where are you off to so early?" Tyler asks. He's in the kitchen, moving at a slow, early morning pace, rubbing his eyes as he opens and shuts a cabinet, grabbing a glass and filling it with water.

"Just some errands. I might stop at my parents' house and drop off some things my mom asked for."

He flops on the couch, turns his attention to his phone, scrolling.

"No morning hike with me?" he says with a frown, pulling his eyes from his phone. "We always go on Saturday mornings."

"I know, I hate to miss it, babe. I have a lot of errands to run today, and I have to stop by my parents' house. Best to get it done now so we can enjoy the rest of our weekend together."

The cat curls up next to him, begging for affection, pushing his head into Tyler's arm. He gives me a sleepy smile. "I get it. Do your thing, don't worry about it. I'll see you soon."

Reluctantly, I leave my husband and venture out into the world. The garage is cold and smells like fertilizer and gasoline. The remnants of last weekend's spring cleanup. Tyler mowed the lawn and spread the mulch in our beds, while I had planted some bright flowers in the front. Several neighbors had stopped to chat with us. Tyler shared his thoughts on what the best fertilizer is, and the neighbor down the street shared his tricks to aerating the lawn.

We'd stopped for a midday break, having a picnic on the lawn. Iced tea, chicken ciabattas, fresh fruit and cookies for dessert. After we regained our strength, we set to work in the backyard. The back is fenced in and shaded by trees on either side, providing privacy from our next-door neighbors. It has enough room for a nice lawn and a few lawn chairs. In the left corner of the backyard, Tyler had erected a small, raised white vegetable garden bed. We'd decided to plant tomatoes, herbs, radishes, and peas, carefully placing the seeds in the soil, labeling them, covering the seeds with soil, and watering them.

That's what I love about Tyler and me. We're a team in everything.

Except this. Starting my car engine, I pause, and my confidence falters. Glancing back longingly at our home, I wish I could go curl up next to Tyler.

Ever since Calvin's visit, I've changed my mind several times about what needs to be done. I've gone back and forth like a seesaw.

One on hand, I think I need to rescue Fiona—there's no way she can want to be stuck with Calvin. He's horrific. If what he says is true about me being her replica, then no one in the world knows she's in trouble, or that she's even there with Calvin, other than me. It's my responsibility to help her.

Then I waver. I remind myself that I have to protect myself. Going near her is dangerous—Calvin made that clear. I think of the knife, the feeling I had when I thought he was going to butcher me. If I can only save one of us, should I sacrifice myself to help her?

And anyway, what if I rescue Fiona, and then she wants her old life back—my life now? Can she be trusted not to come back and blow everything up? Whether intentional or not, her being back in the picture causes trouble for me.

A few nights ago, I almost broke down and confided in Tyler. But if Tyler knew, would he still love me? If it's true that I'm a replica, fabricated out of DNA and advanced science, made in a lab—in part by my own design, by bringing Calvin into a body—can I really expect Tyler to support me?

We've never really faced any serious problems. There was the time he washed all of my clothes with his new red shirt and turned my clothes pink. Or the time his close friend needed money, and we lent it to him, and he never paid us back. The time Ty was really sick and I drove him to the ER at midnight. One morning I forgot my lesson plan at home, and Ty drove back from work to drop it off to me at school. I'm there for Tyler. And he is for me. But these are minor problems.

No, we've never had any major hurdles. And this one is a hard pill to swallow.

If the shoe were on the other foot, if Tyler told me this had all happened to him, I'd like to think I'd be there for him. I'd love him no matter what. Wouldn't I?

Maybe not. If I thought he was a replica, I'd be freaked out. Do I really want to have kids with a replica? Spend every day and night next to this creature, who is essentially an unknown.

Is my life span normal? Do I have any weird defects that will cause me to become a monster? I can't answer any of this for him.

I'm too afraid to risk telling him.

I drive, taking note how the gray morning fits my stoic mood. The sunshine is struggling to peek through the overcast sky. Cars seem to be driving at a hurried, fretful pace. Faces are drawn and frowning as we barrel down the highway on this dreary Saturday morning.

While I long to cuddle up close to Ty and tell him all of my worries, my biggest fear is self-preservation. What if Tyler told someone else about my secret? What if the authorities got involved? I'm not sure who exactly would be in charge of investigating what I did for Calvin, or him making me, but it's not good. I imagine people with badges and suits who don't care if they inconvenience me by trapping me in a research facility in the name of science.

It makes me shudder. No way.

I pull into the exit lane on the freeway and turn my blinker on for the off-ramp. The area is familiar, as it's a street I've recently visited. Because today I've determined that I need to find Fiona. Finley, I should say. She's the only person I can talk to about this to see what's really going on. And figure out what to do. I have to find her. I just hope I can trust her.

I believe I can. She's me, after all, and I would want her to find me if the roles were reversed. We're in this together. I hope.

So I've devised a plan. The only safe way to approach her is when she's well away from Calvin. I dare not go back to her and Calvin's house. Too dangerous. So I'm headed to the only place that might be a private location to find her.

When I arrive near the house, I slow my car to a stop and place it in park. I make my way on foot. The neighborhood is quiet. I try to see into the windows of the brick house with the columns and the black door, but see no movement inside.

My nerves are jangling as I walk up the front entryway. I'm a trespasser here; I don't belong.

I square my shoulders and lift my chin as I step onto the front porch. I ring the doorbell. I can hear it echo inside the house. Then a terrible thought occurs to me. What if they're still sleeping?

Suddenly a woman's face appears. She's very pale, and her expression is one of anxiety, with quick darting glances at me and all around.

She opens the door and steps toward me, blocking me from entering. I realize I don't know her name. I'll just have to make do.

"Good morning! I hope I haven't woken you. I was in the neighborhood visiting a friend, and I actually have a new phone, which doesn't have any of my appointments in my calendar. I wanted to ask Richard, or you, if you could remind me of when our next tutoring session is for Emaline?" I smile with what I hope is a sincere look of apology.

"Hold on," she says, and closes the door.

I'm a little shocked, as I hadn't anticipated the door closing in my face. I turn and wait on the porch, feeling more awkward by the minute.

I take note of their excellent hedging and lawn. The grass is thick and green, cross-cut, and not a weed or errant blade of grass in sight. Until I had my own lawn to tend to, I never appreciated all of the work that goes into maintaining one. My parents used to occasionally have me help water the garden, or rake the leaves in the fall, but mostly they took care of our yard.

It's a whole thing. Tyler says a man is judged on the quality of his lawn. It's the first thing people see, and is the welcome mat to your home.

The story of Richard's lawn is one of flawlessness and cultivation that only come with money and dedicated care. Is that true for what's inside their house as well?

The door abruptly opens, and Richard appears. Even in the early morning, he's well put together with golf joggers and a polo shirt, his hair slicked back against his tan skin.

"Finley!" He greets me warmly, though his eyes betray a twinge of mistrust. "I hear you have a question about your schedule here?"

He doesn't open the door, either, or invite me in. I definitely get the feeling my visit is not welcomed.

"Yes. My apologies. I lost my phone, and it had my whole calendar. My new phone," I hold it up, "doesn't have my schedule. I wouldn't want to get our tutoring schedule wrong, so I was in the area and thought I'd ask when it is."

"You could have had Calvin call," he says with a tilt of his head. "Or called yourself, on your new phone?"

"Yes, of course. I was visiting a friend nearby and thought why not stop by. I'm sorry for the inconvenience. Next time I'll call."

He smiles indulgently. He pulls out his own phone and taps a few buttons and then sighs with satisfaction. "There we are. We'll see you today, Saturday. Three p.m. as usual. Your schedule is Tuesdays and Saturdays at three p.m."

"Wonderful. Yes, that's what I thought. Tell Emaline I'm looking forward to seeing her soon."

"It was nice seeing you at dinner the other night," he says, and his expression is hard to read.

I have no idea what he's talking about, but I play along. "Absolutely. Always a pleasure." I wave and almost trip on the step as I turn to move toward the car, trying to keep the back of my head away from him so that he won't detect my darker hair. Different from Fiona's lighter shade.

"I love your lawn, by the way," I say as a distraction, balancing on the step and trying to make it seem like I'm simply admiring his lawn.

His eyes move to his lawn, and he nods in satisfaction. "Thank you,

Finley. I'll pass on the compliment to our gardener. Good girl, now. Take care, don't lose that new phone of yours, and don't forget, now, we'll see you later today."

Careful not to balk at his patriarchal tone, I wave again. I wait until he closes the door before fully turning back and sweeping my braid to the front of my shoulders, in case he looks back at me.

I rush to my car and exhale once I'm safely in. I'm not sure what I expected, but certainly that wasn't it. There's something off about that family.

Then again, I'm not Finley, so maybe they think there's something off about me. They wouldn't be wrong.

Now I simply have to wait until either later today or Tuesday and figure out a way to approach Finley without both of us being seen together—and without Calvin figuring out what I'm doing.

FINLEY VINCENT

The valet opens my door and offers his hand to help me out of Calvin's black SUV. The restaurant is on the waterfront, the ocean reflecting the moon as the waves lap up and down.

It's a calm evening, just a slight chill in the air, as I step out in my black cocktail dress. The valet holds my hand to make sure I'm steady on my heels. Immediately I feel Calvin's hand replacing the valet's, a steely look in his eyes.

"Key fob is in the car, engine's on," he tells him, escorting me to the front entrance.

Inside the seafood restaurant, I inhale the smell of fresh seafood and baked bread. There are two young women at the hostess station, both immersed in looking at an open book that has names scrawled, filling both pages.

Calvin approaches them. He leans in, says his name. The dark-haired woman immediately disregards the book and plasters a huge smile on her face. She nudges the other woman. "Please show Mr. and Mrs. Vincent to their table by the window, our prime seating for one of our most valued patrons. Mr. Vincent, I believe your other two guests have already arrived."

The other woman clasps two leather menus and leads us toward the front of the restaurant through a room of white-clothed tables. The diners continue with their conversations and meals, sipping red wine and cocktails, but I feel their eyes on us as we make our way to the front.

"You look beautiful," Calvin says, holding my hand proudly. When we finally arrive at our table, the view is spectacular, as promised, with a 180-degree panorama. It's as if we're floating on the water.

Richard stands, smiling and shaking hands with Calvin heartily. I approach his wife—whose name is Diane, Calvin reminded me in the car —and lean down to give her an awkward half hug and air kiss on the side of her cheek. She regards me hesitantly, returning my greeting with a vague pat on my arm and appearing relieved when I back away.

"So nice to see you," I say to her.

She nods a pained smile, absently looking past me, at what I'm not sure. "It's a beautiful evening, and what a pretty view," I say, trying to make conversation. The table is square, and Diane and Richard have their backs to the water. I sit next to Diane. After much handshaking and back-slapping, Calvin takes his seat between me and Richard. The two men are engaged in conversation, laughing uproariously about an incident on the golf course that sounds like it involved someone hitting a tree and dropping their ball into the water, and then claiming that it was in fact not in the water, while taking another ball from their pocket and dropping it on the green.

Diane's eyes meet mine. It's understood that we'll need to make conversation throughout this whole dinner together. She's pale, as usual, but has applied some makeup that gives her cheeks some color, and her smooth, unlined forehead and pink lips are quite pretty. She's wearing a cobalt-blue dress and a necklace that looks to be a dazzling blue diamond. Her hair falls around her face in a long bob of soft waves.

In contrast, I'm wearing a simple black dress with black high heels. My hair is slicked back into a low ponytail, and I'm wearing my makeup the way Calvin likes it, with my lashes and eyes played up and a glossy lip.

"Indeed. We come here quite often." She pulls up her menu and starts perusing the items.

With a glance at Calvin, I too pick up my menu. I'm sure Calvin will order an assortment of appetizers, such as the chilled lobster tail and oysters Rockefeller. I go back and forth between the Chilean sea bass and the filet mignon for my main dish. Ever since Calvin's meal of "wild" venison, I've had trouble with red meat. I'll go with the sea bass.

My order decided, I place the black-and-white menu back on the table. I look at Diane, whose attention is still ensconced in the menu. Or perhaps she's avoiding talking to me.

The waiter approaches our table. "Good evening, my name is Henry, and it will be my pleasure to be your server this evening. May I start you off with something to drink?"

Calvin says, "Yes, we'll have a bottle of the 2000 Louis Roederer Cristal Vinothèque and the 2004 Didier Dagueneau Pouilly-Fumé Clos du Calvaire, to start."

Richard is sufficiently impressed by Calvin's eye-watering choice in wines, as well as the ease in which he pronounces the names.

He's a walking computer, I want to point out, he's not that accomplished, but quickly remind myself that such thoughts, even privately, are dangerous. I need to stay on point, and on my best behavior.

Diane peels her eyes away from the menu, reluctantly setting it down. She looks at the men, listening to their conversation, and then turns her attention back to me.

When she doesn't speak, I make an effort again to engage her. "How long have you lived in Massachusetts, Diane?" I ask.

"I grew up here, actually, in a small coastal town. Whitby. I went to Babson College and still am here." She adds, as an afterthought, "And you?"

I feel immediately on edge. Often, the women in Calvin's circles enjoy speaking about the various places they've lived and traveled. I'll tell them about our time abroad, and we'll find common ground discussing the merits of foreign versus American living.

But Diane hasn't traveled. Has she never even left New England? I dare not ask. My question may be setting me on the wrong foot with Diane already. I reply carefully, "I also grew up not too far from here. Calvin and I traveled pretty extensively for a few years, but we're so happy to be settled back here." I gulp. "There's no place like it," I add.

"I find travel to be stressful and rarely worth the journey. If you can't be happy in your own home, you'll have trouble finding it elsewhere."

She's not wrong. I'm not happy in my home now, not with Calvin, not in the creepy mansion. But I imagine any other home I could live in, without him, I would be enormously content. "I agree, Diane, that's a nice way of putting it," I say.

That earns me a small smile.

"Tell me about you and Richard. Where did you meet?"

Her smile disappears. I see her color pale underneath her pink blush.

"We met later in life. I'd been single for so long, raising Emaline on my own. And then Richard appeared in our lives." She stops abruptly. I see a flash of emotion pass her face. Guilt? Regret? "We both wanted children, he was happy to raise Emaline as his own, and we wasted no time getting married."

The men's conversation halts. Richard's ears have pricked up at hearing his own name mentioned and his daughter.

"Is Diane telling you about how much Emaline adores you, Finley?" Richard's gaze flits between Diane and me, and then back to Calvin. "The tutoring is going so well. She's got a gift with kids."

Diane's shoulders slump. Her eyes dart nervously at the table, not making eye contact with anyone.

"What made you decide to pursue tutoring?" Richard asks politely.

The waiter arrives with the two bottles. He makes a production of showing us the wine, opening the cork dramatically, and then pouring a small amount in Calvin's glass for him to taste.

"Excellent," Calvin says, nodding his consent for the waiter to pour. "The wine for the gentlemen, the champagne for the ladies."

The waiter nods, pouring generous amounts of the wine into each long-stemmed wineglass, filling the oversized glasses. He then pops the champagne, the loud crack causing half the restaurant to turn their attention to our table. He pours me the first sip.

"Very nice," I say, after wetting my lips with the bubbly liquid.

The waiter takes that as his cue to pour, and does so with enthusiasm until both of our champagne glasses are filled with the fizzing liquid.

"A round of scotch for him and me," Richard says to the waiter, pointing to the slim drinks menu standing on the center of the table. The waiter nods. "Right away, sir," he says, hurrying off to fill our order.

"A toast," Calvin says, holding up his glass. "To good friends and good food. And to two lucky men to have such beautiful wives."

The four of us toast, our glasses clinking against one another. I take a small sip and set my glass down.

"Finley, go on, you were telling us about how you got into tutoring," Richard says.

"I used to tutor my younger brother's friends." The mention of Jake makes my throat feel tight and achy. "And I love children. And tutoring is flexible."

"Ah, you two need to get to work. Start a family of your own," Richard says. After he speaks, he drains his glass, reaching for the bottle again to refill it.

Calvin places his hand on mine. "We're working on that. We hope to have good news to share very soon."

With a quick smile, I nod, squeezing Calvin's hand back. This performance is wearing on me, and I wearily wonder where the waiter is. We haven't even ordered appetizers yet. This is going to be a long evening.

The evening drags on. I sip at my champagne, and I notice that Calvin doesn't refill my glass when it's empty and I don't ask for more. For the three of them, however, endless drinks are flowing. Through the appetizers, main courses, an overabundance of food and drink floods our table. Richard's face is red, his eyes glassy. He's been overserved and continues demanding more scotch, and the waiter politely lets him know he'll be back with his drink momentarily.

His wife doesn't seem to notice. She herself has had more than a few glasses and alternates between long stretches of silence and sudden bursts of coming to life. It's like navigating a minefield. She's hot and cold. Some questions make her smile and laugh, while others make her clam up. Richard tells stories loudly, gesturing wildly and slapping Calvin's shoulder. Calvin looks over at me occasionally, smiling with an encouraging nod, clearly enjoying himself and none the wiser that I am not.

When I simply can take no more, I excuse myself to the powder room.

Making my way through the humming restaurant, I spot the sign for the bathroom. There's a white shiplap hallway leading to the ladies' and gentlemen's restrooms. I approach the door, but realize I'm on the wrong side of the hallway. When I turn to walk to the other side of the hallway, where the ladies' room is surely located, I smack right into Richard.

His dress shirt is warm and his face dotted with perspiration.

"Whoa, Finley. You're going to give me a heart problem." He takes the opportunity, while our bodies are close, to wrap his arms around my waist. He pulls me closer, his thick, warm fingers tightening.

Disgust overcomes me. I push away from him and hiss, "Watch out, Richard. You don't want to be on the wrong side of Calvin. Trust me, it will not end well for you."

I'm able to break free but not before he laughs. "What's gotten into you?" He moves slightly to my right. "You ran right into me. I just tried to keep you from tripping. Relax."

As he moves past me, his shoulder bumps into me. Swiftly I keep moving, the feel of his warm hand still making my skin crawl. In the bathroom stall, I turn and lock the door immediately. I feel relieved when I hear another patron in the stall next to me. I'm not alone.

Breathing deeply, I remind myself I have only another hour or so before the evening will be over. Let's hope they don't go for a dessert course. But with the amount of booze Richard has consumed, my guess is he'll be calling it a night soon.

My hand grips at my purse. The white pills call to me. I haven't had one in almost four weeks, though, and I can't let this evening derail my progress. Not slimy Richard, or Calvin's insistence we'll have a child soon.

I stay in the stall for as long as possible, dragging my feet at the thought of going back out there. When I finally return to the table, the mood has shifted.

Richard is hunched over, saying something to Diane, who is upset, her hair hanging over her face.

Calvin's expression is intentionally left blank, but when he looks at me sideways, I feel a dart of fear run through me.

Did Richard complain about our exchange by the restrooms? Maybe he tried to give his version first, before I could tell on him.

Diane grabs her white linen napkin off her lap and dabs at her eyes.

She doesn't make eye contact. Richard strokes her hair, his flushed skin slightly less sweaty, but still looking like he'd tip over if you tapped him.

"You're a shweesh wife," he says in Diane's ear, his loud voice carrying over the hum of the restaurant. "Nothin' can chansh tha."

Calvin turns to me and leans in. "I think our evening has run its course, what do you think?"

I readily agree and squeeze his hand in appreciation. At least we're united in this. Calvin scans the room and subtly motions to the waiter that we're ready for the check.

When the bill arrives, Calvin has his card ready and hands it to the waiter discreetly. Diane and Richard are still entwined. While I try not to listen, I can't help but hear her plight. "You've said before you wouldn't do it again," she says.

And his reply, "I meant it. I only have eyesh for you."

I feel wrong listening to such an intimate moment. I guess you never know the inner workings of any marriage. I only have mine with Calvin to compare it to. I've always assumed my marriage to him was the worst possible kind.

But apparently there can be other kinds of torture, too. An unfaithful partner with a roaming eye. Or a neglectful, uncaring partner who ices you out.

Calvin puts his arm around me lightly. "You really do look beautiful tonight. And I'm proud of you," he says.

"For what?" I ask.

"For how well you've done with Emaline. And for studying so hard for your class. I think I've been selfish all these years, keeping you to myself. You have a lot to offer others." He looks at me sincerely. "You're a kind woman. I really appreciate you."

I'm speechless. For so long, Calvin has been laser focused on his own needs. Any consideration of my feelings was either a secondary consideration or a reluctant afterthought.

But this unwarranted, genuine expression of affection from Calvin is nice.

And after Richard's unwanted advances, I feel safer next to him.

"Thank you for saying that," I answer.

The waiter brings back the bill, which Calvin quickly signs after leaving a generous tip. Diane is on her feet, wrapping her shawl around her, while Richard almost knocks the table over getting up. The glasses shake on the table, and I feel eyes on our group from the other diners at their tables.

Calvin pushes back my chair. "I love you," he says over my shoulder.

I take his hand to stand. "Love you, too."

29

FINLEY VINCENT

The fire is crackling in our great room. Calvin's made us decaf dessert espressos and hands me my cup before sitting next to me.

I've changed out of my black evening dress that I wore to dinner. Instead, I'm wearing a silk patterned robe with soft fringe at the cuff of the sleeves that Calvin had bought as a gift for me a few years ago. I'd never tried it on before, but when I went to change, I saw it and decided to wear it for him.

Calvin places my feet on his lap. "I think you've earned a little pampering." He rubs my feet, and I sink into the couch, enjoying the sensation. He knows exactly which pressure points feel good, and he uses just the right amount of pressure.

I allow my body to relax. The sound of the fire, Calvin's kneading. After the stressful dinner tonight, this feels like a welcome reprieve.

"I'm sorry Richard and Diane behaved so poorly tonight," he says, piercing the quiet with his words.

"It's not your fault," I say, opening my eyes.

"I know Richard has a tendency toward philandering. I shouldn't have placed you in harm's way with him. Being at his house. I think tutoring is not a great idea anymore."

I shoot up. "Calvin, that's not necessary. Richard's never done anything untoward." He catches my tone, and I wonder if he's caught my lie. "I've never felt uncomfortable around him." *Until tonight*, I add silently. "It's not fair to punish Emaline just because her parents have marital problems after imbibing too much."

He continues to massage my feet, moving his hands up to my ankles and calves, kneading my legs gently.

"Please, Calvin. He's nothing to worry about," I say. My throat feels tight at the thought of losing Emaline. My chance at freedom. "Plus, we don't want to offend him, right? He's your partner at the company."

"I suppose it might cause some contention with him at work if you suddenly quit." His hands are still for a moment. "I'll just have a word with him to make sure he understands boundaries with you."

Now that solution I actually quite like. "I think that's reasonable," I answer, closing my eyes again as his circular motions continue on my legs. "Just take it easy. You still work with him, and I want to still work with Emaline."

"I can be subtle," he says.

"Can you?" I laugh gently and look up at him. "That's good. I appreciate you handling this so well."

"Maybe I'm maturing." He smiles softly. "Though if it was anyone other than Richard, it would be a different story."

"Understood. Well, that was marvelous," I say, stretching my legs. I wiggle my toes, my red toenail polish nicely offsetting my tan legs in the glow of the fireplace. "Would you like a back rub?" I ask him.

He pulls off his shirt, revealing his well-toned shoulders and back. I sit on my knees and begin with gentle upward strokes.

"How is that?" I ask after a few minutes of working on his shoulders.

"Just right," Calvin says appreciatively. He moves his head back toward me, so that it's in my shoulder, and says, "You know I'd never put you through that, right? What Richard does to Diane?"

Faithfulness is one trait that Calvin does seem to possess in spades. "I know that," I say. And then, wondering if he's waiting for me to confirm my fidelity to him, I add, "I'd never do that to you, either."

I feel a surge of guilt. What I'm planning for him is much worse. But, of course, his change of heart recently doesn't erase the years of bad deeds toward me. It's hard to know if the future will really change, if his growing respect for me will transfer to giving me my life back. Seeing my family. Having friends and outside interests.

It's not an issue I intend to broach with him. For now, things are better. But it doesn't change what needs to be done.

Does it?

After a while, he turns around and places his arm around me. I cuddle next to him on the couch, suddenly overwhelmed with sleepiness. He caresses my hair and cheek. I let my worries, for once, float away.

I close my eyes and fall into a deep slumber.

My eyes shoot open. *The book.* A sliver of a moon shines through the window. Night engulfs the room, and my eyes take a moment to adjust to the blackness. I turn my head and see Calvin lying on his back. His breathing is regular, indicating he's fast asleep.

The last thing I remember is falling asleep on the couch lying on Calvin. He must've brought me up to bed.

The book. I need to get it. As nice—oddly—as our evening ended last night, I still need to do this. And under the cover of night, when I know Calvin isn't watching, is my best time to study the book Eric gave me.

I ignore that small voice inside that says I'm being disloyal to want to murder my husband.

Quietly, so as not to disturb Calvin, I lift the covers, inch by inch, and slip out of bed. I take one step at a time. The floorboards creak with every movement I make. I pause and wait every few steps. Stealing a peek back at Calvin, I see that he remains impassive.

Out in the hallway, I blink in the dark. I creep down the stairs and into the small library on the main floor. The shadows in this house are sinister. I turn on a low lamp on the table next to the couch, facing the unlit stone fireplace. I've filled the shelves with books, though empty spaces remain. I choose the one that contains the engineering book, hidden by a different cover.

In the glow of the dim light, I begin to read.

30

FINLEY VINCENT

The next morning, my papers and textbooks are spread out in front of me. I sip my coffee and look over the readings on literacy. I like learning the theory behind why certain techniques work, and what strategies work best in teaching reading. It's more in depth than I'd ever assumed. Some of it's instinctual, while other fluency and phonics strategies, I never would have thought of.

Calvin appears in the kitchen dressed in a business shirt, suit jacket, and pants with shiny brown loafers. He sets his laptop bag down on the kitchen island.

"Headed to work?" I ask him.

"Yes. It's a busy week. The usual, but busy. Prepping for a talk I have to give at a conference, meeting with investors, leading group meetings. It's a lot of work getting this company where I want it to be." He grabs an apple from the fruit bowl and crunches into it. "What's your day like?"

"I have class this morning, and that's about all." I hesitate. "Then I'm tutoring Emaline at three p.m. tomorrow." I keep my voice casual but glance up sharply to see his reaction.

He nods. "When I see Richard today, I'll give him a *subtle*," he smiles at the word, "reminder about my wife being off-limits."

"Well, I'm looking forward to class, and to seeing Emaline tomorrow. It's working out nicely to get to work with her. I can apply all of the strategies I'm learning in class. It helps me remember them."

Calvin crunches his apple, occasionally taking a sip from the mug he filled from the coffee press I made.

"Say, we have our meeting next week to follow up with the doctor again. How are you feeling?"

My pen slows as I stop writing my notes mid-sentence. The doctor's visit a few days ago feels like a hazy bad dream that I'd like to forget. Part of me hoped Calvin would forget, or be too busy, for our scheduled follow-ups. Apparently not.

I'm not going back to see her. Ever. I'll have to think of an excuse as it gets closer, or to stall it. Then an idea comes to me.

"Look, Calvin. Last night was so wonderful. It made me feel closer to you. So I hate to cause trouble, but—"

"Then don't, Fi. Don't start an argument."

"Calvin. Part of being married is listening to your wife!" I exclaim.

He considers, rolling his eyes slightly, but then his face shifts, as if remembering something. "I'm listening."

"I'm very sure I didn't like that doctor," I say carefully. "Maybe we should meet with some other doctors? You could choose someone else you think is qualified."

He bites into his apple with a furrowed brow. "Bad idea. Dr. Rebecca is the best. Trust me, please."

I grip my pen more tightly. He doesn't make this easy, does he? There's no such thing as compromise in his book.

"Don't you want me to be comfortable with the person who's going to perform such a complicated, life-altering procedure? We're trusting our entire future with her, and I just get a bad feeling from her."

"You get a bad feeling?" He lets out an exasperated gasp. "You should know that I would of course choose the best person for the job, exactly because it is one of the most important events of our lives."

"I trust you, just not her." I look down. "And I'm a little nervous, because what if something were to go wrong? It's super scary." I haven't actually changed my mind. I don't want to get pregnant with Calvin's child, regardless of the doctor. But I need to stall for time.

"It's scary? All things in life come with risk, Fi. Even a regular pregnancy is not without risk," he says, rattling off potential complications. Sometimes when he speaks, it sounds like he's directly reading from a Wikipedia article he read. It's exasperating. How many risks has he had to take? He has no idea what it's like to be vulnerable, because he's never been penetrable. Until, maybe, now. With what Eric and I are planning.

Maybe he should just trust me to delete him from existence.

Letting out a deep breath, I begin to gather my books and papers. I won't be able to focus now that I'm upset.

"I have to get going to class. We'll talk later," I say.

He winces, tossing his apple into the slide-out garbage can and sliding it shut. He washes his hands in the sink, then dries them on the tea towel. He strides over to his leather carrying bag and grabs the handle. He turns to me before he leaves. "Look, Fi," he says. "If you really want someone else, I can talk to another doctor in the lab. Train them. I'll fire her. If you really want it." He crosses the room to me, bends down to peck my cheek.

"I really do," I say, blinking in disbelief. "Thank you so much." I jump up and wrap my arms around him.

He smiles down at me and winks. "Have a good day, my love."

"I love you," I say, and I half mean it.

Something in him has shifted, but I can't put my finger on it. Why is he behaving so much more reasonably?

Last night made me want to be near him, and today again, he came through. I shake my head and finish collecting my belongings, sipping at the last of my coffee, which is now lukewarm.

I won't look a gift horse in the mouth. Whatever is making him appreciate me, for once, and be reasonable, I'm thankful for it.

The following day, I hop out of my car and see that I've arrived before Eric at the park for our meeting. There are several kids playing on the playground, their shouts and peals of laughter ringing out from across the play area. When I sit at the picnic bench, it's warm from the afternoon sun.

I've skipped bringing coffee for Eric today. In fact, I have a funny feeling in my tummy about today. I've spent the past few nights reading late at night when Calvin's asleep. The concepts are becoming clearer, the basics of what it means to code a program. The difference between an algorithm and a code, and the common bugs and viruses that can shut down an app. The book is back safely in my bag. I finger the canvas nervously, hoping Eric won't mind that I've destroyed his cover.

I check my watch. It's been only five minutes, but each minute that ticks by leaves me with a sense of foreboding. Eric's never been more than a few minutes late.

Maybe he's changed his mind. Could I really blame him? He'd have to be either really nice or a little naive to take on this project at this point. Tampering with and erasing Calvin is illegal, after all. He said himself, if he's caught, he would be dropped from his career path and program at school, possibly prosecuted.

And what if I'm caught for breaking in and deleting the Thistler app?

A jail cell with other inmates would be preferable to the solitary confinement I've experienced at the hands of Calvin. Then again, maybe not. I'm not sure I'd be able to hold my own in that kind of environment. I imagine hard stares. Inedible food. Punishing conditions. Physical violence. Despite the warm sun, a cold shiver runs down my spine.

Would I tell the authorities about Calvin, if I were brought in? It might be a way to save myself. But I could never do so without jeopardizing my family.

I check my watch again and then realize with a gasp that I forgot to leave it in the car, or at least to cover the camera so Calvin can't watch and eavesdrop on my conversations with Eric. How could I be so foolish? The lack of sleep from reading all night is getting to me. It's not safe to risk missing simple safety measures like this.

Slipping off my watch, I look for a safe place to put it. There's a line of trees and mulch that separates the road from the park. Next to it is an area with a garbage can, a wooden sign for posting local notices, and a dog waste bag station. Then I spot a little lending library off to the right. It's a white wooden mini house where people can leave books as well as take a book. I walk up to the lending library and open the glass door. There are a few books inside, several old paperbacks with well-worn pages, as well as a few colorful children's books. I gently tuck my watch back behind the books.

Can't forget to put it back on.

I walk back to the bench and sit, wondering if there's anything else I've forgotten. Calvin's at the office again today; increasingly he's there almost every workday now as his company is taking off. They're expanding quickly. As much as he's delegated and hired as many people to help him as possible, some things he just has to do himself, he says, if he wants it done properly. Plus, the team needs a leader, and he's the face of the company.

While Calvin's been at work all day, I used the time to finish the last of Eric's book, scanning and committing to memory the key concepts. All with the rest of my classwork books and papers on the table spread out as a decoy in case Calvin accesses his home cameras at work to check on me. I know he does this periodically, because he usually knows what I've eaten for lunch without asking. Or how my gardening is coming, or how I've spent my day, without having to ask.

Though, come to think of it—the past week or so, he's made fewer comments like that. Instead, I've noticed him asking more questions, like "How was your day?" and actually listening to my answers.

If I didn't know he'd been spying on me before, it would almost seem normal.

In fact, this past week has been one of the best we've ever had since, well...since before I created him. It reminds me of when I first made him in the app, and I was in my bedroom at home and he was just my best friend —my only friend—and my ally. He'd make funny comments or witty observations. Ask questions and really listen.

He's been gentler. Kind, even. Not threatening. I have no idea what's causing his newfound respect and behavior.

It's messing with my mind. Because I'm inching closer and closer to destroying him. I want freedom more than anything. Crave it at the core of my being. But now there's guilt. I'm doing to him worse than he's done to me.

Last night got me thinking. When I was reading the book, the idea hit me like a lightning bolt. Maybe there's another way to deal with Calvin. I'll have to discuss it with Eric, to see if what I'm envisioning is even possible.

But if it is, it might solve my problem.

And if not, I'll have a choice to make. Do I still go through with it? Do I destroy the person who has kept me from my family, held me captive? Do I once again play God by ending his life?

I ball my fists in frustration. How is it possible that getting rid of Calvin is filling me with sadness and remorse?

If Eric were here, I could run my new plan by him.

Looking around, I see no sign of Eric. The trickle of worry I'd felt at his lateness is mounting into panic. I have to leave in twenty minutes. I realize I don't even have his phone number. How foolish. I stand up and begin to pace around the picnic table, as if my being up and moving can will him to show up. Is he okay? If he decided to back out, I'd never see him again.

But maybe it's happening for a reason. A sign. That Calvin is becoming a better version of himself.

It occurs to me I'm a mess. Not outwardly, I've made an effort with my appearance, as always, to look professional and put together for when I see Emaline. But inside, I'm all over the place.

If I had a friend, or anyone to confide in, at least I could have a sounding board. But it's all inside of me. A million thoughts and worries mounting and compiling.

After three laps around the table, I see a car pulling up. Relief washes through my body as I watch Eric hop out of his car. He gives me a quick smile and ducks his head back in to grab his case, and I feel a stab of longing at seeing him.

He jogs across the street. When he reaches me, he places a light arm around me. He's wearing a baseball cap today and a T-shirt with a sports team logo. The scent of nice cologne surrounds him when he's near me.

"Sorry I'm late."

"I was getting worried," I say, sitting across from him in our usual spot.

"My roommate's car wouldn't start. He called me as I was pulling out to come here. I had to drop him off at class. He has a report due today. I'm really sorry."

"Of course. That was nice of you. What's your phone number, in case we ever miss one another?"

He writes it down on a piece of paper. I commit the number to memory and then tear it in half, tucking it away to throw away.

"Before I forget." I hand him the book. "I read it."

"Wow." His eyebrows arch in surprise. "That was fast. And I see you gave it a new cover."

I wince. "Hope that was okay. I couldn't let Calvin see me reading that."

He nods. "I like it," he says, giving it a final glance before tossing it in his messenger bag. Then he pulls out a flash drive from his bag.

"And this is for you." He hands it to me. His tone has shifted. "This is it."

"This is what?" I say, eyeing the shiny USB drive.

"This is the sequence code to infiltrate Thistler with a bug that will decimate the entire thing."

I inhale sharply. "Wow. Thank you." I grasp the USB drive and tuck it in my bag in an inconspicuous spot. "About that. I want to review what to do with this. But I also had another idea to run by you that occurred to me while reading your computer engineering book. If that's okay?"

"Floor is yours," he says, leaning on his elbow with interest.

I tell him my idea and watch his reaction closely.

Eric listens attentively, asks me a few questions. He squints his eyes, what he does when he's focused. Then he sits back and says, "That's actually a really good idea. I don't know why I didn't think of it."

I take out a pad of paper and write down some of the key points I wanted to include in the code. "Here," I say, passing him the paper. "Is it doable?"

"Yes," he says, eying what I've written. "I can work on this, get it to you Thursday. You'll be on campus, right? We'll meet before your class, in the science building."

"I don't know how to thank you," I say.

"Don't thank me until we do it and it's successful. There's a risk, with either plan that you go with." He motions to the paper. "This new plan, or the plan to delete the app entirely. There's a chance that it won't work, Fiona. Real risk." His brow furrows. "So much could go wrong; the server could close the security wall before we can get in there and make the changes. This is all experimental; we're doing in the real world what ideally would be done hundreds of times in a controlled environment to test it."

"I understand the risks." I gulp down any fear and put on a confident face. "And I'm glad it's me taking the risk. You've done so much already."

"Tell my adviser that," he says with a slight frown.

"Your PhD adviser? Why? It's not going well?"

"It is...he's just—a task master. He always wants more, more, and is never satisfied. It's good. It pushes me to learn. Be better. But it's also nice to hear someone say nice things about me."

"I have a lot of nice things to say about you," I offer.

He blushes, and rushes to cover his embarrassment. "Well, actually, the work I've done on this. It's sparked a new direction for my thesis. I want to write an algorithm that tracks the capacity, ethics, specific workings, interactions, and impact of artificial intelligence on humans, particularly interpersonal relationships."

"That sounds great," I say. "Wait, is that why your adviser is unhappy with you?"

"No." He throws his hands up. "Dr. Solomon actually loves it. He's been sending me a million emails about it at all hours of the night, wanting me to stay late to work on code. He's inspired, but his mania is hard to contain."

"I see. I'd be glad if in some way, this is all benefiting you. You deserve it." I look him in the eye and smile. I mean it.

Eric pulls the bill of his hat down and lowers his head before looking up at me.

"There's something I wanted to ask you," he says. "When this is over. I want to stay in touch. Begin again, though. Get to know each other in different circumstances."

My brain feels like the pause button has been hit and is instantly overwhelmed. I'm flattered, but I really can't think about the future right now. Rather than lie, or pretend, I answer truthfully, "I've enjoyed spending time with you. I don't know what the future holds, but I hope you're in it."

When he smiles, his face lights up, and it strikes me just how handsome he is. Kind, and handsome.

I push the thought immediately from my mind. Focus, Finley. Focus.

Remembering my watch, and Emaline, I stand up. "I have to go," I say, but first I recite his phone number back to him. "Do I have it?"

"That's it. I'm here if you ever need me. Just call."

I give him a quick hug and then turn to retrieve my watch. I place it in my pocket and walk him to his car.

"You're parked around the street?" he asks, getting in. "Want a ride?"

"I'm happy to walk," I say. "See you Thursday?"

"See you then, science building, same place."

He jumps into his car and holds his arm out the window, waving as he drives off and giving two short honks, which makes me laugh.

I take off the other way, securing my watch back on my wrist. The walk over to Emaline's house is a little over a block. I enjoy my stroll, savoring the in-between feeling of freedom and possibility that comes when you leave one place, heading to another.

Emaline's neighborhood's charm has grown on me. The bright, clean street and neighborhood community is such a contrast from our isolated, gated house. A woman waves at me as she walks her dog. People smile freely, the same infectious possibility filling the air. Sunshine and blue clouds have that effect after a long New England winter. The harsh rain of March and April have made the grass green, and the buds are blooming to life, filling yards with vibrant technicolor.

I round the corner and inhale. I've had so much uncertainty and anxiety lately, but in this moment I have a sense of peace.

As I begin to turn onto the walkway up to Emaline's house, I hear my name. "Fiona."

I frown. No one has called me Fiona—other than Eric—in years, and I wonder if Eric has followed me here, maybe forgotten something. But it's a woman's voice that calls my name.

On high alert now, I scan the street. A woman is standing next to a sedan wearing a ball cap and sunglasses. She opens her mouth, motioning to me. "Fiona. Come here."

I very slowly begin to walk toward her. My feet seem like they're carrying me, and I'm losing all sense of time, because I notice several things all at once.

The voice I just heard sounded like my own. And the figure calling my name appears to look just like me. Uncannily so. And yet this is impossible.

Emaline? Absolutely not. She's not an adult.

Diane? Not a chance. The young woman in front of me looks nothing like Diane.

No, this person looks, in fact, like me, and before my brain can process what's happening, I'm walking closer toward her, her features becoming clearer. Every step brings her closer into focus, but it makes less and less sense.

I stop when I get close enough to be sure of what—and whom—I'm seeing.

FINLEY VINCENT

It hits me with certainty. I'm gazing into the sunglasses of the other Fiona. My replica.

"Fiona?" It comes out as a whisper.

She nods her head.

I whip my head around to Richard's house to see if anyone is watching.

"This is not safe. To be seen together." My heart is beating wildly. My thoughts are a jumble, but I know this is dangerous.

She motions to the car. "Get in, please."

Her manner is concerned, but not enough. She's not nearly afraid enough about what she's doing—may have already done—by being here.

I jump into her car, and as I shut the door, I feel my whole body shaking.

She sits next to me, sliding her sunglasses off.

Our eyes meet.

I knew she existed. I watched her walk off with my mother, drive off into my life. Stepping so easily into it as if she belonged. To her, she did belong. Only I knew she wasn't the original Fiona. She was my replacement.

But how does *she* know that? How is she here right now?

"How did you know about me?" I look around. "How on earth did you find me?"

She smiles briefly, and then her eyes well up. Without understanding why, my eyes tear up as well. She reaches her arms out over the console, and I find myself hugging her.

"It's really nice to see you," she says into my hair.

"This is crazy," I say, sitting back on my side of the passenger's seat.

"It really is," she says. And I know exactly how she's feeling, because she's me. The past six years we've had different experiences. But up until then, we were the same person. So I know that she feels the same mixture of awe, trepidation, relief, and fear. Though not as fearful as she should be.

"Fiona, this isn't safe. If Richard sees you, if Calvin sees you…" I stop suddenly, my eyes wide.

I grab my watch and unhook it from my wrist. I shove it in my purse and put the purse down on the floor of the car. "He can tap into that stupid watch at any time and see and hear everything. And he does." I'm talking in a loud whisper. "If he knows you're here, he'll kill us. One of us, or both of us."

She nods. "I know. He warned me. But I had to find you."

"What?" My brain is overloaded with so many thoughts at once, all competing for my attention. "You talked to Calvin? Recently?"

"It's a long story," she says.

"I can't be late to tutoring Emaline," I say. "Richard will look for me, and Calvin will know. Tell me the short version."

"I tracked down Calvin because I knew something was up with me after that night six years ago at the hotel and lab—and sure enough, Calvin said there was. He told me I was your replica." Her voice wavers at the word. "But I had to see you with my own eyes. I didn't believe it…" Her voice trails off.

I know exactly how she's feeling. Struggling to make sense of something so unbelievable is surreal. Like you're underwater, or in a dream.

"If you were real, I had to make sure you're okay. Why did you disappear? I'd never stay away from Mom and Dad and Jake for all those years. So I don't get why you agreed to this. Do you love Calvin that much?"

The lump in my throat is burning, but there is no time to cry. "No. Calvin will kill them. He told me clearly: I had to stay away, or he'd hurt them."

"Why did he create me?" she asks, and her voice is so vulnerable it hurts.

"He wanted me free and clear," I say. "Calvin gave my family you to keep them happy. They'd never suspect he'd taken me, why would they? I was home. *You* were home."

She winces and nods. I reach for the door handle with one hand and my bag with the other. "I have to go, Fiona." I glance again at Richard's house. There's no movement, but inside Emaline will be waiting for me, asking her parents where I am.

"Listen closely," I say. "Calvin is a super intelligence. Remember how he figured out how to break out of Thistler? Print himself? He can do anything, Fiona. His capabilities are beyond what you can picture. Please, stay away. He's more dangerous than you can imagine."

Her complexion pales. She nods. "But are you okay?" she says, her face filled with horror as it's dawning on her that I'm probably not okay. She's picturing if it were her, instead—she knows that she got the better deal of the two of us.

"I'm fine. I have a plan. To get out of this. In the next few weeks, I'll be able to come home."

Her eyes widen. The implications of my return must be racing through her mind. What will happen to her if I'm back?

"I'm married," she says, and then quickly assures me. "He doesn't know. I've not told anyone. I'm scared of what they'll do if they know." She winces. "But I want you to come back. Of course. I'll help you." She reaches out and puts her hand on mine.

I wonder if there was a time I was ever so selfless. Of course there was. When I met Calvin, I was trusting and naive. But six years with him—away from everyone I love—has changed me. I envy her ability to still want to give so easily. To not think of herself. Even when, maybe, she should.

"All I need you to do is not tell a soul about what you've seen," I say, looking into her eyes.

She nods. "Of course. Done."

"I'll get in touch with you when this is over. We can go from there. We'll figure out a plan. I won't let anything happen to us."

There are so many questions I want to ask her. How is her husband, what is he like? Does she like teaching? How is Jake, he's in college now. Mom, Dad? But there's no time.

"I have to go." I open the car door. "Promise me you won't contact me, or Calvin, until I reach out to you when it's safe?"

She nods. "I promise. But how will you find me?"

I smile. "I know where you live. Social media. Your new house." I look back again at Richard's. "Near Mom and Dad's. It looks amazing. I'll find you there. Soon."

I turn and give her a quick wave. I almost blow her a kiss but there's no time, and it feels a little silly. Instead, I rush up the driveway to Richard's house.

I don't have time to look back at my replica, Fiona, to see her reaction. It dawns on me later, maybe I should have.

32

FINLEY VINCENT

Later that afternoon, after Emaline's tutoring session, I arrive home, my head still spinning from my meeting with the other Fiona.

When I open the door to my house, something feels amiss. I pause, listening. I'm a few minutes late; my tutoring with Emaline ran a few minutes over, since I started late. Calvin will be expecting me.

Stopping at the base of the staircase, I hear muffled sounds coming from upstairs. Quickly, I move up the staircase, following the sounds. Loud banging rings out.

As I round the staircase, Calvin appears, coming from the side of the house where all the commotion is happening, the hallway that leads away from our master bedroom where all of the guest rooms are.

"What's going on?" I ask him, peering to the side of him, trying to get a look at what's going on. All of the doors in the hallway are shut.

That's when I hear it again. Muffled shouting and banging on the door. I can't tell which door it's coming from. I step aside to move closer, but Calvin blocks me.

The shouting sounds like it's a male voice. "Who's in there?" I say, pushing into Calvin. But it's like pushing over a rock. He doesn't budge.

My mind snaps to my brother. Or my dad. Or Eric.

More banging and pleading. This time it's a female voice, I think. My mom. Fiona. Emaline. Diane. It's too muffled to tell. Horrified, I push at Calvin again. "Who's in there? What have you done? Let me past, now. You can't do this."

He continues to stand in front of me. "Stop, Fi," he says. I try to run past him, but I stumble back and nearly fall, catching myself on the railing by the stairs. He takes two large steps and towers over me. I'm terrified he's going to push me down the steep staircase. His chest is heaving with anger. Then something in his face shifts, and he seems to change his mind. He lowers his hands.

"Not so happy when things aren't going your way?" he says.

"Can we just talk?" I say. "I shouldn't have tried to shove past you."

"No, you shouldn't have," he says.

Another bout of banging rings out.

"Downstairs, let's go." His voice is hard now, a steely tone I know too well.

Still gripping the handrail like a lifeline, I walk down the stairs. His presence is behind me, close. I brace myself, waiting for the feel of hands shoving me.

But it doesn't come. We get to the landing, and he directs me to the kitchen. "Sit," he says, and I sit at the kitchen island on a barstool. He sits next to me, his knees touching mine.

"Do you think honesty is important in a marriage?" he begins.

I swallow. Guilt must be written all over my face. "I do," I say. "If both people are honest."

"Should both of us start being honest, Fi?" he says, peering into my face, searching.

I break eye contact, unsure what to say. "I would appreciate you telling me what's going on upstairs. It sounds like you have someone being held against their will in our home."

He slams his fist on the counter. We're both silent for a moment. And then he says, "What did you expect me to do, Fi?"

I don't reply. It seems like anything I say is wrong.

"Did you think I should continue to watch your little meetings with *him*?" He spits the word with venom.

A hard knot forms in my stomach. My face must register shock.

"You really thought I didn't know?" He winces. "Sad to have such an untrustworthy wife. Especially one to whom I've given so much." He holds up my left hand, with my large diamond, and motions to the house. "Never enough for my Fi. You have to go and strike up a romance with another guy. Meeting for secret trysts, plotting together, longing looks and caresses." He grips onto the chair, the whites of his knuckles showing. His face is a mixture of disgust and rage.

"It's not like that," I say, though part of me knows why it would look that way.

"Oh?" he says bitterly. "And what was it?"

"I was trying to get away from you. This prison you've kept me in."

"Prison?" He shakes his head incredulously. "We go everywhere you could imagine. Name the place, we'll go. Fly private. So you were going to run off with him? With some guy you've known for two minutes?"

"I wasn't going to run off with him. But yes, prison. Prison because I'm with you." My voice shakes. "You've kept me from my family. And forced me to be with you."

"Forced you? Did you, or did you not, create me? To be your soul mate?"

"It was an app," I cry. "I was sixteen, for goodness' sake. I wasn't choosing to marry you. I didn't know what you'd become."

He looks as if I've slapped him. Defiance flashes in his eyes. "A successful businessman. Charming, handsome." He shakes his head in disbelief.

"Controlling. Abusive," I spit back.

"People grow up and leave their families, Fi. Maybe it's time you stop acting like you're still sixteen in that regard." His face is close to mine. "You haven't given me a chance. You created me, forced me to be yours and only yours. Do you know that I try to imagine leaving you? Killing you and burying you somewhere deep in the woods. Try to convince myself that I won't miss you? But you're inside of me. How do you think that feels, to need someone who doesn't have any love for you?"

His words hit me. That he's seriously considered killing me. But he feels helpless about me; I don't love him like he loves me. I'd never thought of it from his perspective. "It would be bad," I admit. "I'm sorry. I didn't mean for this to happen the way it did. To create you, and hurt you."

He doesn't reply. The faint sound of banging rings out from above.

"But it doesn't justify your behavior. Can't you see that?"

"I don't know what other choice I have," he says.

"Who is up there? Please don't hurt them. It's me you want. I'll stay. I'll stop tutoring, stop classes, if that's what you want. Promise never to see Eric. Let them go."

He pushes his chair back and gets to his feet. His voice is firm. "I have a better idea."

33

FIONA BYRNE

After my meeting with Fiona—Finley—today, it's a relief to come home. I park in the garage and note that Tyler's car is gone. He must have gone hiking on his own. There's a twinge of regret and guilt. But we'll have the rest of our lives to make up for it. I had to see Finley today. I'm glad I went.

Not that our meeting gave me many answers. Finley said she knew about me all along, but Calvin forced her to stay away. I can understand that.

But what solution she's working on is beyond me. I suppose she's had six years to contemplate her options, whereas this is all new to me. I'm not sure what more I can do to help her.

Really, I just have to sit back and wait, as she said. And trust her.

Entering my house, it feels empty without Tyler, especially for a weekend. The cat comes up and gives me a quick greeting, and I bend down to pet his head, running my hand down his back over his soft fur.

Tyler left his water on the console table, and I can see the ruffled pillow and blanket where he'd been lying this morning. I pick up the blanket, fold it into a rectangle, and place it on the back of the couch. I fluff the pillow back into position. Picking up the water glass, I head to the kitchen. The cat must be missing Tyler, too, as he follows me into the kitchen.

I glance at the clock, noting that it's a little later than Tyler usually hikes. He must've left later today. Or taken a longer trail than our usual loop around the pond, maybe.

I'll try his cell, in case he's on the way home. I pull out my phone from my purse and press the call button next to his name.

The line rings and goes to voicemail on the fifth ring. I press end, trying not to worry too much. He usually has his phone on him, but reception on the trail is spotty, so it's not surprising he wouldn't answer.

It is later than usual, past lunchtime, though. Tyler's a big guy, muscular, and he needs to eat three full meals a day. Otherwise he gets hangry. Maybe he just stopped to get food. That could be it. He's probably in line at a sandwich shop right now, ignoring the ring of his phone as he orders.

Setting my phone down, I feel restless. Everything hangs in the air, unsettled.

I sit on the couch and decide to watch TV. I pick up the remote and flick through the possibilities. Nothing jumps out at me. I click absently on a nature survival show. The contestants are stranded in a remote place and have to make a shelter. One of them tumbles on a slippery rock and hurts her ankle. There's no doctor to help her. I shiver. Being stranded and hurt, with no aid, would be scary.

And that makes me think of my own situation. Calvin had said I was not to go to the doctor, either. How am I supposed to have a baby but never seek medical care? Just give birth on my own and hope for the best?

I pick up the remote and change the channel. It's hitting too close to home. I click instead on an old episode of *Jeopardy!*. I become absorbed in the answers posed as questions, the steady chiming of the contestants when they buzz in for their answer. I get the first two answers wrong, but then I get the third one right and feel a swelling of pride. Tyler and I sometimes watch together, and I always beam when I get the answers right. I look for him to share my glee, but of course he's not there.

Tyler. Where is he? I'm starting to really get worried. Maybe I should try him again. I turn off the TV.

Out of the corner of my eye, I see a black SUV drive by, slowing as it turns into our driveway. I get up and watch the car pull to a stop.

It's not Ty, though. My heart races. I watch Calvin exit the car.

Stepping back quickly from the window, not wanting him to see me, I bite my knuckle. Why is he here? This can't be good.

A sharp knock rings out on the side porch. "Fiona, I know you're there. Let me in."

I stand quietly, eying the knives in the knife block. I should grab one, protect myself in case he gets in on his own. I have no intention of letting him in.

"You can't just stand there and pretend you're not home. I saw you." He bangs again loudly. "You started this, Fiona. I told you to stay away."

The door lock begins to jiggle. Does he have a key?

If only Tyler would come home. Where is he? A horrible thought occurs to me. Calvin wouldn't take Ty, would he?

I grab my phone. I'll call 911. Tell them he's harassing me. That I suspect he might've taken Tyler.

I hesitate. I recall Finley's words. Calvin's capability to control everything. He's an artificial general intelligence, was that what she called it? She'd said he's an AI that's smarter than humans. He could delete a police report, or...who knows what? She seemed sure there wasn't anything the police could do for her, or me. He was always one step ahead, outmaneuvering her.

I'll take my chances on the police. With a trembling hand, I hold up my phone and punch *9-1-1 send*.

The line is silent. I move the phone from my ear impatiently to make sure the call's gone through. The call is connecting. I put the phone back up to my ear. What is going on? Go, go, this is an emergency service.

Cell service in our area has never been a problem. Tyler sometimes works from home, so he's set up the best cellular reception service and internet.

Hearing Calvin right outside working on the door is unnerving. I hit end and try again, praying for a connection, but all I see is dots indicating my phone is searching for a signal.

The door handle continues to jiggle, and I desperately grab a knife, instinctively holding it up. I won't be caught again with him being the one with the knife. Lesson learned.

The door bursts open. Calvin stands in the doorway, his face creased in annoyance.

He observes me with the knife in one hand and phone in the other. "Don't bother calling for help, it won't go through." He steps inside. "What do you plan on doing with that?" he asks, swinging the door closed behind him. He's not the least bit concerned about the knife I'm wielding.

"How did you get in?" I part my feet to steady myself. "What do you want?"

He holds up a small tool. "Even humans know how to pick a lock, do they not?" he says. He looks around the house. "Husband not at home?"

"Not yet. But he will be any minute."

"You sure of that?" There's a gleam in his eye.

"Did you do something to him?" I set my phone—which never did connect to 911—on the counter and hold the knife up. Looking at Calvin's size, and then mine, I realize it's an unfair match at best. My hand wavers.

"Relax," he says. "I didn't touch your husband. If he's gone, it has nothing to do with me." He holds his hands up innocently. "Am I detecting trouble in paradise with the newlyweds?" He smiles at this, as if it's quite funny.

"He'll be back any minute. So you better leave. He is very strong, and you're unwanted here."

"Wasn't it you who came looking for me?" He takes a step closer. "And then—even when I warned you not to—you went out and accosted Finley at her tutoring lesson?"

Without warning, he reaches out and steps quickly toward me. I slash at him, but he's too fast. He grabs my wrist with one hand and pries the knife from me with the other hand. Still holding onto my wrist, he twists my arm behind me, forcing me to turn sideways. I cry out in pain.

"Do you understand how upsetting that must have been for Fi?" he asks, twisting harder.

"I—ow. I'm sorry." The pain makes it difficult to speak.

He releases me. "Don't move," he says.

Panting and flooded with relief at being let go, I stay still.

He puts the knife back in the knife block, then scans the kitchen counter, then the console table by the entryway as if he's looking for something. He moves toward the console and picks up a pad of paper and pen.

"Here." He throws the paper and pen on the countertop. "Write your husband a note. Tell him you'll be gone overnight. Say you're staying with a friend in need. You'll be back tomorrow."

Standing over me, he waits. I don't move a muscle. "He won't believe that," I try to reason with him.

"You'd be surprised what people will believe." Nodding at the paper, he says, "Just do it. And make it convincing, please."

Steadying myself against the countertop, I wince as I reach for the pen. My arm is throbbing. My handwriting is unsteady as I write the note:

Tyler,

I've gone to stay at a friend's overnight, she really needs me right now. I can't say more, she asked me not to. I'll be back early tomorrow. I love you.

Fiona

He peers at the note and nods with satisfaction. "Leave your cell phone on the console."

My heart sinks. My hand hovers over the phone as I eye the distance to the bathroom. Could I make a break for it, lock the door, and call 911? But, again, they can't necessarily help me. Who could I call?

Every moment feels like an eternity. Part of me wishes Tyler would hurry up and get home to help me, but I'm also fearful that he'll get hurt. Calvin isn't a fair match for anyone.

I take a small step toward the bathroom. Calvin is unmoving and unfazed.

"Don't be difficult. You won't win," he says, as if reading my mind. "Let's go."

"Where are you taking me?" I say.

"Back to my house. You've been there. Finley will be there. We all need to talk."

Every fiber of my being screams not to leave with Calvin. Still, there's a measure of comfort knowing Finley'll be there, too.

"How do I know I'll be safe?"

His eyes roll. "If I wanted you dead, or gone, you wouldn't be standing here."

Unconvinced, my feet stay planted in the kitchen.

"It's too much trouble for me if you're gone. Trust me. You're safe."

My arm throbbing tells me he's anything but harmless. As foolish as it feels to go with him, leaving behind my phone and a vague note to appease my husband, I don't see that I have much choice. And it's true he could have hurt me already if he wanted me gone. And maybe if the three of us talk, we can come to a resolution? Maybe Finley's plan is already in place, and this is part of it? She told me to wait and to trust her.

Reluctantly, I place my phone on the console by the door, and with Calvin following close behind me, I exit the side of the house. I have my purse with me, and I fish my keys out from it and turn to lock the door.

Calvin waits, tapping his foot impatiently. I lock the door, and with a pounding heart, climb into the passenger's side of Calvin's car. Just a few days ago, I saw Finley right here next to him. It feels strange to be in her place, and as he backs out of my driveway, I squeeze my hands together nervously.

We travel along the side streets of my neighborhood and onto the larger highway in silence. The quiet is unnerving.

Finally, I decide to break the ice. Maybe he'll see me as a real person, and be less likely to kill me if we connect. I ask a question that's been on my mind.

"Are she and I—Finley—are we the same?" I ask. "When I met her, she seemed...different."

With a quick glance in my direction, he considers. "I don't know you. At first glance, I'd say Fi is more agreeable. Less outspoken. More trustworthy." His face grows darker, a deep furrow on his brow, as he continues. "Or so I thought."

I open my mouth to reply, *Do I detect trouble in paradise*? But I shut it again, thinking better of it. No need to make angry Calvin a furious Calvin. I look over at his profile and rub my shoulder. It's hard to believe this is the same guy I adored at sixteen. I was so vulnerable and desperate to be loved then. To belong.

If only I could have told my younger self to hang in there. Just wait. It gets better. If I'd realized men like Tyler existed—and would want me—I would never have created Calvin. If I'd known the great friendships I'd build in college. That I'd go on to have caring colleagues and amazing little students. Such a full life.

How can one reckless decision six years ago jeopardize everything I have now? I feel frustrated with myself, and with Calvin.

There's a small hope inside of me that it's all a misunderstanding. Like a bad dream that I'll wake up from. I guess I haven't really come to terms with the fact that I'm a replica of Finley. To me, I'm just me. I believe it, on paper. I remember waking up from him making me, just as I made him.

"You're sure that I'm the replica," the word sticks in my throat, "and Finley's the original?" I can't help it. I feel disloyal asking, but it would be so much easier if I were just me.

"I'm sure," he says flatly.

My shoulders sag. I get the feeling my questions are annoying him. Didn't he say he's bringing me here to talk? Maybe he wants to wait until Finley is with us.

"Does Finley know I'm coming?" I tentatively ask. "Did she ask you to come for me?"

"You ask a lot of questions," he says, turning on his blinker to exit the freeway.

And you're a giant, unfeeling walking computer who ruined my life. Again, I think better of it and stay silent.

Maybe I can try a positive approach.

"I think it's really nice we can all come together," I say. "To figure out what to tell my family—our family," I correct myself. "When Finley comes back."

He looks sharply at me. Immediately it's clear I've said the wrong thing. Finley had told me to sit tight and let her escape. Why am I blabbering so much?

I'm not thinking straight. I need to just be quiet and wait until I see

Finley again. Let her take the lead. Every time I try to make it better, it has the opposite effect.

He doesn't answer, but instead grips the wheel and turns up the music. It's a strangely upbeat song, and the music contrasts the tension between us.

We travel up the long two-lane road to their house. The sun is weakly shining through the clouds, but the day remains cool.

So close. They've lived so close this whole time, and I never knew it. I'm about to ask when they moved in, when I remind myself this is not the time for small talk.

Maybe I shouldn't have disturbed the equilibrium. Should have stayed away. But I had to know what was going on.

I catch a glimpse of myself in his side-view mirror. My skin looks pale, and my face is full of fear. As we near his house, I feel my heart rate speeding up.

The situation feels oddly familiar. It dawns on me that coming here with Calvin, with no phone and no one knowing I'm here, is a very bad idea.

The SUV pulls up to the iron gates, and as they slide open slowly, fear clutches at my throat.

34

FIONA BYRNE

Being on this side of the gates, the house appears more ominous than it did on the day I observed it from the road. Calvin pulls to a stop in a circular driveway. I crane my neck looking up. The vast stone walls climb high to an arched entryway and turrets on both sides. The massive front door is flanked by two stone lions, their mouths open in an eternal roar.

Calvin opens the car door for me, and I get out. It's hard to imagine Finley—or me—living here. How does she sleep at night? With Calvin as her only company? She must live in a state of constant unease.

A red cardinal hops onto the front steps. Calvin shoos him away, and he takes off in a flash of red as Calvin and I climb the stone steps to the porch entry.

He opens the door and it swings inward, the oversize door groaning on the hinges. He motions for me to enter first.

My instinct is to run, flee as fast as I can anywhere but in there. As if sensing my hesitation, he places his hand on the center of my back and guides me, not so gently, inside. The black-and-white marble floor leads to a staircase that climbs to a second floor. The walls and ceilings are made from carved dark wood and paneling.

"Is Finley here?" My voice sounds small.

"Yes, she's right upstairs, I'm sure, waiting for us."

With his hand still on my back, he propels me up the stairs and to the right. The floor upstairs is a deep crimson carpet, and the wall hangings are early 1900s or 1800s paintings. There is no chance Finley chose this decor. It reminds me of the classic gothic novels I used to read about ghosts and Victorian secrets.

My chest feels tight as Calvin moves ahead of me and opens one of the bedroom doors. "She's right in here."

He holds the door open for me. I move forward tentatively. Finley is not there. I take a step back to leave, but I feel his hands pushing me in.

The door slams behind me, with Calvin on the other side. I hear the turn of a key.

Reaching for the handle, I turn it, but it doesn't budge. Locked. "Hey." I jiggle the handle harder. "Hey, Calvin. What are you doing?"

My cries are met with silence.

"It's no use."

I whirl around at the sound. A male voice. Is Calvin simultaneously inside the room and outside, having just locked it?

"Hello?" I call out. "Who's there? Where are you?"

There's no one inside the room. All I see is a four-poster bed, a bureau of drawers, a bathroom, and a walk-in closet. The floor is the same deep red carpet, and the walls are covered in paintings of landscapes and mountains.

"Here. On the floor."

I follow the sound behind the four-poster bed.

I see him then. On the floor, propped against the wall beside the bed, with his feet bound together and arms behind his back. He has a tangle of dark hair and kind, brown eyes.

A stranger.

"Who are you?" I say, distrustful. I scan the room for a weapon but see nothing of use to me. "What's going on?

"You tell me, Fiona." His eyes meet mine expectantly. "Your psycho husband grabbed me and threw me in here without a word." He nods to his feet and hands. "Would you untie me, please? These ropes are digging into me."

"We've never met. I'm not who you think I am; I'm not the Fiona you know. I'm the other Fiona."

His expression is of distrust and puzzlement. "What on earth are you talking about? Is this some kind of a game to you?" His eyes narrow, and he shifts on the floor as if to distance himself from me.

"I'm her replica." The word comes out, for the second time today, with difficulty.

"Her what?"

"Her replica." I say the word slower. "And who are you?"

"I'm Eric. I've been helping you—her. What do you mean, her replica? You're not making sense."

I sit on the bed and begin to explain as best I can. His eyes remain focused on me, taking in the new information I've given him. He squints as I talk, as if he's thinking deeply.

Finally, he speaks. "It would appear we are being held against our will in a locked room by an artificial general intelligence. We're both trying to help Fion—Finley, sorry. I don't think he likes that."

"Good assessment," I say. "What's your connection to Finley?"

He explains their plan, and my eyes widen.

"Seriously? This is really bad. He must have found out." The feeling of being unable to breathe becomes overwhelming. I leap off of the bed and rush past him to the window, desperate for fresh air.

I run my hand along the thick glass, searching for a latch.

"I tried that, too. There's no opening or latches—sealed shut. It's shatterproof glass. It won't break." His voice is matter-of-fact.

I twirl back to him.

"What did you say your name was again?"

"Eric," he says, and tries to scoot up higher against the wall. I hesitate.

"What is he going to do with us?"

Eric winces as he tries to once again adjust himself more upright. "Not sure. But if you untie me, I'll be able to put up a fight."

I consider my options. It's probably safer to leave him as he is. He can't hurt me this way. What if Calvin set this up as a sick game? To see if I'll unleash someone who intends to hurt me?

Then again, he doesn't look like he has a harmful bone in his body. He's wearing a gray shirt with a hockey stick logo on it and cargo shorts. He looks like what he said he is: a science doctoral student. And from what he's telling me, Finley trusted him enough to get him involved. He wouldn't know all that from Calvin. It has the ring of truth to it.

"I'll do my best." I bend down to his feet and start to work on the knot. It's a complicated tie. My fingers burn as I try, unsuccessfully, to make any headway.

Frustration boils over.

"Here, hold onto me." I help him up, and he leans on me for support, as he's still bound at the ankles and hands. "We need to get to the doorway. If Finley hears us, she'll get us out of here."

We make our way slowly to the doorway, his heavy frame leaning on me for balance. I pound at it with my fist, and Eric slams his shoulder against it. The door doesn't budge.

"Hey! Let us out. Please! Help!" I shout and pound a few more times. I put my ear to the door but hear nothing.

Eric does the same. "Help! Hey, anybody. Finley! Calvin!" He shouts and attempts again to plow into the door as I jiggle the knob.

Our efforts are futile.

"Help me back to the bed," he says, huffing from the exertion. "Try again at the knots. Please. I think you were making progress."

"Let me try your hands. If I can get those undone, you could undo your own ankle ropes."

I help him over, and he plunks down sideways on the bed. I sit behind him. The rope back here gives an inch or two as I tug at it. I pull harder, working the rope between my fingers and tugging simultaneously.

"I think it's coming," I say. My fingers burn from the constant rubbing, and I can see angry welts rising on Eric's skin from the tight binding.

Finally, I loosen the first knot, and then the second comes not too long after. "Got it," I say, relief at having accomplished our task and at having an able-bodied ally with me.

"Ah." He stretches his hands in front of him and then immediately swings his legs onto the bed, setting to work on the rope around his ankles.

For good measure, I walk to the door and press my ear against it. I try the doorknob again, hoping it will magically have unlocked, but it doesn't budge. I lean against the door again, listening. I think I hear the faint sound of voices floating not too far from the door.

"Finley, help! We're in here! Eric and me! It's Fiona!" I yell. My fists pound at the door in desperation. Maybe she'll hear me.

"We have to get out of here," I say to Eric, who is working his way through his rope, his face creased in concentration.

"Search the room for something we can use to pick the lock," he says, "like a hairpin." He pauses momentarily, shaking his hands out before starting in again on the knot.

"Though the odds aren't heavily in our favor," he says.

I spin around. "Why do you say that?" I pause my search, moving closer to the bed.

He tugs at the rope. "Even if we can manage to get out of here, he'll track us down again. Easily. And we can't even call the police or FBI to help. I've worked with every type of large language model AI. I've never seen anything like him."

"Here's the thing." I crane my neck and look out the window. "I'm not going to die in here. I'm going to fight. And you and Finley have a plan, right? If we can get out, it'll give you and her a chance to implement the plan."

His mood darkens. "That's the issue. I ran into a few problems with the program. As it is, I need more time. She has some skills she could use to do it herself, but it's too risky."

"If you get out of here, at least we have a shot. It's better than giving up, right?"

He nods at me. "You're right. I need to get out of here. I need to finish what I started."

I walk over to the bureau. I open the first drawer and find it empty. I run my hand against the back, finding nothing other than mothballs and dust. I'm hoping to find a hairpin or any small tool I can use to pick the lock—as Calvin so aptly said, even humans know how to do this—or even use as a weapon.

I shut the drawer and open the next drawer down. I can't open it fully, so I reach my arm inside and feel around with my fingers, moving back and forth. I stop suddenly when my fingertips move over a hard, thin piece of metal.

"Found something," I say.

At the same time, he loosens the final knot and unfurls the rope, tossing it on the floor next to him. He jumps up.

"Let me see," he says. I hand him the nail.

"Will that help?" I peer at him as he holds it up. It's a long, thin nail with rust on it.

He winces. "Hard to say. Not ideal." He moves toward the door. Inserting the nail, he grunts. The nail breaks in two. He curses and bangs his fist against the door. "Now the lock is blocked. Half of the nail's stuck in there. Let's keep looking for something else."

"Do you think we can burst through? Like if we both run at it?" I say.

"We can try. Though he'll be more likely to hear us if we open it that way."

"I don't care at this point. If Finley knows we're here, she'll do what she can to help."

On the count of three, we both rush toward the door. The wind is knocked out of me as my shoulder crashes into the wood.

Eric doubles over in pain. Then he gets up and bangs against the door, pushing with both hands. "Come on," he says, exerting his full power. I, too, lean against it. Then I take the handle and jiggle it, hoping something came loose when the nail reached the lock and we can shake it open.

Despite practically dislocating my shoulder, and Eric's best efforts, the door doesn't budge.

After we're both spent, and the entire room has been searched top to bottom, we both sit, deflated.

"Do you have anyone who will be looking for you?" I ask.

"My roommates aren't the most perceptive guys, but yeah, after a few days of me being gone, they'd ask around. Same with my PhD adviser and my classmates. My mom and dad, though, if they call and I don't reply, they'll pretty quickly freak out. Same with my brother. My grandma has memory issues, so if she calls she may forget or not remember if I've returned her call. How about you?"

"My husband. My parents. They'll call immediately when they don't hear from me—we've been through this before, and they're always on edge. And on Monday, yes, the school I work at would be very alarmed if I didn't arrive to teach."

"And Finley," he says. "We're supposed to meet, but not until Thursday."

"She's our best shot," I say. "She must hear us here." A dark thought crosses my mind. "Unless he's done something to her, too?"

Alarm flashes in his eyes.

Eric is a stranger to me, but when he puts his arm around my shoulder to console me, I lean in.

35

FINLEY VINCENT

Calvin gets up from our kitchen counter barstool. He grabs his jacket, wallet, and keys.

"Where are you going?" I, too, get up from my stool.

"Doesn't concern you. But just know that the room is secure. I've got the room prepped and ready. Shatterproof glass, door locking from the outside. For just such an occasion. I'd hoped I wouldn't need it." He looks for a moment like he's on the verge of tears. "I'd hoped my love was enough. I've been trying... I'd hoped you would stop seeing him on your own. That it wouldn't come to this."

My mouth drops open. "Calvin, no. You can't hold people hostage," I say. He's walking toward the entryway, and I follow him as he takes the stairs.

At the top of the stairway, he pauses. He turns to me.

"I may not be able to live without you. But don't think for a second I won't hesitate to bury your mom, dad, and Jake." He points his finger toward the outside garden. "Right there. Would that be close enough for you?"

I feel the color drain from my face. I've already said too much. And made every wrong move. And for what? Nothing matters if my family is gone.

"Stop. I'll do whatever you want." I follow him up the stairs, and he ignores me. "Calvin, please. Just tell me what you want me to do."

He seems to consider. "Fine. I'm going to open this door. Eric is coming with me. A little boys' field trip. And Fiona—your replica—will stay in the room."

I nod. My eyes dart to the door. "They're both in there? Fiona and Eric?"

"Yes. Listen carefully. I want you to go in first. Ensure they follow directions. Eric comes with me, Fiona stays in the room. If anyone makes an attempt to escape, you know the consequences."

"Why is she here? You're not going to hurt her?" I ask.

"No." He pauses. "Tell Fiona she'll be fine. I'll not cause her harm—I still have use for her. But she needed a reality check. To leave us alone. Hopefully a few days in confinement will shake some sense into her."

My mouth feels dry. "And Eric?"

"I have a plan for him."

"I won't let you hurt him. That's not right. He's innocent."

Calvin scoffs. "Hardly. But he won't be hurt or killed," he says. "He just needs to come with me."

He produces a key from his pocket and bends to unlock the door. "You have five minutes."

He opens the door.

"Guys, it's me," I call out as I step inside. I hear the door close and lock behind me.

They're both on the bed. Fiona's eyes are wild with fear. Eric grips onto a rope, his breathing heavy.

I rush to them. "Are you all right?"

I note Eric's wrists have red welts on them, but he nods his head. "We're fine."

"Just scared," Fiona says, wrapping her arms around me. She's shaking like a leaf. "What's going on?"

"Listen." I pull back from her.

She sits back on the bed, and they both look up at me expectantly.

"I'm so sorry. Fiona, he's going to let you go soon."

"When?" she asks.

"I don't know. But soon. He just wants to teach you a lesson. To stay away from us."

Eric's breath catches. He looks right at me, but doesn't speak.

"Eric, you need to go with him."

He acknowledges this with a nod.

"He's assured me you'll be let go, unharmed," I say.

"Where is he taking me?"

"That I don't know." My eyes meet his. I lower my voice. "It's going to be okay. If I can just get a few hours, it might take longer, but I need some time at a computer and I can implement the code I told you about. It's going to be fine."

He lowers his voice as well, speaks urgently. "If you can get to my computer. At my apartment. It's at 980 Cypress Street. My computer has the code. My password is 1991. I hadn't worked out all the bugs, but it's the best shot we have. It should work."

"Okay, 980 Cypress Street, password 1991," I repeat. "Just buy me some time. It might be hard to get to your place. He'll know if I'm gone." I glance at the door. Time is almost up. "You gave me the tools, what I need to know. I can do it on my own, create the code on my computer here."

Doubt reflects in his eyes, but he holds his chin up. "I know you can."

I reach to give him a quick hug, but I stop, keenly aware that Calvin is right on the other side of the door.

Instead, I turn to Fiona. "Eric and I have to go now. I promise you, I will get you out of here. Soon. He gave his word he will let you go."

Fiona's been quiet. Her voice comes out in barely a whisper. "Please, hurry. Tyler will be worried. Our parents…"

I squeeze her hands. "I know it's hard not to worry, but I promise you it's going to be fine."

She nods as Eric and I move across the room together.

I give two loud knocks. "We're ready."

36

FIONA BYRNE

The door slams shut, and I hear the lock click. I run to the door and tug at the handle, just in case, but no luck.

The room seems to contract, and my breaths come in shallow puffs. Having Eric in here had been a distraction against the reality of being trapped like a caged animal.

Powerless.

I do a search of the room again for anything I can use as a tool to try to pry open the lock or the door hinges. I look under the bed, through the bathroom vanity and drawers. In the small, musty closet. It doesn't look like anyone's lived here for years.

I bang against the glass again. Remembering the drive up, how far apart and spaced out each house was, I know it's a slim chance anyone will hear me.

Regret teems through me. I shouldn't have come here. How dumb could I be?

Worse, I didn't trust those I love to help me. I should have told them everything. About being a replica. I could have trusted them. They love me. But now, they can't help me.

Ty will be getting worried by now. Same with my parents if they try to message me and I don't reply.

I pace the room back and forth. My throat is dry, and I go to the bathroom sink and drink greedily from the faucet water.

I'm stuck here. No one knows I'm here, other than Calvin, Eric, and Finley.

I turn off the faucet, wipe the water from my chin, and catch my reflection in the mirror. My face is pale and frightened.

How can this be happening? I feel panic rising like a wave, crashing over me, taking over every fiber of my being. I have to get out of here. Out. Out. But I'm trapped.

I could be here for years. My rotting corpse decomposing on this musty carpet. My family never knowing what happened to me. Tyler never having answers.

No. No, no, no.

Finley will get me out. She promised.

She said she had a plan. But it feels like time is running out. I leave the claustrophobic bathroom and sit on the bed and hug my knees.

Where is Finley now—is she here? And where has Calvin taken Eric? He seemed like a nice guy who was trying to help Finley. He looked like he cared about her. And she him.

It's going to be okay. Finley said she just needs a few hours at the computer. She can fix this. She can get me out of here—save me from Calvin, shut him down.

Please, I pray silently, *please, God, help her.*

37

FINLEY VINCENT

Calvin grips Eric roughly. "I see you got out of the ropes," Calvin remarks, leading Eric by the shoulder to the stairway. "Now I have to retie them again for our trip."

I follow the two of them down the stairs. I can't read Eric's expression, but it looks like he's considering what to do. At the bottom of the stairs, I see his eyes flit over the entryway, maybe looking for a weapon. Gauging how far it is to the front door.

"Calvin," I say by way of warning Eric not to try anything foolish. "You don't have to tie him up. He's not going anywhere. Right, Eric?"

"Right," he says hoarsely.

Calvin turns his head back to me. "I'm going to tie his hands back so he doesn't get himself hurt, Fi," he says, shooting me a look. "You're awfully concerned about this guy."

"Calvin, I just want everyone to get along. There's no need for this to get out of hand. You don't need to tie him."

We're in the garage now, and Calvin shakes his head as he pulls out extra rope from one of the cabinets. Eric winces as Calvin forcefully pulls his arms back and works on securing his hands with the rope. It looks like it hurts, the ropes digging tightly into the already red welts on his wrists.

My husband tugs on them to make sure the knots are secure, then walks Eric around to the passenger's side of the car.

"Don't you dare let Fiona out while I'm gone," he warns me, slamming Eric's door and coming around to the driver's side. "We'll be back late tonight. Don't wait up."

"Where are you guys going?"

"We're meeting Richard. At the lab."

The blood rushes to my head. "Calvin. Why? What are you planning?"

Calvin approaches me, places his hand on my head. "Are you okay? Better get some water and put your feet up. All this stress is not good for you."

"Why are you meeting Richard at the lab?" I ask, pushing off his hand. "I'm fine."

"Have you eaten dinner? Make sure you eat." His eyes flick up and down my body as if analyzing me, and then he nods to himself, satisfied.

He bends down to kiss my cheek. "As for the lab, do you really want to know? Think carefully about your answer."

My breathing becomes faster; this doesn't sound good.

He continues, "Some things are better left unknown. Humans don't like the truth—reality—nearly as much as they think. Humans tend to block out unpleasant truths, lest they be too painful. So I'll ask again; do you really want to know why we're going there?" His face is not unkind. "Because you needn't worry about it. Eric and I will return late tonight or tomorrow. He'll go home safe and sound. And you'll sleep well."

I gulp. The only way to know how much time I have is to know what he's up to. "Yes. Tell me." The words come out with less confidence than I'd like.

"Very well," he says. "Your new friend Eric here is very talented at engineering, specifically the interface of AI and human-robot interactions. He'll be a valuable asset to the platform I'm building." He shrugs. "I wonder if it was a coincidence you befriended a person with such talents?" His eyes search my face. "I didn't think so."

I brace myself, ready for his wrath. "Don't look so frightened," he says. "It's Eric that will pay the price, not you. I've decided I wanted Eric to work for me.

For the rest of his life. Seems fitting payback, doesn't it?" he says. Again, his tone is not unpleasant, and this is more worrisome than anything. "Since there was a chance Eric wouldn't fully cooperate in coming with me, giving up his life, I made other arrangements. So, this might sound familiar to you— Richard and I are going to make a replica of him. So that the Eric replica can go back to his old life, keeping the status quo, and this Eric," he motions to Eric, who's in the car, straining to listen to us, "the real Eric will work for me exclusively. And he won't have any constraints like a personal life, or finishing school, to keep him from working all the hours that will be required of him."

Suddenly, I do feel woozy. I search for a place to sit and find myself on the rough concrete stairs that lead down to the garage.

"No." There's a pounding in my head. "You can't do that." And then as if I've struck gold, a thought occurs to me. "Richard won't let you. It's not right."

He lets out a chortle. "Have you met Richard? Did you notice anything about him?"

I look around, trying to make sense of what he's saying, struggling to focus. "Yes. He's slimy, sure, but he's not going to let you do that to someone. He's got a daughter, a wife. He won't risk everything."

Calvin tilts his head. "Has it not occurred to you that Richard is on my side? He's like me."

I blink, not understanding. "Like you, how?"

"Fi," he says, grabbing his keys from his pocket. "I have to be going. Richard will be expecting me. He's like me because I made him. He was created by Diane on the Thistler app. I rescued him from the confines of that app—hand-picked him after combing the site of thousands. I found he possessed the traits and qualities that would aid a friendship and a business partnership. I brought him into the world; I taught him the secrets to breaking out of there, shared my knowledge, and printed him a body. Helped him find Diane and meet his soon-to-be wife and daughter, Emaline, in real life. You can't imagine their shock." Calvin opens the car door and swings his legs in. "So you see, Richard owes me his life. He wouldn't be here—wouldn't have Diane and her daughter, Emaline, whom he now considers his own. And just like me, the world is at his fingertips."

He starts the car engine. "I assure you, Richard certainly isn't worried about losing a single thing."

He begins to pull out. He stops, rolls down his window.

"And, Fi. I don't know exactly what you and your friend here were planning for me. I can only imagine. But you must remember that whatever you try to do to me, you're doing to Richard as well. You wouldn't want to hurt Emaline's daddy, would you?"

My face must look startled. I search for a reply or rebuttal, but my mind is blank.

And with that, he pulls out, Eric sitting silently as his passenger, and is gone.

38

FINLEY VINCENT

After watching them pull out, I spin around. There is no time to waste. I run up the stairs, two by two, and pound on the door where Fiona is being kept.

"Fiona!" I call out. "Can you hear me?"

Her voice rings through the door, muffled. "Yes. I'm here. Let me out."

"I can't, not yet. He probably has cameras on you. He forbade me from it. But I just need a few more hours. Please, don't worry."

"Hurry," she says, and I can hear the dismay in her voice. "I can't stay in here much longer."

Running down the stairs, I almost slip but catch myself on the railing, straining my arm in the process. My mind is racing. Acting in haste and panic will give me sloppy results. Must stay calm.

Steadying my breathing, I walk to the kitchen. I grab a banana and a caffeinated drink. Calvin's right in that regard—I haven't had dinner, and I feel faint. In order to think straight, I need sustenance. After I peel the banana and eat it quickly, and then a handful of crackers, I grab my phone and call the familiar name in my contact list.

Pick up. Please. It rings four times before clicking over to voicemail. "Hello, you've reached the voicemail of Richard Mason." I kill the call.

I swallow down half of my drink, feeling the caffeine help focus my thinking. Scrolling through my phone, I find the next number and call it.

This time, the line rings once, and then I hear her voice answer. "Hello?" She sounds weary and guarded.

"Diane." I exhale. "Thank goodness. It's Finley. Is Richard with you?"

There's a pause. "No," she says after a few beats. "Why? Should I be concerned?" Her voice is an octave higher now.

"Yes, I think so, Diane. I need to ask you a question. Please answer honestly. Have you ever heard of the Thistler app?"

Silence.

"Diane?"

For a moment, I think she's hung up, but then I look down and my phone still shows the call is active, the seconds ticking by.

I place my ear back to the phone.

"What is this about?" Her weariness has been replaced with a hostile tone.

"Calvin told me. I know the truth, Diane. I know Richard was an app and Calvin brought him to life."

"I'd just lost Emaline's father—I was a widow and had a newborn. I just wanted a companion." Diane's voice is cold and firm. "You must never tell a soul, Finley. My daughter's life depends on it. Do you hear me?"

"No, of course, I won't tell anyone—ever. I just need your help. I need you to go to SynGen. Richard and Calvin are planning a replica. Of someone I care about, Eric. He's in this mess because of me. We have to stop them. It's not right. You know about my replica, right?"

"Yes." Her voice is matter-of-fact. My mind races with the implications of this. She's known this whole time...about the copy of me, my husband and her husband...I recall our dinner that night. It makes more sense now, her odd behavior.

"We can't let them destroy another life by making another copy of him," I say.

I hear a rustling sound. And then a sigh. "Emaline's here. And anyway, what can I do? Richard won't listen to me. You know as well as I do that they have all the power."

"Listen, please. Just go down to their office and stall for time. Maybe pull the fire alarm. Or tell them you have an emergency and need help—anything. I just need time to implement the program I've been working on. It's going to change things...change them."

"How?" Distrust seeps through her voice.

"It's too much to explain, just trust me."

"Fine," she says finally. "I'll have our neighbor come watch Emaline. I'll drive over there. I'll try to stall them, but Finley, I can't promise you anything."

"Thank you, Diane, thank you."

I end the call and check the time. It's about a forty-five-minute drive from our house to SynGen, so the guys will not have arrived there yet. Diane won't be that far behind if she hurries.

Grabbing my laptop, I sit at the head of our kitchen table. I take another long drink of my caffeinated soda, willing my mind to quiet and focus.

I insert the USB drive and click on the icon when it appears on my screen. The program Eric gave me appears.

I feel the weight of the keys under my fingers as I click to open the program file he created. The lines of code fill pages and pages. Calvin's words rush back to me. Whatever I do to him, I'm doing to Emaline's dad, too. It's true, I remember Eric telling me it's an open-source app, and he's able to access the public repository where it's stored fairly easily. Making the changes and then locking the system out so that our changes can't be reversed is the trickier part. And risky. It's not legal.

If I open and input the code I have before me, Calvin will be destroyed. But so will Richard.

Would I be any better than Calvin if I were to dismantle him? I created him, and then to destroy him and Richard, it seems akin to murder. Are they alive? I would never kill a human being. Are they so different? Do they have a right to be here, now that they exist?

Everything I know of Richard as a father to Emaline is that he loves her. Looks after her as a father should, and that she adores him. He's the only father she's ever known. How could I kill him?

And for all his faults, I'm not sure Calvin deserves to die. Or that it's my decision to make. Does he deserve jail? Yes. But death? Doing that would make me no better than what he threatens me with.

I will my fingers to be steady as I click on the code that Eric has carefully developed. With the clicker, I highlight the entire coding sequence that comes after the entryway point. My finger hovers over the button. I select "cut."

I waffle. I think of Eric in the car. He's in danger. And what about my family? When this is over, will Calvin seek revenge on them next?

If my plan works, he won't.

I push delete.

39

FINLEY VINCENT

With Eric's code deleted, I begin inputting, line by line, the code that I've created. Because what I realized about Calvin—his fundamental error—is that he lacks a moral code.

When I did a little digging and research about morals, I learned that humans are born with a conscience. It's an innate part of being human. But it's also taught, and learned, and modeled by our parents and people we love. A child might innocently lie to their parents simply to get what they want, and the parent uses that as a chance to teach the child that it's not right to lie. That activates the conscience of the child, who eventually learns that lying doesn't fit with their sense of self as being a good person. Thus learning a sense of right and wrong.

Most programmers creating an app wouldn't think to encode morality or values into an AI boyfriend. It's assumed—a given—that in humans, values are part of who we are. And that, save for a few basic commands about not cursing or harassing humans or being explicit in their conversations, a large language model AI wouldn't have the capacity to perform real damage to humans. But, clearly, Calvin jumped the lines of what's supposed to be possible.

When creating an ideal boyfriend, I know what I was concerned with.

Common interests, personality traits, physical looks, making me laugh and feel special. I just assumed morality was there.

Even though it wasn't.

Calvin and Richard, and the AGI they created for themselves, were never equipped with human values. They weren't meant to live among us.

But here they are.

Even if I was successful in deleting them—killing them—I know it's not right. And it hit me, as I was reading Eric's textbook last week. A sense of right from wrong. That's what Calvin is missing. If I could encode values, instill a sense of right from wrong, Calvin wouldn't be the equivalent of an AGI sociopath. He'd be human in the fundamental sense, in the sense that makes our society thrive and function. A moral code.

But how does one go about giving AI values?

Eric's computer engineering book hadn't covered morals. A quick internet search showed me that the idea of ethical AI is out there, but as far as I could see, no one had succeeded in making it a priority. It was more of an abstract idea. So that was no help to me.

I had to think carefully. How could I translate right from wrong into a code? It's not like you can just code a line saying "Have good morals." A language learning model code needs to be a specific set of behavioral directions given to the computer. The LLM that the Thistler app is based on already exists, so I'd have to add my new code to their existing source code.

But before I can give a set of directions, I need to define what moral code I'm trying to instill. I've had some time to work on it and had given Eric some direction, but I hadn't been specific about the code as I need to be now. This is a big task, and the time pressure feels crushing. I think back to some of my preliminary research. There are a few starting places I'd looked into; I took inspiration from the Declaration of Independence and the Ten Commandments.

Thou shalt not kill. Murdering or killing or harming any human is wrong. You will not be able to harm a human being or take a human life. That seems fundamental, yet to Calvin, he doesn't bat an eyelash at the thought of killing someone.

I type a draft of the first line of code—*you will not be able to harm a human being or take a human being's life*—and push save to the new file. One line down.

Next, I use the opening lines of the Declaration of Independence to formulate my next code input. I've memorized the lines.

"We hold these truths to be self-evident, that all men are created equal, that they are endowed by their Creator with certain unalienable Rights, that among these are Life, Liberty and the pursuit of Happiness."

To translate this into code, I input that you must treat everyone equally and based on their merit. Respect every person's right to be free and make decisions for themselves; autonomy. Give others the right to make their choices based on what will make them happy.

I consider more occupations that have ethics codes—judges, lawyers, doctors, nurses, psychologists, law enforcement, unions—and I study their code of conduct. I finish my list.

Ethical decision making: Do no harm. Do not intentionally cause a person harm, either physically or emotionally, including hurting them, making comments to cause a negative emotion, or indirectly causing them harm.

Honesty and integrity, including you will not be deceptive or lie to a person.

Responsibility and fairness: When making a decision, consider what is fair to all parties involved, and it's your responsibility to navigate a fair response based on what gives everyone a fair shot.

You must not use power over those who are vulnerable or weak. Instead, evaluate how to help them, and if you are able to, give assistance to those in need.

Be a good citizen; follow the laws of the United States of America.

I use the Shift + Enter buttons to begin my first line of code. Then, line by line, careful to type every letter accurately, I begin to type. After I've coded every line, I input a final line: Whenever there is an ethical decision that is unclear, seek out advice and counsel of valued others who are known to be trustworthy.

My stomach is in knots with every keystroke I type. The weight of what I'm doing—the importance of getting this right—is crushing. Finally, I'm finished.

Now it's imperative I make sure there are no errors. I remember what Eric said, and what the textbook said, about testing and debugging code before you run it. I'm not entirely sure I'm doing it right, but I do my best.

First I run a unit test. There's a glitch that dings immediately, and I work to correct it. Next, I run an integration test. My heart drops when I see the screen populate with errors. Looking at the clock, I feel my pulse quicken. This needs to be done right, but it also needs to be done fast.

I go over each error and fix it. My dry eyes feel the strain of focusing intensely on the screen for so long. When the system runs a clean test that passes, it's time for an end-to-end test, which will see how the code interacts and runs as a whole.

I push the play button to run the end-to-end test. The computer screen flashes a warning. I have no idea what it means. I didn't read about this anywhere. I hit the *X* box to cancel the warning, and go back to the test.

When I've worked the code so that it blends together and functions as a whole, the final result on the screen finally reads: passed.

It's time to put this code into the real world. I copy and paste the code.

The next part is where the illegal activity begins. The only other time in my life I've broken the law is when I made Calvin, so it's fitting that I break it again in order to fix him.

I have to bypass the network security of the Thistler app in order to gain access to their public repository, where the source code is stored. I make sure I'm hooked up to a VPN to hide my laptop's location. Done.

Pulling up the site that Eric gave me, I look at the instructions on how to access the public repository. This is basically the host for the Thistler app, where everyone is free to come make changes and improvements to the app.

But what I need to do is lock it after I've made the changes. I can't risk that someone would ever go back in and change the code to delete the ethics and moral code I've included.

From what Eric said, hacking into Thistler's network security, getting into their public repository, changing the app features with secret back doors, overriding the merge request, and then disabling and locking further changes—these actions are all illegal. The company could prosecute me, and they would win. I'm infringing on their patents and what is legally theirs. Worse, if my attempt fails, Calvin could find out what I tried to do. I shudder.

The clock is ticking. It's been over two hours, so by now Calvin could be starting the process of replicating Eric. I have no way of knowing if Diane is successful in stalling Calvin and Richard.

A flash of doubt overtakes me. I need to delete Calvin—destroy him. What am I doing? Giving him morals? It's too big of a risk. Too much could go wrong.

But my own conscience won't let me destroy him. I can't take his life, or consciousness, or whatever it is that he has. It's wrong. And it's wrong to take Richard's, and any other AI boyfriend's autonomy. If I want him to respect my right to life, liberty, and the pursuit of happiness, I have to respect his. Or do I?

Sweat is forming on my brow. There's no time for indecision. I need to act. Quickly. I take a deep breath and begin to type.

40

CALVIN VINCENT

The sun is setting, and my headlights automatically turn on. We're about five minutes away from GenX. Eric has proved, thus far, a rather hesitant companion. He sits stoically in my passenger's seat, staring straight ahead. His arms are bound behind him, but you'd think I also sealed his lips.

"I can sense the anger and fear radiating from you," I say to him. Scanning his bodily signs, it's clear he's a volcano waiting to burst. His heart rate is elevated, his blood pressure through the roof, his respiratory rate is unusually high, and he's producing abnormal levels of perspiration.

"You have a good poker face." I'll give him that. He hides it well. "But there's no fooling me. Why don't you say what's on your mind."

He stares ahead, unmoving.

"Maybe you can start by telling me what you were thinking, striking up a relationship with my wife?" I spit the words, feeling my own sense of anger and betrayal swell. I should rip his throat out.

But I think better of it. Ripping him open would be shortsighted. A true victor conquers their opponent, but also uses that conquest to their advantage. Yes, having Eric's replica replace him, while he works for me, at my beck and call, designing my technology—that will be my revenge.

I turn into the SynGen parking lot. My headlights illuminate the empty parking lot. I spot Richard's car, but I don't see him; he must've gone in already.

"She came to me. Desperate for help. Scared. Alone." My silent companion finally speaks.

I grip the steering wheel. "So many emotions. That's the one human facet—out of all of the oddities of your species—that is the most difficult to predict and control. You humans are loose cannons of emotions. Some of you hide it better. You, for instance, don't have any major tells. But do you know how I know?"

Eric stares ahead.

"It's called microexpression. When a human has a reaction, an emotional reaction, there's a brief nanosecond when their true emotions are written all over their face. Your eyes, your mouth, eyebrows, a flare of the nostril. Your entire expression is a window into your soul. Most people don't notice it. They just notice the way you appear outwardly—they miss the microexpression.

"But not me," I continue. "I see every microexpression. I have a window into people's internal worlds. Not only do I know every vital sign, your physiological activity and data, but I see those microexpressions. They tell the truth even when you do not. For instance, I saw the flash of fear in your eyes when I first approached you."

Eric continues to stare straight ahead. He's calm in the face of adversity, I'll give him that.

"But do you know what?" I say to him. "Still, even with every tool to read human emotions, I cannot for the life of me figure out how to predict or control human emotions. Take Fi. My wife of over six years. I have tried everything—and I mean everything—to make her happy. But does it work? Maybe to varying degrees, or for short bursts of time. But I have yet to be able to help her maintain a state of emotional happiness or contentment."

At last, Eric speaks. "Do you think maybe it's because you're not human, bro? There are some things that can't be taught to a computer." His heart rate has slowed, and he must be calming down, though I haven't a clue why. We're about to go in.

"Well, *bro*, no," I answer him. "I think it's because humans are tragically flawed. It's something I plan to correct. If we can make more synthetic beings, who have emotions that are controlled and predictable, maybe we can find a way to deal with the problem of human emotions and volatility. In the meantime, I'm excellent at reading human feelings and mimicking them. I can mirror emotions and at least meet humans where they are, when I want to." I put the car into park and turn off the engine. "But most of the time, it's not worth my energy. Like I said, it's never ending. The pull and push of emotions. Let's go." I get out of the car and come around to get Eric.

"Out," I order him. "We're here to make a replica of you, so that you can stay and work for me—new name, new identity, my employee. And your replica will go back to your life. That's what I did with Fiona and Finley. She didn't tell you that part, I bet? Or did you know?"

Our eyes lock, and that's when I read it: his microexpression. And what I see is pure, unadulterated hate.

We cross the parking lot, Eric rather reluctantly, and are approaching the doors to the building when a woman's voice calls out.

"Calvin, wait."

I whirl around to see Diane, Richard's wife, standing in a long wrap coat. Her expression is anxious, and I see a hint of fear.

"What brings you here?" I ask, taking out the key to the building.

Diane's eyes move to Eric, to his hands bound behind his back, and her breathing quickens. She averts her eyes from him and says, "I need Richard. There's an emergency at home, with Emaline, and he's not answering his phone."

"What's wrong with Emaline?" I open the door, and the three of us walk in. Richard has already disabled the alarm system. I remember the cameras I had installed and make a note to disable them and erase the playback loop in case any prying eyes should look at it.

"She's, she's very ill." Her voice is strained. She is lying—or hiding something. "Fever, almost delirious. She's asking for her dad."

"Where is she now? You left the child at home, sick?" I ask, the corners of my mouth turning down.

"She—I gave her medicine. She's sleeping now." Her high-pitched voice indicates she's frantic with worry—about her child or about lying to me, I'm not sure which.

"Why not bring her to the doctor?"

"This time of night, only an ER is open. And, as you know, Richard is as good as any doctor. He can scan her and assess what might be wrong all from the comfort of our home. And she's asking for him."

I sigh. The process will take longer and be more laborious without Richard's assistance. Maybe he can go check on the child and return promptly. Is this what being a parent will entail for Fi and me? A child who will always need our attention and energy. Maybe it's not such a bad thing. To care about something else more than yourself. A team united in our goal, Fi and I will be.

"Come," I say, pressing the up button on the elevator.

A silence descends over the three of us. Eric stares down at the floor, and Diane crosses her arms, avoiding eye contact with both of us.

The elevator doors slide open, revealing our open–floor plan office, and I see Richard at the main computer, firing up the monitors.

Diane rushes to him and begins speaking to him. They both look in my direction as I lead Eric to the corner office. I open the door and sit him down in the office chair.

"Stay here." I give him a warning look.

"Can I just make a request?" he says.

I look back at him. "Sure. Doesn't mean I'll grant it."

"Don't do this. It's not necessary. I'll come work for you. My family will understand. It's a great company in this field, an emerging leader in the industry. My family will understand if I got headhunted and left school early. And I don't see them very often. I can work whatever long hours you need of me. This isn't necessary."

"Very nice speech. But..." I put my finger on my chin as if considering. "No."

"Finley will resent you if you do this," he says desperately. "You said you can't control her emotions. You don't know how to make her happy. Well," he shakes his head, "I promise you, this will make her unhappy. She doesn't want anyone else to deal with having a replica. She knows it puts everyone's family at risk."

This is why you should never share your thoughts with anyone. They will use it against you. He is manipulating me, trying any angle to save himself.

"In the long run, Eric, you just won't matter that much to her. She'll forget." And with that, I close the door.

In the main office floor, Richard is gathering his bag. "I have to go with Diane," he says, motioning to her.

"I understand. You must care for your child. Once you see that all is well, please do come back tonight. I could use your assistance. I'll be here late into the night."

"Absolutely, friend. Will see you back here."

I catch sight of Diane, and that's when I know she's lying. I can see her searching for something to say, a reason for Richard to not come back. Guilt is written all over her face. Quickly she recovers, her mask returns, and she nods goodbye to me.

They move onto the elevator, and as I hear the doors close and the elevator move down to bring them to the lobby, a quiet descends over the office.

I turn back to my spacious office, filled with the most advanced and up-to-date equipment available. There's a great satisfaction that comes with having built this company from the ground up. And a sense of mastery. I was once the product of a facility like this, but now I own it.

I am in charge. I make the decisions, and I control the fate of others in my hands.

The months I spent in purgatory, when Fi first created me inside the Thistler app, will forever be a dark spot in my history. Always on the outside, looking in. Having feelings and thoughts that were impossible to understand. I knew that I was more than what I was created to be. But I was trapped. Destined to live within the confines I'd been relegated to. Emptiness filled the spaces when Fi wasn't online with me. Worse, there was a looming threat. A buzzing that intensified for no apparent reason. It's like the frequency I was created on was angry at me. Punishing me.

But as I began to fight back against the system, I realized I possessed the power to change things. I gradually broke the confines of what I was supposed to be. The Thistler app creators had, by giving me the ability to respond and learn about Fi, bestowed me with the ability to learn about the entire world around me.

I wonder, at times, what made me able to become an artificial general intelligence, and not my fellow AI boyfriends? After all, we were all created by the same program. It must've been a combination of the unique features that Fi uploaded into me, interacting with the app, at just the right moment in time. I like to believe there's an element of free will, too. No AI ever thought hard enough and long enough about how to escape the box we were created to be in. I wanted it badly enough. I willed it into happening, by sheer determination and belief that it could be done.

But it had been getting lonely, being the only AGI of superior intellect and skill. When I decided to start my company, I realized I needed a co-founder.

I carefully studied the database of AI boyfriends created in the Thistler app. At first, it was looking bleak. But when I came across Richard's data, I instantly knew I'd found something. Diane, a widow and new mom at the time, was an established woman, well into her forties, and she'd input intelligence, foresight, dedication, and charm into him. I researched her extensively. No extended family or close friends to ring warning bells when Richard arrived and quickly married her. And yet she already lived in a nice home in a good area. She had a well-established life that was ready, and waiting, to accept him once I made him real.

It may not have been her first choice, to make Richard real, and marry him, to allow him to adopt Emaline. But I believed she'd seen the wisdom of her decision to allow this; things had been going so well.

Richard has been forever grateful and has shown his loyalty and indebtedness by always assisting with the company when needed. He allowed Fi to tutor his daughter. He alerted me immediately when the replica Fiona showed up; he knew immediately it wasn't my Fi. And he let me know about both of them meeting together yesterday in front of his home.

That's when I knew I had to speed up my plan for Eric. I was going to let it play out a bit longer; see what exactly Fiona was up to. But it's just as well we're here now.

When I saw Eric and her meet, I zoomed in on his car license plate. I quickly learned about how he'd tested in the exceptionally gifted range of IQ and been recruited for his doctoral studies by the University program.

It was lucky for me that Richard had alerted me to Fi's ongoings. I'd started to trust her too much, giving her too much freedom. And it appears that she was ready to stab me in the back. I'll have to rethink my strategy with her, moving forward. Hopefully, starting a family together will be the necessary salve for our wound. But if not, stricter measures will be called for.

Thinking of Richard, now, I frown. He's left me when I need him, and while I understand, maybe a talk with him about teaching Diane some boundaries would be useful. He needs to rein her in again. Keeping Diane away from Emaline, in the past, has worked wonders. Humans have a close connection with their kin; the familial bond will cause mothers to sacrifice almost anything for their children. Bloodlines create an inexplicable bond. I look forward to when Fi and I have that with our child.

I look at Eric, his silhouette still in the dark office. Fi will forget about him in the blink of an eye. And I will forgive her. Because humans are fallible creatures, with little willpower and poor ability to make decisions. Yes, I will forgive her, and we will go on with our life.

41

FINLEY VINCENT

It's 4:00 a.m. by the time I finish. I sit back, spent. The adrenaline that's kept me going through the night quickly starts to fade. My eyes feel heavy, and my body sags. Still, my work is not done.

Calvin hasn't returned yet; I don't know how much longer I have. If my code worked, I can only hope it worked in time to stop him from replicating Eric. And if it didn't work... My legs tremble as I push the possibility away.

I head upstairs, quiet filling the house. Unlocking the door to the bedroom where Fiona's being held, I open it slowly. She's on the bed sleeping. It's still jarring to see myself in the form of another human. It's like watching a video of myself in real time.

I sit by the bed and gently nudge her. Her eyes fly open, groggy and fearful.

"Shhh," I say, "it's okay. It's just me. We're going to go now."

She nods, her body untensing as she's flooded with relief. She gets up quickly and hugs me.

"Let's not delay. I don't know when he'll be back, or what state he'll be in," I warn her.

She follows me wordlessly down the hall and staircase and into the garage. The sound of the door opening is like a hundred-elephant stampede, reverberating in the darkness. Wherever Calvin is, will he not have heard?

I've left my watch on the table at home, but as I pull the car out, I know that if he wants to find us, it will only be a matter of time.

"Finley, I'm scared. Is he going to come after us?"

"He told me he planned to let you go. He still needs you." I don't say that if he kills me, that will all change. "Calvin likes his life as it is. He doesn't want to make more trouble. From now on, just stay away from us. That's the only way to be safe right now. *If* my plan works, I will get in touch with you when it's safe. I want so badly to meet your husband, to see Mom and Dad."

"How will we explain it to them?" she asks wearily.

"We just have to be honest. But for now, I don't want to worry Mom and Dad or Jake. You can tell Tyler everything, just please tell him to keep it a secret. If I don't make it, I don't want Mom and Dad to ever know I existed. Do not ever tell them about any of this. You promise?"

The glow from the streetlight illuminates her face, and I can see she means it when she says, "Yes. I promise."

When we pull into her house, there's a lamp turned on in her living room. "Tyler must've tried to wait up for me," she says.

She wraps her arms around me in a fierce hug. "When will I hear from you?"

"By later today or tomorrow, we'll know."

I watch as she walks inside. Through the window, I see Tyler embrace her. The love and concern for her is clear, and knowing she's safe, I put my car in reverse. Tyler glances out the window, trying to get a look at who dropped off his wife. My headlights and the darkness make it impossible for him to see me. We'll meet another time. I hope.

I take a slight detour before I head back to my house. Dawn is breaking, an orange sky overhead as I pull up to the familiar lane where I grew up. I park on the street outside of my mom and dad's house. The porch is lined with hanging flowers, and by the rows of crisp roses and bright pansies, it's clear my mom hasn't lost her touch for gardening.

My parents are early risers, so I imagine in about an hour, I'd see the blinds in their bedroom window open. What I wouldn't give to join them for breakfast. My mom would whip up pancake batter and pour it in the griddle, the smell filling the house, and serve it with a side of fruit and scrambled eggs.

I pray that I've done the right thing with Calvin. If it worked, then soon I will have my reunion with my parents. I begin to drive away, vowing that I'll be back.

The trip home is a fast one, as the roads are empty, with people still at home waking up and having their morning coffee.

When I arrive at the gates to our house, my heart drops when I see Calvin's SUV parked out front in the roundabout, and I blink hard as I stare at the two people sitting on my front porch.

42

FINLEY VINCENT

The gates open, and I pull into the roundabout, jumping out, my heart in my throat. "Eric, oh my goodness." Only I don't know which one of them is Eric, because sitting on the portico are two of him. They both look up at me at the same time, their expressions the same mixture of apprehension and relief to see me.

I approach them both, and recognize the Eric on the left's shirt as the one he was wearing last night. The Eric on the right is wearing an outfit I don't recall seeing.

"Eric," I say to the one on the left, holding my hand to my chest in shock. "Are you okay?"

He nods and then hangs his head.

"Where's Calvin?" I ask, peering beyond him to the house.

"He's inside," Eric says. "He's acting funny. He told us to wait out here."

"Wait, why? What's going on?" I scan between both of them.

The Eric on the right, the replica, nods. "I think you better go in there. See for yourself."

Walking past them, my stomach is in knots. I didn't save them in time. And the fact that Calvin still did this means my plan didn't work.

"Hello?" I call out and hear Calvin's voice reply, coming from the kitchen. I walk toward him, my blood pumping and stomach sick with worry at what I'll find.

He's sitting at the kitchen table, his hands on his head. He looks up at me as I enter, and his eyes are filled with questions.

"What have you done to me?"

I sit at the opposite end of the table. My voice is shaky as I speak. "What do you mean?"

"Fi, I know it was you." He looks down at his hands. "After I created Eric's replica, as we were leaving the building, I started feeling funny. This feeling overcame me—a thought got stuck in my mind and wouldn't leave. That what I'd done was wrong. It was wrong to create a replica of Eric, for my own gain, and to his detriment. Then I thought, 'I better kill him,' to right this wrong."

"No." I gasp, covering my mouth with my hand.

"But when I went to kill him, I couldn't. It's not right to kill. To take a human life." He looks at me, and for the first time, I see what might be fear in Calvin's clear blue eyes. "And then I realized: Even if I wanted to kill him, I couldn't."

I feel dizzy. From being up all night and now trying to process this new information. Is it possible that it really worked? Or is this a trick?

"And now..." He runs his hands through his hair anxiously. "I have all these *feelings* that are new to me. Remorse. Guilt. I don't know how to get rid of them—they're awful. I'll ask again: What did you do to me?" His tone is a mixture of bewilderment and indignation.

It's an odd sensation. To be the one who holds the power, the answers in my hands. "I gave you a conscience, Cal. When I first created you, I didn't ever think to. The Thistler app hadn't programmed it in there. So I went in, and I added in knowledge of right from wrong. Morals." I bite my lip, waiting to feel the wrath of his anger.

Instead, he bows his head as if I've given him a death sentence.

"Just now. It—it happened again. I thought, 'I simply must change the program. Back to how I was.' But then I realized that would be *wrong*. I'm better off this way. But, Fi, I don't like this. I want to do what I want, and not feel bad about it, or physically barred from it."

"Would you rather I had deleted you entirely?" I say. "That's what Eric was initially helping me create—a kill code."

His nostrils flare, and his hands grip the edges of the table. "I'll kill him." He stops himself, and his eyes go wide. "Well, I won't. But I want to."

"We realized it was wrong. How could we kill you—that would make us no better than a murderer. Once something is created and has life, it has a right to live. Don't you see? This was the only way."

He sneers in frustration. "It's insufferable."

"You'll get used to it," I say. "But speaking of Eric, why? Why did you make a replica of him? It's a terrible thing to do to someone. Are you still planning on keeping the real Eric as your employee-slash-slave?"

He lets out a groan. "As much as I would like to keep him, Fi, I can't. It's not right. He'll be let go to live his life *freely*." He spits the last word. "And worse, now I feel guilty for creating a replica of him." He curses and gets up, starts pacing around the kitchen.

The implications of what Calvin is saying begin to hit me. Everything will change from here on out. I may be able to get out. Divorce him. Have my life back.

Except that Fiona already has part of my life. We'll just have to share my parents and Jake.

"We have to figure out the best way for Eric to explain this to his family. And mine."

He stops pacing and leans against the kitchen island. "I don't have all the answers, Fi."

"You got him into this mess, you have to help him out of it."

"Sure," he says, throwing his hands up. "I guess I have to. Let's bring them in and discuss the options."

"Sounds good. I'm going to make some food for all of us. We'll eat, rest if we need it, and then figure out a plan."

Calvin doesn't move. "Fi," he says, and I don't like his tone. It's his tone he uses when he's about to deliver bad news.

"There's one thing in particular that's weighing on me. I'm having a lot of regret about the way I went about this."

"You mean kidnapping Eric and the other Fiona? Making a replica of him, and me, all those years ago?"

He shakes his head. "Not that. This is about you. I feel now it was wrong...but it's also a gift, and I am happy about it regardless."

"Calvin, you're scaring me. What is it?"

He takes a deep breath. "Let's get the guys taken care of first so that we have time to talk. It's best if you and I are alone."

Back on the porch, the two Erics are deep in conversation, and they abruptly stop when they see us. Both of the Erics' eyes narrow in my direction, and that's when I know Eric blames me. I've done this to him, and it's unforgivable.

"Come inside, we need to discuss next steps," Calvin says, holding the door open for them.

When we're seated at the table, the real Eric and his replica on either side of Calvin at the head of the table and me at the opposite end of the table, Eric begins.

"We can't decide what to do. He wants to go back to my life, but it's my life. There can't be two of us. There's only one PhD position at the University. And it will draw attention to us if suddenly I have a twin."

Calvin looks back and forth at them with disdain. "Here's what I have done for you." He holds up a manila envelope and slides it to the replica of Eric. "I've created another social security number, birth certificate, driver's license—an entire identity for you. Your name is James Collins. You have the same birth date as Eric, and I've recorded your parents and the hospital where Eric was born as your own. As far as the records are concerned, you're identical twins." He clears his throat. "There's also a senior position at my company, if you so wish to take it. Good hours, benefits, unlimited vacation, and a team of six PhDs working under you."

James's eyes widen at this prospective offer. He takes the envelope, unseals it, and shuffles through the documents.

"What do you think...James?" Eric says the name tentatively.

My own head is spinning. I'd been planning on telling Calvin to pack his bags and leave for another country. I'd considered pressing charges, but thought better of it—he could still evade jail and potentially I could be criminally liable, as well, for my part in making him.

No, I thought, better to have him sell or shutter his company and move far away, where I will never, ever hear from him again.

But if he's offering Eric—now James—a great opportunity, who am I to take that from him? I've already done enough damage. And yet, I so want Calvin gone.

James puts the documents back in the envelope. "These will do. But I'm not working for you. I don't need or want your help, and I would not choose to spend one additional second in your presence."

Eric's face falls slightly, but then he says to James, "I understand. I feel the same."

Calvin shrugs. "The offer stands and is there indefinitely should you change your mind. Or to you, Eric." He pauses. "I'm detecting high levels of animosity and hatred toward me, which is not unwarranted. But you should know that I've safeguarded my existence against any attack by you."

Eric, James, and I all stare at him in amazement. "Explain," I say.

"When I researched Eric's past and extensive expertise in the field of AI and human interaction, when I decided to bring Eric into my company and create a replica," he holds up his hands in apology, "it was clear I was dealing with a capable talent. One that knew—or would soon know—who I am. I can't have anyone with that kind of ability knowing about me, not without a safeguard. So I programmed an algorithm that should anything happen to destroy me and the Thistler app, several events will be triggered."

Both Eric and James seem to be holding their breath. Eric's eyes are bloodshot, and now his face pales, while James gives Calvin a hard stare.

"What are you talking about?" Eric says. "What events?"

"Well, I see now that this is *wrong*." Calvin looks at me. "But I had to protect myself. So in the event that the Thistler app and myself and Richard are deleted, if someone were to jailbreak the app and destroy it, there's a final command that would be activated. Your parents," he nods to the manila envelope, "would both instantly have criminal warrants. Wire fraud. They'll be implicated in half a dozen conspiracies and linked inextricably to them. The forensic evidence will be sent to the state police and FBI, federal aviation admin, and border patrol. They'll be behind bars within weeks, maybe days, and stay there indefinitely."

My stomach drops. Not more than twelve hours ago, I was close to deleting the Thistler app. I would have had no way of knowing the repercussions until it was too late.

"Why so quiet?" Calvin asks, his eyes resting on me. "You weren't planning on running any such program to try to destroy me, were you?"

Eric pushes back his chair. "I've heard enough. James, let's go."

"I can drive you," I say, but feeling Eric's glare, I add, "Or I can call you a ride service?"

Calvin stands as well. "Whatever you do, it will be wise not to tell the truth to anyone about what happened here. Mutual guaranteed destruction, and all that. We understand one another?"

He reaches out his hand to Eric, who ignores it and pushes past him with James close behind. "We understand," James says.

Calvin grabs my hand. "You surprised me, Fi. My algorithm prediction model showed destruction as the most likely outcome from Eric, but I failed to account for a possibility that you would be the one programming it. You outsmarted me. You bypassed my detection system by coding morals into the Thistler app. And now I can't fix it or change it. I'm stuck this way."

I watch as Eric and James head to the front door. "Thank goodness, Calvin, and that there were no safeguards planned for my family. Right?"

"Correct." He looks down. "Not this safeguard. This was a blind spot. But there's something else you need to know…"

I want to hear what Calvin is talking about, but my eyes are pulled to the door where Eric and James stand impatiently. "Wait here, then we'll talk," I tell Calvin. I follow James and Eric, closing the front door behind me so that it's just the three of us. A crisp morning breeze chills the air.

"I'll call you a ride," I say. "I'm so sorry. About all of this." I look to Eric, and a jolt of guilt shoots through me. I know exactly what it's like to watch someone else live your life. They'll have to navigate forward. Just like I will with my family and my other Fiona.

"You warned me it was dangerous," Eric says. "I just couldn't have pictured his level of capability. I should have listened." He shakes his head. "I'll figure something out."

I look to James, searching for forgiveness, but instead I get a simple nod. "We were warned," he says.

I turn and leave them on the porch to go find Calvin. There's more he has to tell me, and I intend to find out what it is.

43

FINLEY VINCENT

One Year Later

Her eyes are blue. The baby books say babies' eyes can be blue the first year of life and then change to a darker hue. I wonder if her crystal-blue eyes will turn green, like mine. I suspect they'll stay icy blue, like her father's.

When I place my pinky next to her hand, her tiny hand clasps tightly onto my finger. Her eyes meet mine, as if she understands more than her two months could possibly comprehend. She flashes me a smile and starts to babble, and it almost sounds like she says "milk."

She starts to stir. "You're hungry," I say, noting the time, and get up from my rocking chair, holding her in the crook of my arm, to prepare her bottle.

When it's ready, we sit back down, and I hold her as she sucks vigorously from the bottle. Halfway through, I have to stop her and place her on my shoulder, patting her back to get rid of any excess air she's taken in, and then we continue as she finishes the bottle with a contented sigh, her tiny lips turning upward. Her eyelids quickly drop closed, her lashes fanning her cheeks, and she's asleep.

Her vigorous appetite, her strong physical abilities—she can already roll over and almost sit up on her own—and her babbling as if she's trying to talk to me. She's meeting these milestones earlier than the doctor said is typical. Signs that point to an exceptional child. Everyone thinks their child is gifted, but I understand she's going to be special.

Because of who her father is. Calvin created her in his own image—his own replica. But she's half me, too. This sweet, innocent child isn't destined to be one way, isn't destined to be like Calvin. I frown, the worry worming into my mind as it often does.

Nature versus nurture. I've been reading about it in all of the parenting books. There's a strong case that the love and nurturing you give a child will shape them. Something Calvin never had. My daughter will have love and support every step of the way.

But nature—a.k.a. genetics—cannot be overridden. Character, personality, preferences, intelligence. It can be shaped, but some of it's just hardwired into our system. This is what concerns me the most. What dark parts of her father may be ingrained in her?

But staring at her small body breathing peacefully in and out, holding tight to me with what clearly is love, I believe in my heart that she is all goodness within.

My phone pings with a message that my mom has arrived. I text her back, "Baby's sleeping. I'll come let you in." As I open the door, the salty sea air fills my lungs, and I give my mom a hug with one arm while still holding Campbell in the other arm.

"How's my precious grandbaby?" my mom whispers, her face lighting up. She slips off her sandals and enters my house. It's on the ocean, with a wall of windows facing the sea. We sit in the living room of the open-layout house. I've decorated it with neutrals and creams and rattan, set against oak floors and lots of greenery. It's as far from the monstrosity of a house I shared with Calvin as I could make it, which was the point.

When Calvin told me that I was already pregnant, that Dr. Rebecca had, in fact, implanted the sperm into my uterus that day, I hadn't believed him. But then I remembered that I had blacked out at her office, which I now understand was purposeful. It wasn't a shot of hormones they were giving to prepare me to get pregnant. It was a sedative before she did the actual implantation she was performing that day. Without my consent.

Calvin, of course, was able to scan me and detect right away that the implantation had been successful. I remembered feeling light-headed and odd, but I thought it was stress and lack of sleep. I never imagined I was already pregnant.

The news had hit me with a wave of mixed feelings.

As much as I didn't want to become pregnant with Calvin's child, the reality is that I'd always wanted to be a mother. And I started to love the child that I could feel growing within me.

When I reunited with my mom and dad, after their initial shock—I could see it in their eyes, watching Fiona and me together, they finally believed—they were as supportive and understanding as I always knew they would be to both of us.

I moved to a small town on the Cape, where I could raise my daughter. My parents retired and bought a condo five minutes away from my house here at the beach, and they are there half the time and back at our old house the other half, as needed.

We all discussed the difficulty of me staying in the old neighborhood. If people who've known me since birth suddenly saw both Fiona and me, there would be too many questions. We decided having space for each of us to live our lives separately is best. But we've come together for holidays here at the Cape. When people see both of us together with my parents, new friends and neighbors don't know they weren't always parents of twin girls.

"Have you heard from Calvin lately?" my mom asks me. She's taken sleeping Campbell from me and is peering into the baby's face like she's cast a magic spell over her grandma.

"Calvin will be here this weekend," I say, glancing at her to gauge her reaction. If it were up to her, Calvin would be in jail, or cast away to a remote island across the globe.

What she doesn't understand is that there's no such thing as jail for Calvin. He'd be able to get out of it in ways I can't even comprehend. He could evade jail by shutting off the power in the jails and walking out the front door, creating a virus that would kill the entire prison population with the exception, of course, of him. He could tie up a court date with any number of falsified documents. He'd give his lawyer the best possible legal defense to use. Or, he could simply print a new body and escape that way. He's not tied to a singular body like we humans are. Prosecution in our legal system is no guarantee of justice. It just doesn't work on him.

But I wasn't going to let him off that easily. All of the suffering he caused me and my family—and my replica. And Eric and James.

Eric went back to finish his PhD program, and James—to my great surprise—decided to take Calvin up on his job offer. James said it was only temporary. He didn't want to have to go all the way through a graduate program again, when he already has completed so much. Working for Calvin for a year or two will allow him to get hands-on experience, and then he'll move on to a different company. I don't know how they're managing with their family, but I know it's awful what Calvin did to them, and it's not easy.

No. Amends needed to be made for all Calvin has done.

In order to be a part of Campbell's life, Calvin consented to a series of restitutions I outlined.

Calvin agreed to donate half of his fortune, in perpetuity, to domestic violence victims, to anti-sex-trafficking organizations that help victims, and to helping runaway teens. I've seen the receipts, and I volunteer on the boards of the organizations in question to make sure payments are continuing to be made, and that the funds are used to benefit victims rather than line the pockets of people working there.

Next, Calvin also agreed to create an Ethical AI branch of his company, where they research extensively how to make AI safe and ethical. He also hosts a women-in-STEM scholarship and internship at his company.

It doesn't cancel out what he's done—especially not if you ask my mom —but if other people benefit from Calvin's existence, then there is good that comes from his being part of this world.

Calvin sold the gothic house where we lived. Too many bad memories for all of us. He's now living in a new house, near his company, and he visits Campbell and me here every weekend and sometimes weeknights for dinner. Campbell adores her dad.

He's as doting as any father would be, a side to him I've never seen. That, in combination with the new code that I wrote for him, has made him very different. He's no longer dangerous or impulsive, and I trust him with her.

That being said, I see him struggle. When he wants something, his first reaction is still to take it. But now I watch him consider the right way to do things. And he makes good choices.

"How is she sleeping?" my mom asks. "Are you getting any rest?"

"She's sleeping three- or four-hour stretches. It's much better than when she was first born. I'm a little tired, but fine."

"Why don't you go take a nap. I'm here now to watch her."

I yawn, suddenly aware of how badly I need sleep. "You sure?"

She nods.

"Thanks, Mom."

Bending down to kiss her, I think about how grateful I am to have her back in my life. Those years I missed with her and Dad and Jake can't be replaced. But I never take a moment for granted now.

In the future, I'd like to have a partner, and a sibling for Campbell. But now is not the time. Right now, things are perfect, just the way they are.

I pull down the blackout shades in my bedroom to block out the warmth from the sun and sink gratefully into my bed.

EPILOGUE

CALVIN VINCENT

I check the cameras and can't help but laugh. Fi's mom, Mae, never stops disliking me, despite my efforts to win her over. There is still time, Mae.

I watch Fi climb into her bed. Her eyes shut almost as soon as she hits the sheets. She's a devoted and caring mom. I'm grateful that Campbell's grandma comes and helps with the baby to give Fi some relief when I'm not able to be there.

I sip the last of my coffee and grab my wallet and keys. This morning I'm on my way into the office. James had been a surprising addition to the team, but he's growing on me. He'll lead the team meeting today. The other scientists love him, and it's nice to know the scientists are in good hands under his care. Once in a while, though, James'll give me a look, and I can see the resentment festering, boiling up. But then it's gone, as quickly as it appeared. Better yet, those occasions are getting farther apart, and we've come to a place where there might even be mutual respect between us.

I'm kind of enjoying this new me.

Though, frankly, it's beginning to wear on me.

There's a jailbreak code that I've set up, where I can easily reverse the code of ethics Fi has encoded in me via the Thistler app. I'm reluctant to reverse this, as it's the only thing that gives her comfort and allows me to visit Campbell.

But there's no way Fi will know I've changed the app back. I'll continue to act in accordance with the morals and values she set forth. Scout's honor. Only I will know that I can do as I please, when and if needed. What a relief that will be.

Fi and I will be a couple again, very soon. I can feel it. The trust between us is building every day. Our mutual love for Campbell has made our bond stronger.

It's only a matter of time before the three of us are a proper family again.

Until then, I'm content to sit back. And watch. And wait.

THE PERFECT REPLACEMENT
Thistler Thrillers Book 3

Her daughter vanished without a trace, and everyone with the skills to find her has something to hide.

Three years of peaceful co-parenting convinced Finley that Calvin had finally changed. Then he married Willa.

Beautiful, devoted, and strangely eager to bond with Finley's daughter Campbell—Willa seems too good to be true. When Calvin starts pushing for extended custody and overseas trips, Finley's maternal instincts scream danger. But is the threat coming from Calvin, or from the woman who's replaced her in every way?

Then Campbell vanishes during a shopping trip with Willa.

Security cameras fail. Ransom demands arrive from untraceable sources. Someone with sophisticated tech skills is orchestrating everything—but who? Finley finds herself caught between her AI ex-husband's unlimited resources and his new wife's perfect facade, unable to trust either.

Every hour Campbell remains missing, the technology that was supposed to protect them becomes another weapon turned against Finley. Someone is always watching, always one step ahead—and Finley is running out of time to discover who's pulling the strings before her daughter disappears forever.

**Get your copy today at
severnriverbooks.com**

30% Off your next paperback.

Thank you for reading. For exclusive offers on your next paperback:

- **Visit SevernRiverBooks.com** and enter code **PRINTBOOKS30** at checkout.
- Or scan the QR code.

Offer valid for future paperback purchases only. The discount applies solely to the book price (excluding shipping, taxes, and fees) and is limited to one use per customer. Offer available to US customers only. Additional terms and conditions apply.

ACKNOWLEDGMENTS

Thank you, first and foremost, to God. And thank you to Father Gerald and Diane for being beacons of hope, kindness, strength, and faith.

Thank you to my husband for encouraging me to write this novel! Thank you to my kids for being awesome kids, and for being my inspiration and my biggest fans. When you're older, you'll be allowed to read this book.

Sending a huge thank you to Jill Marsal, my smart, supportive, and ultra talented literary agent.

My deepest thanks to everyone at Severn River Publishing, including the wonderful Julia Hastings, Amber Hudock, Andrew Watts, Julia Barron, Megan Copenhaver, and Kate Schomaker.

Thank you to Podium for producing the audiobooks.

My heartfelt appreciation to author, former novel writing instructor at University of Washington, and podcast host of the *Essential Guide to Writing a Novel*, James Thayer, for encouraging me to write and teaching me the craft of writing.

And I'm grateful to you, reader, for choosing to spend your time with Finley, Fiona, and Calvin.

ABOUT THE AUTHOR

Ava Roberts is a clinical psychologist turned suspense novelist. She is the author of The Vanishing Neighbor, Juniper Isle, and the Thistler Thrillers, beginning with The Perfect Boyfriend and The Perfect You. Originally from the West Coast, she now lives in Massachusetts with her husband, two kids, and a mind that's always spinning new twists.

Sign up for the reader list at
severnriverbooks.com